...d to the Spirits
Rattling Chains

Bound to the Spirits

RATTLING CHAINS

T. STRANGE

Rattling Chains
ISBN # 978-1-83943-987-2
©Copyright T. Strange 2021
Cover Art by Louisa Maggio ©Copyright June 2021
Interior text design by Claire Siemaszkiewicz
Pride Publishing

This is a work of fiction. All characters, places and events are from the author's imagination and should not be confused with fact. Any resemblance to persons, living or dead, events or places is purely coincidental.

All rights reserved. No part of this publication may be reproduced in any material form, whether by printing, photocopying, scanning or otherwise without the written permission of the publisher, Pride Publishing.

Applications should be addressed in the first instance, in writing, to Pride Publishing. Unauthorised or restricted acts in relation to this publication may result in civil proceedings and/or criminal prosecution.

The author and illustrator have asserted their respective rights under the Copyright Designs and Patents Acts 1988 (as amended) to be identified as the author of this book and illustrator of the artwork.

Published in 2021 by Pride Publishing, United Kingdom.

No part of this book may be reproduced, scanned, or distributed in any printed or electronic form without permission. Please do not participate in or encourage piracy of copyrighted materials in violation of the authors' rights. Purchase only authorised copies.

Pride Publishing is an imprint of Totally Entwined Group Limited.

If you purchased this book without a cover you should be aware that this book is stolen property. It was reported as "unsold and destroyed" to the publisher and neither the author nor the publisher has received any payment for this "stripped book".

RATTLING CHAINS

Dedication

For M.

Chapter One

Harlan stared at the scuffed, dented metal strip across the bottom of the doorway. Behind him was worn linoleum, with a pattern so familiar that he could have drawn it from memory. Ahead was a concrete sidewalk. It was scribbled with cracks, and there were piles of sodden leaves gathered anywhere the wind couldn't touch them, dark spots where people had spat out their gum, cigarette butts, candy wrappers and so many *people*.

Inside—order, sameness, routine.

Outside—chaos, change... Excitement.

Harlan wasn't looking for excitement or change. He wanted very much to turn around, away from the physical and mental threshold the doorway represented and vanish into the building that had housed him since he had been five years old.

"Do you need a push?" Tom asked, gently.

It was still difficult for Harlan to think of him as Tom. He'd known the man since he was eight as 'Mr. Addison'.

Mr. Addison had called Harlan into his office a few days before. There had been a paper on his desk with an official-looking stamp that Harlan hadn't been able to identify before the man had covered it with his broad, hairy hand.

'Am…am I in trouble, Mr. Addison?'

Mr. Addison had laughed and said, *'No, of course not! Please, call me Tom. You're an adult now, and I'm no longer your teacher.'*

Those words had dropped something heavy and poisonous deep into Harlan's guts and it had stayed there for the last three days. It had been there while he'd packed his few belongings, while he'd said goodbye to everyone he'd ever known his whole life — everyone who gave any kind of shit about him, anyway.

Harlan shook his head. No, he didn't need — didn't *want* — a push. He wanted that letter to have never arrived. He wanted to stay in the Centre, the only home he could really remember.

After leaving him there, his parents had visited for a few years, and it had been strained for all three of them. Then Harlan's parents had had a new baby, one without 'the' ability. They'd visited once a month, then twice a year — his birthday and Christmas — then just sent cards. And after a few years…nothing. He couldn't remember the last time he'd heard from them, but it wasn't a relationship he intended to pursue, in or out of the Centre. They'd made it clear that they wanted nothing to do with him — and the feeling was mutual.

He didn't really consider anyone at the Centre his family, but it was his home, and he was being forced to leave with only his tiny, overstuffed duffle bag. Most of the things inside were just silly little presents the other kids had made him, not even personal items. He was also holding an envelope that Mr. Addison—Tom— had pressed into his hand with great importance, telling him there was three thousand dollars in it.

Harlan had never had to worry about money before. The resident children were given allowances, to spend or save as they chose, and some kids snuck out of the Centre to buy candy—or cigarettes and alcohol when they were older—but Harlan had never been tempted to leave. He'd been given everything he needed there, and they'd kept him safe. A cigarette that smelled bad and made him cough or a beer that made his head swim and made him sick in the morning weren't worth the risk of stepping beyond the Centre's encircling walls. He would have been happy to stay forever, maybe even eventually become a teacher like Mr. Addison... Tom. But apparently that wasn't his decision to make.

"Harlan? Is everything all right?" Tom asked.

No. Everything was *not* all right. It would never be all right again. "Fine, Mr.— *Tom*."

Tom grinned at Harlan—the smile of a man who would, in just a few minutes, be shutting himself back in the safety of the Centre, closing out the rest of the world.

Harlan tried to return the smile, close-mouthed, afraid that if he opened it, he'd throw up.

Looking past Harlan, Tom waved. "Ah! Your ride's here!"

A sleek, black car with tinted windows drew up beside them. The driver climbed out, circled the car and opened the door closest to Harlan without speaking.

"You've got everything?" Tom asked. The too-enthusiastic, bubbly voice that had encouraged Harlan as an eight-year-old didn't have the same effect at twenty-one.

Harlan shrugged, throwing his bag into the back seat and climbing in after it.

Tom sprawled one elbow on the roof of the car, leaning way down until his face was uncomfortably close to Harlan's. "Great! And don't worry — the car's been specially treated. Didn't want to stress you out too much on your first day! Give me a call if you need *anything*." His voice was positively saccharine, and Harlan wanted to punch it.

Tom slammed the door and rapped on the trunk as though he were dismissing an ambulance.

Harlan didn't look back.

He closed his eyes when he saw the first ghost. He'd seen plenty, first as a kid, then when his parents finally realized what was going on, in the controlled environment of the Centre. As a child, he hadn't understood that other people couldn't see his 'visitors.' They'd been excellent playmates, until one *wouldn't* go away. Harlan had been too afraid to sleep, jumping at noises no one else could hear, having screaming fits with no apparent cause.

His parents had taken him to psychiatrist after psychiatrist, desperate to deny that their son might be a medium. They'd wanted something medical, something they could cure with pills and therapy. They hadn't wanted their son to be one of *those* people.

Answering the doctors' questions, Harlan realized for the first time that he really was the only one who saw the 'see-through people'. He'd always thought his parents were just ignoring them.

The psychiatrists tried to convince Harlan—and his parents—that it was just a phase, imaginary, nothing to be afraid of. The ghosts didn't go away, no matter how hard Harlan tried not to believe in them. Finally, the Centre had called Harlan's folks. He'd found out later that one of the psychiatrists they'd seen had taken pity on Harlan, contacted the Centre and informed them she had a patient who was potentially a medium. The Centre had invited Harlan and his parents for a tour. His mom and dad certainly didn't *believe* in that sort of thing, despite the overwhelming scientific evidence, but they had run out of options and Harlan wouldn't even go into his bedroom without screaming. He hadn't slept in days, and the whole family had been desperate.

Young as he'd been, Harlan remembered his first step past the threshold of the Centre. It was…silent. There were no voices here—unlike everywhere else, where they surrounded him like a wall of sound, people he could and couldn't see clamouring for his attention. There was no one but those he knew were really there—him and his parents. He realized he'd never felt this blissfully alone before. There had *always* been ghosts. And now they were gone.

He closed his eyes and breathed it in—the silence, the solitude.

He startled when he felt a soft touch on his shoulder. A few minutes of peace had been wonderful, but he knew it couldn't last.

An older man—even older than the grandparents Harlan was no longer allowed to see after he'd frightened them by passing on messages from people who'd died long before he was born—was kneeling in front of him.

"You must be Harlan."

Not wanting to speak, to shatter this beautiful silence, Harlan nodded.

The man smiled. "Do you like it here, Harlan?"

"Yes! Very much!" Harlan had said. He'd been afraid that if he didn't speak up, didn't answer this man's question, he might have to leave. He'd wanted to stay...as long as possible. Just a few more minutes.

"There's someone I'd like you to meet. If I'm right, she won't be much of a surprise to you. And if I'm wrong, you can go on home."

Harlan nodded again, fighting to keep his face blank. He didn't *want* to go home, where it was always noisy and crowded with people only he could see or hear, never mind the *thing* in his bedroom—

The man offered Harlan his hand to shake, just as seriously as he would an adult.

Harlan shook, just as solemnly. The man's hand was pleasantly cool and dry, and he didn't squeeze too hard. Harlan wished his own hands weren't so clammy.

"I'm Dr. Cunningham, the director here at the Centre. It's a pleasure to meet you, Harlan."

Harlan tensed—just another doctor, more tests to see what kind of crazy he was. And that was a pity, because it was so *lovely* here. Harlan didn't think he was crazy, but his parents did, so he must be. They just hadn't found anyone who could prove it.

Dr. Cunningham laughed. "Don't worry. I'm not... This test will be different than any you've done before. I promise."

Standing, Dr. Cunningham gave Harlan's parents a reassuring wave before immediately returning his attention to Harlan. "Would you like to come with me?"

Harlan had heard plenty of stories from ghosts about how to tell if someone was dangerous, what would get a person killed and who to trust. Dr. Cunningham felt safe and genuine.

He nodded, allowing Dr. Cunningham to take his hand and lead him deeper into the building. They left his parents behind, but he didn't mind very much.

This part of the building was different. The front part, where they'd come in and where they'd left Harlan's parents, had carpets and art on the walls, like a hotel lobby. Here, the floors were bare concrete, the walls plain white with pipes visible overhead.

Dr. Cunningham's shoes clicked as he walked. The sound, the way the doctor walked with confidence, as though he belonged here and expected everyone to know it, made Harlan feel special. He belonged here, too, and he'd take any test they wanted to prove it.

Maybe reading Harlan's excitement as nervousness, Dr. Cunningham gave his hand a gentle squeeze. "Don't worry. The dormitories are far more comfortable. This is the lab, and you won't be spending much time here. That is," he said, smiling down at Harlan, "if you pass this test, which I very much think you will."

The doctor winked, and again Harlan felt as though he was being included in a wonderful secret, one not even his parents knew.

"We have a ghost in here."

Harlan stiffened. He'd never had a grownup talk about a ghost like it was real, and he felt a surge of bitterness when he realized the doctor had just been making fun of him like everyone else did.

Dr. Cunningham gave Harlan a reassuring smile. "Don't worry. She's quite safe. She won't hurt you." He laughed. "She actually used to work here, in the lab. She always talked about becoming a research ghost when she died." His face turned grim. "She should have had many years ahead of her, but… Well, she still works here, just in a different capacity. You don't have to be afraid."

"I'm not afraid." He was, though—afraid that Dr. Cunningham was teasing him and afraid that he *wasn't*. Ever since that horrible woman had taken over his bedroom, ghosts weren't fun anymore.

"Good lad." Dr. Cunningham gave Harlan's shoulder a brief squeeze. "I'll be right here with you the whole time. When you're ready, step onto that pad." He pointed at a metal circle set in the concrete floor. "This whole building is warded against ghosts, except for a few select places like that one. You won't run into any by accident here…if you choose to stay."

Harlan bit his lower lip, hard, so he wouldn't cry. He wanted to stay. He *had* to pass this test.

"If, at any time, you get scared or you want to stop, just step outside the circle and she'll disappear again."

"W-what do I have to do?"

"Just talk to her. Say 'hi'. It's only polite. She'll tell you a special word that will let me know you've really seen her."

"I just have to talk?"

Dr. Cunningham nodded.

Harlan drew in a slow, deep breath and briefly closed his eyes. He could do that. He'd always found it easier to talk to ghosts than to 'real' people. He could never tell what the living were thinking or feeling, but ghosts kind of…projected their feelings, whether they meant to or not.

Breath hitching in his chest, Harlan stepped forward onto the pad. He realized he had his eyes closed and had to force them open. His hands were trembling.

She appeared slowly, not just popping into his view the way ghosts sometimes did, and he suspected she'd done it on purpose so she wouldn't scare him.

"Hello. Are you Harlan?"

He nodded, just a tiny tilt of his head. He'd learned to hide when he was listening to a ghost, and he almost never spoke to them out loud anymore. He glanced back at Dr. Cunningham, but he just gave Harlan an encouraging nod. He didn't look at all angry or mocking.

"It's very nice to meet you. I'm Gwen. Are you ready for the word?"

He nodded again, a little more confidently.

"The word is 'ludicrous'. Ludicrous. You'll remember?"

"Yes," he said, shyly.

She waved and started slowly fading.

He stepped out of the circle and turned to face Dr. Cunningham again. "She said…ludicrous."

Dr. Cunningham beamed. "You passed the test."

Chapter Two

Harlan kept his eyes closed during the drive. He'd hardly left the Centre since he'd arrived, and he wasn't used to so much...*everything*. Ghosts aside, and even with his eyes closed, it was a complete sensory overload of unfamiliar sounds and smells. Every time a noise startled him, which was often, he had to squeeze his eyelids tighter, and before long, he had a headache from the strain and the constant, too-loud sounds of the city outside the car.

The driver was silent as he navigated the winding streets, and Harlan was grateful. Listening to someone and having to respond coherently would have been beyond too much.

"We're here," the driver said, the first time he'd spoken. There was the sound of his door opening. A pause. Then Harlan's door opening.

The open car door let in a rush of hot, stinking air that made him gasp. Exhaust, rotting garbage and cheap, greasy food... His stomach lurched. He popped open his eyes. Looking directly at him was a mostly decapitated ghost standing halfway through a parked car across the street, and that didn't help his nausea any.

He swallowed, hard, forcing a mouthful of bile back down his throat.

He knew he couldn't get out of the car, grab his bag and walk into a strange building with his eyes shut, but he truly wished he could.

The driver was staring at him impatiently—an expression Harlan was familiar with when dead people distracted him from the far-less-patient living, though he hadn't seen much of it since he was a child. He hadn't missed it. The driver had probably asked his question several times already, and Harlan hadn't heard a word.

"Sorry. What was that?" It had been an all-too-familiar question as a child, and he was fully aware of how stupid and spacey it made him sound. He suspected he'd have to ask it more often again, now that he'd been forced to leave the Centre.

"Your keys...sir." The last word came after a pause that was slightly too long, making it sound mocking.

Thinking back to his Life Skills classes, Harlan wondered if he was supposed to tip the driver with some of the money from his envelope, and if so, how much, but that comment made up his mind. He took the keys from the driver's hand. They were on an ugly, heavy plastic keychain shaped like the Tasmanian Devil's head. He'd never liked Bugs Bunny.

That didn't matter. He had money now. He could buy a new keychain—though it was hardly worth the effort of going out in public where he'd encounter both ghosts and living people just to replace it.

Gripping the key tightly, hard enough that the cut edges dug into his palm, he stared up at the building that he now, apparently, would call home.

It was old but fairly well maintained. The age didn't necessarily mean more ghosts. He was sure people had died in this place long before there were buildings, and this probably wasn't even the first structure that had been here. But there was a certain truth to the cliché of spooky old places being haunted. Harlan had been taught that old buildings tended to collect or concentrate spirits. When a building was torn down, any resident ghosts usually dispersed. Apparently, there weren't many ghosts from before the arrival of buildings in the world. While ghosts could remain for hundreds of years, most disappeared—or were removed by mediums—within their first century.

The driver already forgotten, Harlan grabbed his bag from the back seat and paused just outside the building, trying to get some sense of the place, which was silly, of course. His talents lay with the dead, unlike some of the other kids, who could do things like touch an object and see what its owner had eaten for breakfast.

The red-brick building was attractive enough. Its name—Parkview—and address were spelled out in brass letters above the front door. It was four stories high, plus it likely had a basement. The window frames were painted white, and none of the paint had peeled or flaked off. Rain, wind and the dust of years had worn the bricks' edges smooth, and the concrete accents sported spots and lines of green growth.

So far, so good. Harlan liked the look of the place. It was certainly more attractive than the practical, utilitarian buildings of the Centre. All that remained was to see if there were any restless former residents roaming the halls and if he could tolerate their company.

A curtain twitched in one of the windows, and Harlan caught a brief flash of a pale face before the fabric settled back, covering the window again.

It was a living person, Harlan thought, not a ghost, but he couldn't be sure at this distance and after such a short glance. He knew ghosts could do far more than ruffle a flimsy curtain, if only from training videos and half-forgotten childhood memories.

The driver stared at him, as well as a woman wearing a navy-blue dress and a grey-green beret. She unlocked the front door of the building, fumbling with her keys in her distraction as she watched Harlan instead of what she was doing. Not sure what else to do, Harlan flashed his new keys like an ID badge and strolled past her once she got the door open. He was sweating and breathing hard, and he took a moment to lean against the wall beside the door with his bag on the floor, pressed tightly against his feet as a very ineffectual shield.

The woman strode past, still eyeing him warily. Her heels clacked on the black-and-white tile floor.

Harlan closed his eyes, slowed his breathing. That was one of the first things he'd been taught at the Centre, when the sight, sound or touch of even the most benign ghost had sent him into what he now knew was a panic attack. He'd been so haunted—no pun intended—so on edge, that even a loud, sudden, but completely mundane noise or someone touching him unexpectedly could bring one on.

In. Out. In, slow. Out, slower.

He opened his eyes. The lobby was small and pleasantly dim. It was lit by an overhead chandelier, sconces and a few floor lamps, all casting a warm, soft glow. There was a bank of locked mail slots beside him, made of brass like the lettering on the building, each marked with a unit number. Several black leather benches — a little shabby, but clean — stood against one wall. One of them held a small stack of old paperbacks, apparently there for whoever wanted to take them. He liked that. It gave him a sense of the others in the building. Apparently, they were generous and liked to read. *Good people.*

The place felt welcoming, despite the translucent teenage girl who stood peering out the front door, anxiously waiting for a ride that would never come — or had arrived years ago. She was quiet, a simple repeater — a ghost caught in an infinite loop, not interacting with anything or anyone, growing fainter and fainter until she finally vanished completely.

She stood at the window, took a few steps — away from Harlan, toward the elevator — paused, bit her nails and briefly flickered out of existence before reappearing in her original position. The loop didn't show how she'd died, and aside from being able to see a painting of a lily through her, there was nothing to indicate she actually was dead — no blood, no missing limbs, no bloated, distorted features. This moment had been important to her and close to her death, and now she played it out over and over again.

Her clothes — bellbottoms and an orange sweater — looked at least a few decades out of date, but it might have just been her personal style.

He wondered why exactly her spirit, her essence — whatever was still present here — had chosen these few seconds to repeat. She looked to be about sixteen, though she could have been a few years older or younger. Harlan wasn't great at estimating people's ages.

Maybe she'd gotten pregnant and was waiting to tell her parents or boyfriend. Maybe she'd been waiting for a friend to pick her up, they'd gotten drunk and ended up in a fatal collision. Maybe her friend had survived and thought about the dead girl to this day, however many years or months ago the accident had happened.

They'd been encouraged to do this sort of speculating at the Centre, guessing what a spirit's motivation was. They'd mostly worked from videos, a flat, monotonous-voiced narrator stating the facts of the haunting before each clip—male, age thirty-four, died of cirrhosis. Reason for haunting—his ex-wife's new marriage.

Even as a child, Harlan had found the exercise pointless and a little stupid—*Why guess what a ghost was thinking or feeling when you could just ask?*—but here he was, out from under the watchful eyes of his teachers, not even *in* the Centre and still doing it.

Harlan risked a glance at the rest of the lobby, but it was fortunately empty of persons living or dead. He exhaled, slowly. He could live with this sad, silent ghost. Of course, she wasn't guaranteed to be the only spirit haunting the building—or even the lobby. Ghosts could appear at any time, not only after dark—though many spirits kept 'haunting hours' and were only visible during certain times of day. They could only be sensed as a cold spot the rest of the time.

So, that was the lobby.

Harlan took one last look back, just in time to watch the spectral girl blink out of existence, reappearing a moment later a few feet away.

Realizing he had no idea where he was going, Harlan looked at the key he was still holding, hoping it had some sort of clue. The key itself had only the manufacturer's name stamped on it, but taped to the back of the ugly keychain was a piece of paper with 'seven' written on it. The building was only four stories tall, so it was probably — *hopefully* — the suite number.

Sighing, Harlan decided he'd start on the lowest floor, likely in the basement, and work his way up.

The elevator was out of the question. Shortly before his parents had sent him to the Centre, Harlan had been trapped in an elevator with an angry ghost who didn't speak English. He'd eventually ended up curled in a corner, screaming until his voice gave out, much to the embarrassment of his parents, who couldn't see or hear anything but Harlan's hysterics. They had no idea why the elevator had really stopped, why their son had screamed, *'Stop, please. I don't understand!'* over and over again.

Taking the stairs was healthier anyway, right?

There was no suite seven in the basement. The last apartment was six. Beyond that were two labelled doors — a boiler room on the right and a laundry room on the left.

Harlan had never done his own laundry. Every Thursday morning at the Centre there'd been an announcement, reminding everyone to put their dirty clothes and bedding in the hamper before leaving their rooms for breakfast. After dinner, when he returned to his room, his clothes were neatly folded and put away in their drawers, his bed made by unseen hands. He'd tried to stay, once, hiding in his closet with the door open a crack, to see who took the laundry away. He liked to imagine Dr. Cunningham doing it, groaning as he lifted the baskets of clean laundry, grousing about Kleenex left in pockets and socks without mates.

Harlan had been missed at breakfast roll call and found before he could see who handled his clothes. Dr. Cunningham had died a year later. Harlan hadn't seen his ghost, but he had seen the body being wheeled out.

As promised, he'd never seen any ghosts he wasn't supposed to at the Centre, a luxury he'd come to rely on and was sorely missing already.

The key slid into suite seven's lock on the first floor but didn't turn. He jiggled it, just in case it was sticky or there was a trick to it. It'd be annoying to have to try every floor, hauling his bag up and down the stairs, only to learn that he belonged on the first floor after all. The key didn't budge, and Harlan left before someone came out of another apartment and found him trying to unlock a door he didn't have the key to.

The same thing happened on the second floor, and this time, Harlan hurried away when he heard the elevator door open and voices approaching. He felt like he didn't belong there, and anyone who saw him would immediately know it. They'd know he was one of those damn kids from the Centre, and they'd call to complain, and the Centre would send a car to pick him up—probably just have the same driver who'd dropped him off turn around, if he'd even left. He was probably just waiting outside for Harlan to fuck up—then he'd have to bear the driver's judgmental silence and he'd have to sit through a lecture from Tom about his failure to perform his civic duty and about how even though the Centre was always open to him, they encouraged him to live independently.

Harlan's hands were shaking and he felt his consciousness start to slip, as though he were watching himself move rather than being in control of his body. His teachers had called it 'disassociating' and encouraged him to tell them whenever it happened. Personally, he'd always thought it helped him understand ghosts. What, after all, were ghosts but the ultimate form of disassociation?

He half-ran up the stairs to the third floor, as if someone were chasing him. He didn't usually run. He was self-conscious about the way his body moved. That, and rapid movement tended to attract ghosts' attention.

Harlan had barely slid the key into suite seven's lock on the third floor when it opened, jerking the plastic keychain out of his hands and startling him so badly that he yelped. He found himself facing a large, angry-looking man.

"S-Sorry!" he managed, attempting to pull the key free—or close the door so he'd have a barrier between himself and the man. "I'm new to the building! Must have been the wrong door!" His voice felt too high, too shrill, but he couldn't stop talking.

The man slammed the door, catching the keychain and snapping it cleanly in half. The Tasmanian Devil's forehead and eyes were still attached to the key ring, but the bottom of it was still inside the apartment. A tiny, subversive part of Harlan liked that thought, of the Devil's mouth grinning, madly, at the man who'd separated it from the top half of its face.

He grabbed the key from the floor, where it had been jarred loose by the impact of the door closing, turning the broken keychain over and over in his hand. Now he had an excuse to buy a new one, or maybe he'd just keep it this way. The number was still taped to it on three sides, the fourth piece of tape hanging over the edge.

Harlan left before the man saw the broken piece inside his apartment and decided to throw it at Harlan's head.

He passed a shuffling, mumbling ghost in the stairwell on the way to the fourth floor, but they ignored one another—just the way Harlan liked it. If he could ever find his suite—and barring any unpleasant surprises on the way there or inside—he could stand to live in this building.

When the door to the fourth and final door marked with a brass seven refused to open, Harlan was ready to huddle in the nearest corner and shake until someone noticed him and called the police or the Centre. He was almost ready to call them himself, never mind that the asshole driver who'd dropped him off would probably be the one to come for him or his shame at not lasting more than... He glanced at his phone—two hours on his own.

He gave the key a vicious, frustrated jerk, hard enough that he worried about snapping the fucking useless piece of metal off in the lock—not that it would be his problem, because apparently this wasn't his apartment, either, even though he'd checked all of them and was this even the right building—or had the driver dropped him off here as a cruel joke?

Soft, friendly laughter. The good kind—laughing with him, not at him, or that was how it sounded.

Harlan kept his head down, twisting the key one way, then the other, as though repeating the same motion over and over would change what happened. He wished the door would open and he could step inside, proving he wasn't trying to break into the apartment.

And close the door behind him. And disappear.

"There's a trick to it. You mind?" A large, male hand reached between Harlan and the door, hovering just short of touching the key.

Harlan shrugged.

"You've got to kinda…" The man jiggled the key, simultaneously pressing a certain spot on the doorframe. "And…voila!"

The door swung open, but before Harlan could dart past the stranger into the safety of his new apartment, the man closed the door again, swiftly turning the key in the lock.

"Whoa, not until you can do it yourself. Teach a man to fish and all that." The stranger gestured at the key with a flourish, stepping back and out of Harlan's way. "You can tell management about it, if you want. Maria—the woman who lived here before you, who taught me the trick so I could feed her cats whenever she was out of town—always said she was going to complain about the lock, but she never did." He shrugged. "Maybe she just got used to it. Maybe you will, too."

That sounded slightly, vaguely ominous.

Harlan was exhausted, overwhelmed and overstimulated. He wanted to get away from the living and the dead and just be alone in an apartment he hadn't even seen yet. He twisted the key the way his neighbour—he assumed the man was his neighbour—had demonstrated, pushing on the doorframe. The door creaked open.

"I've got some oil for the hinges, if you want."

"Thank you. Do I have to do that when I lock it, too?" Harlan was a little surprised he'd spoken, never mind asked a question. Questions only made interactions with people last longer, and that was something he tried to avoid.

"Nope. It just locks. Not sure why. Here... Try it."

Harlan had been borderline rude, but it didn't seem to faze the guy.

Harlan locked the door and turned to the man with a smile he hoped didn't show how worn out he was. "Thank you, again...for your help." Jiggle, twist, push — the door opened. Snagging his bag by the strap, he slid inside and pulled it in after him.

As he closed the door, he heard the man say, "I didn't catch your name. I'm Jared — " The last name was cut off by the surprisingly soundproof door.

Harlan knew he probably wouldn't remember the man's name, anyway.

Locking the door, Harlan gave a deep sigh he hoped the man in the hall couldn't hear. Sound could be funny like that sometimes, only going one way.

He slid down the door, painfully bumping his kidney on the knob as he passed it, until he was sitting on the golden hardwood floor with his legs sprawled in front of him, his head down and bag clutched to his chest. He still felt vulnerable and exposed, so he drew his knees up until he was a complete, self-contained ball.

The apartment smelled like artificial lemons and ammonia, the chemicals burning the back of his throat with each deep, heaving breath.

Something crinkled behind him when he leaned forward. Reluctantly setting his bag aside, he reached back, lifting himself a little, until his questing fingers touched paper. It was an envelope, he saw as he brought it into view. Judging by the piece of tape trailing from it, it had been stuck to the inside of the door, and he'd knocked it loose during his slide. Trying to ignore the spike of dread radiating from the horrible little knot that had taken up residence in his gut since he'd found out he was being forced to leave the Centre and had only gotten worse since he'd crossed its threshold, Harlan opened the envelope. Inside was a typed sheet of plain printer paper, with *Tomas Addison* signed at the bottom. *Huh.* Harlan would have assumed Tom spelled his name with an H, if he'd ever thought about it.

Too tired and jittery to focus, Harlan scanned the letter—his apartment had been ghost-proofed, the bed was freshly made, there was food in the fridge, here's the number of a grocery store that delivers—but he should *try* to get out on his own—his rent would be automatically deducted from his earnings, blah blah blah. Nothing urgent. Nothing that couldn't wait until the next day.

Chapter Three

There were sheets on the bed, nicer ones than he'd ever had at the Centre. They were decorated with paisleys and whorls rather than being one solid, institutional colour and they were soft, too. Harlan had hardly noticed the night before. He'd been so exhausted that he'd simply collapsed on the bed, fully dressed, and fallen asleep almost instantly. That was rare for him. Typically, it took hours for him to fall asleep naturally — or the help of a sleeping pill.

Even safe within the ghost-warded confines of the Centre, his mind wouldn't easily switch off at night.

He hadn't closed the curtains — soft blue, with a subtle design that matched the sheets without being identical, and much more decorative than the beige plastic blinds in his old room — and the sun was shining directly on his face. He groaned and rolled over, covering his head with a pillow, but he knew it was useless. Now that he was awake, he'd stay that way, no matter how much he wanted to block out the world and sleep and sleep and sleep.

Rolling over again, he glanced at the alarm clock, which had glowing, red LED numbers, rather than the old-fashioned analog one he was used to. He'd have to find a way to cover the clock's face or the light would bother him at night—when he didn't simply collapse from exhaustion, which he hoped wouldn't become routine. Blackout curtains, too—the blue ones were pretty but thin and wouldn't block out much light. And a new keychain. Just like that, he had a shopping list.

Harlan was shocked to see that it was after eleven a.m. He was used to his day beginning at eight-thirty, nine at the latest, and that cycle was so ingrained in him that he usually woke at that time on his own, even on 'free' days. That he'd slept more than two hours late, with an uncovered window no less, was a testament to how tired he'd been. He considered lying in bed, simply because he could. No one was going to come knocking on his door, telling him he had to be in class in half an hour, and he'd already missed breakfast. He wasn't expected anywhere. No one would be looking for him. And wasn't that a frightening thought, one that propelled him out of bed, stumbling into the bathroom. Also, he really had to pee.

He'd packed his toiletries, but everything had been provided for him here, neatly laid out and still in its packaging.

He cracked open the new tube of toothpaste—a different brand than the half-used tube he'd brought with him—and squeezed some onto his old toothbrush then glanced at the new, unopened one, dropped the used one in the wastebasket and instantly regretted it. He hadn't had it that long. The lines on the bristles that indicated when it should be changed hadn't faded yet. He'd also wasted toothpaste, but he couldn't quite bring himself to fish the old one out of the trash, even though it had an empty bag and the plastic bin itself looked brand-new.

Unwrapping the fresh toothbrush, he carefully dropped the package so it landed directly on top of the old toothbrush, deliberately hiding it.

His teeth clean, bladder empty, face freshly shaved, hair brushed into some semblance of order, Harlan considered himself in the mirror — or rather, considered the shower behind him.

Deciding he wasn't up for the task of facing his new residence wet, he shuffled out of the bathroom, through the bedroom and into the main room he'd hardly glanced at the night before — hadn't even seen with the lights on. A couch, two armchairs, a coffee table and two end tables — clearly, whoever had furnished the suite had expected him to be a regular, social human being, who enjoyed being around other humans and willingly brought them into his living space. He considered selling the furniture or giving it away, but that left the question of what to put in its place. And he'd have to deal with whomever came to pick it up.

There were even paintings on the walls — generic, inoffensive abstract shapes and colours that Harlan took an immediate and irrational dislike to, much like the keychain.

If he closed his eyes, Harlan could see the ghost-wards protecting the apartment. They were well done, carefully scripted in a tight, professional hand, without any added flourishes or personal flair. They'd hold just about anything out. He'd be safe here — from ghosts, anyway — not from helpful neighbours, who might not be so helpful now that he'd closed the door in their faces.

Harlan wasn't especially hungry, even though his internal schedule told him it was almost lunchtime, never mind breakfast. He needed to eat so he could have his pills without feeling sick. A generic brand, of course — they were paid for on the government's dime, after all. Not that he cared, as long as the pills worked. Taking away the constant, uncontrolled ghostly invasions in Harlan's young life had mostly preserved his sanity but hadn't touched his depression. He vaguely remembered, from the note he'd barely scanned the night before, something about calling *any* time, day or night. Harlan could hear the emphasis in Tom's voice, even in writing. Tom had also listed several mental health support groups he could join. *Right.* Listening to a bunch of people talk about their mental illnesses was definitely going to make him feel better.

Finding the note discarded in the middle of the floor, where he'd dropped it the night before, Harlan crumpled it and threw it into yet another spotless wastebasket, satisfied by this small act of defiance and the way he'd successfully made the shot.

That was the note taken care of, but where had he put the key? He was still wearing the same clothes, and it wasn't in any of the pockets. Frantic, he raced back into the bedroom, the bathroom…nothing. He went back to the living room and impulsively opened the front door. There was the top of Taz's head, Harlan's key still firmly in the lock. At least the building seemed crime-free, if he could get away with leaving his key in the lock overnight like a fucking idiot.

Setting it on one of the end tables and thoroughly disgusted with himself, Harlan stalked into the kitchen. The last few days had been hard enough on him without missing his medication. The fridge — besides being glistening white and clearly brand-new, like everything else — was full of staple foods — milk, eggs, cheese, apples. There was nothing he particularly liked or disliked. The cupboards were the same—cans of soup, boxes of cereal, flour and other baking necessities, nothing exciting. Whoever had bought it, like everything else in the apartment, hadn't been shopping for him in particular, just for food in general.

Harlan poured himself a bowl of cereal, added milk and sat on the couch to eat it. The apartment didn't have a dining table. He kept getting distracted, thinking of things he wanted to buy with the money in his envelope, and the cereal got mushy. Stubbornly—it was the first meal he'd prepared for himself, *by* himself, dammit—he forced himself to choke it down.

He spent the weekend rereading books on his old e-reader and learning to live alone. His Life Skills classes had fallen somewhat short. He had to make food for himself, multiple times a day, *every* single day? The thought was strangely depressing, and he hadn't even attempted anything more complicated than reheating soup. First, he'd tried it in the microwave, then, to mix things up a bit, on the stovetop. He'd had to rummage through every cupboard and drawer until he finally found a pot under the oven. At least he didn't have to leave the apartment.

On Sunday afternoon it hit him, abruptly, that this was his space, which meant he could masturbate where he wanted, whenever he wanted. The thought was oddly more horrifying than arousing—too much freedom. He'd had to be furtive and awkward at the Centre, where he'd constantly been surrounded by other people and had to snatch whatever moments alone he could. Looking back, he was a little amazed he'd never been caught masturbating, never mind the few times he'd managed to have full-blown sex.

He tried the shower first, because that was familiar and he was naked anyway. Then a short nap. After dinner — more soup and some crackers he'd found hidden behind the canned goods — he cautiously entered the main room, holding some lotion and Kleenex. Being naked outside his bedroom was odd and terrifying, yet also exhilarating.

He lay on the couch, the soft white leather clinging unpleasantly to his skin as he squirmed, trying to find a comfortable position. He almost gave up and retreated to the bedroom with his tail tucked between his legs, but he stubbornly pressed on. He thought about what he nearly always thought about when he jerked off — rough, masculine hands holding him down, spanking his upturned ass while another man fucked his mouth. His climax was satisfactory but not earthshattering, and he decided that — empty apartment or not — he'd stick with the bedroom from now on.

Chapter Four

Monday morning, Harlan was woken at nine-o-six by the phone ringing—a landline beside the bed that he'd seen but ignored, assuming it wasn't connected but was simply set dressing like the rest of the furnishings. Harlan had a cell phone, a few years out of date but still perfectly functional.

"'lo?" he mumbled, tentatively, after fumbling for the receiver long enough that he worried he'd accidentally hung up on whoever was calling him. It was probably someone checking in on him.

"Where the fuck are you? You're five minutes late!" a curt voice barked in his ear.

"S-sorry. I think you have the wrong number..."

"Harlan Brand?"

"Yes." No one used Harlan's last name. He sometimes went years without hearing it.

"Then I have the right fucking number! Get your ass down here in twenty minutes, or I'm coming up to get it!"

Click.

Shaking and wide awake now—it was amazing how, after only a few days out on his own, his internal schedule had shifted so he slept later—Harlan lay frozen in the still-unfamiliar bed, clutching the receiver. An aggressive stranger who knew a number he hadn't given out—hadn't even known existed—who also knew his full name. Reaching for his cell phone, he hovered his finger over the number Tom-without-an-H had programmed into it, then he moved it away again.

He didn't think the stranger was bluffing.

Groaning, he rolled out of the bed he didn't think of as his yet and pulled on one of the nearly identical outfits he'd been provided with. These, at least, were his size, and he wasn't used to variation in his wardrobe, anyway. Jeans, T-shirt, underwear, socks... The shoes were his own, brought from the Centre. He didn't have another pair but wasn't sure why he'd need more than one, anyway.

Glancing at the alarm clock that he still hadn't gotten around to covering—though it hadn't bothered him at night as much as he'd expected—he weighed his options. He could brush his teeth and shave, but he'd be cutting it close to the twenty-minute deadline. *Fuck it.* The man had woken him up, rudely. He'd just have to deal with Harlan's morning breath and stubble.

There were no people waiting outside the apartment building. No cars parked nearby, either, on either side of the street, except for a police car with its lights off.

Maybe it was a joke. A prank. One of the newer kids at the Centre—who would probably never be allowed to leave its ability-dampening confines, and Harlan wasn't *at all* jealous—could manipulate electronics. Someone must have put her up to calling him. The landline probably wasn't even really hooked up.

"What the fuck are you doing?"

Harlan looked around, hoping the unfortunately familiar voice was addressing someone else.

The police car's driver side door was open. A scowling, uniformed cop leaned on it, staring directly at…Harlan.

Of course.

"Get in here!" He jerked his finger at the car.

The speaker was on the short side, at least a few inches shorter than Harlan's own six feet, but lean and without an ounce of extra fat on him. His hair was dark blond and cropped almost to his scalp. His eyes were hidden behind dark sunglasses.

A small but vocal part of Harlan wasn't surprised. There had been a mistake. He wasn't supposed to have been let out of the Centre. His weekend out on his own was over. He hoped the food in the fridge wouldn't go to waste, that whoever was assigned the apartment after him would use it.

Personally, he thought sending a police car rather than the car he'd been dropped off in by an equally sunny individual was excessive, but the kids at the Centre had whispered stories after lights out, about psychics who went rogue when out on their own, who had to be taken down by the police, by SWAT teams, by *helicopters*. When powers were involved, the authorities couldn't be too careful. Still, he found it strange that no one had tried to contact him, either on his cell or the landline, before bringing him in, but bureaucracy, he supposed.

After crossing the street reluctantly, Harlan tried to open the rear passenger door, putting as much space between himself and the angry man as possible, but it didn't open.

"What the fuck are you doing?" the cop repeated, so eerily similar to the first time he'd said it that, for an instant, Harlan wondered if it was a recording.

The cop reached out with the arm that wasn't leaning on the car door, almost violently, slapping the roof of the car and startling Harlan. "Get in, now, before you make us any fucking later."

Later? Late for what? And it occurred to Harlan that, on the phone, the man had told him he was already five minutes late.

Harlan stumbled the two steps to the front passenger door and opened it on the first try. He'd half expected it to be locked, too, or, if the man had been sitting in the driver's seat, for him to pull the car ahead a few feet. Harlan hadn't known the man for even two minutes, and he already suspected that was the sort of humour he appreciated.

He slid into the passenger seat without incident, closed the door as softly as possible and carefully buckled his seatbelt. He stared at the policeman expectantly, warily. The car smelled like sweat, coffee and a gag-inducing artificial floral scent emanating from a blue, pine-tree-shaped air freshener hanging from the rear-view mirror.

Ignoring Harlan, the cop turned on the car engine. "Your door's not shut." Had the cop's voice softened just a fraction?

Face bright red and hot, Harlan opened his door again, then closed it more firmly.

His companion grunted and put the car in gear. Twisting the wheel violently, he pulled away from the curb much more sharply than Harlan thought was strictly necessary. He gripped the door handle in his right hand and curled the left as far beneath his seat as it would go, as though that would do anything to keep him safe if they got into a collision. *Police officers take special driving training, right?*

"The Centre is that way," Harlan pointed out, softly, after a few silent minutes passing other cars at an alarming speed. They were headed north, rather than southeast, where they ought to be going. Harlan didn't know Toronto well, despite having lived there most of his life, but he knew that much.

"Why the fuck would we be going *there*?"

Harlan discreetly glanced over, but he couldn't see the officer's name embroidered on his uniform without leaning noticeably farther forward. He hadn't thought to look at it before he'd gotten into the car, and he regretted that now. He might be able to get his cell phone out of his pocket without the man noticing, could maybe call someone for help, but having a name would probably help them track the car.

"Where *are* we going?" Harlan asked quietly, sinking into his seat.

The officer rattled off an address that meant nothing to Harlan. After seeing what the obviously blank expression on Harlan's face, he glanced over at him, sighed, clenched and unclenched his hands on the steering wheel. "You seriously have no idea?"

Harlan shook his head, nipping at a loose, dry bit of skin on his lip.

"It was supposed to be in the letter they gave you." The officer frowned.

The blood rushed away from Harlan's head so quickly that he felt faint, leaving him pale and trembling. *Fuck.* He was such an idiot. That stupid letter — He'd hardly glanced at it the night he'd been dropped off at the apartment, then he'd thrown it out without looking at it again.

He felt sick. He was distantly aware that the officer was speaking, but it hardly registered as noise, never mind words.

"You know about police mediums, right?"

Harlan nodded. He *was* a medium. Of course, he knew some mediums worked with the police.

"Well, congratulations. Now you are one." The officer made a grand gesture, taking both hands off the steering wheel.

Harlan clenched his teeth together so hard that he almost drove his lower molars into his sinuses. He'd always been a nervous passenger, and this man's driving style certainly wasn't putting him at ease.

Police medium. That was actually a pretty good job for him — away from people, low pressure. Violent deaths tended to create ghosts, and mediums were dispatched to crime scenes to send victims' ghosts on their way. He'd been taught a wide variety of skills at the Centre for exactly that purpose — psychology, grief counselling and — for extreme cases — exorcism rites from a dozen different cultures.

After several years, a medium might join the regular police force — solving crimes rather than cleaning up after them.

"So...you're my partner?" If this were a movie, the cop's gruffness wouldn't last. Harlan would save his life and they'd become a mismatched pair of friends, cracking wise and sharing a beer after work. It seemed unlikely. Also, Harlan didn't want to be responsible for saving anyone's life, his own included.

The officer snorted, shooting Harlan a withering, lingering glance that took his attention off the road for far too long. "Partner? Not fucking likely. Look... Here's how it goes." He held up his hand horizontally, near the car roof. "You've got the cops, up here at the tippity-top"—he lowered his hand a little—"then the crime scene techs, then the crime scene clean-up crew, then you. You're a fucking ghost janitor."

Well, that was how crime scenes worked, chronologically. Seeing as this particular cop's job was, for the moment, babysitting Harlan, he couldn't help but wonder where the man fell in his own hierarchy. He knew better than—or at least, wasn't confident enough—to voice his thoughts. He nodded meekly, sitting in silence for the rest of the drive.

Eventually, his companion turned on the car stereo, which blared to life so loudly that it startled a sound out of Harlan. It was a country song Harlan had never heard before—not that Harlan listened to country music.

The car stopped in front of a nondescript, derelict brick warehouse, with nothing to distinguish it from a dozen others they'd passed.

Harlan undid his seatbelt and touched the door handle. The policeman didn't move or speak. They stared at each other for a moment, Harlan's eyes quickly dropping to the level of the man's chest. The officer took a long swallow from the coffee cup that was sitting in the cup holder between their seats then turned off the car but made no move to get out.

"Right." Harlan was the first to break the silence between them, which almost never happened. "I'll just..." It didn't matter, he tried to convince himself, that this would be—presumably—his first solo ghost. He'd trained and studied for years for this exact moment. Still, he felt woefully unprepared.

He opened the door, got out, the wet gravel—it had rained the night before, the soft patting of drops against his window helping him sleep, but giving him strange, furtive dreams—crunching beneath his feet, stone against stone, mixed with cigarette butts and other small bits of trash. There were several sheets of corrugated metal leaning against the building, large pieces of machinery Harlan couldn't identify, and some lumber haphazardly stacked on a broken pallet.

He couldn't see a ghost, not yet, but there was a kind of sparkle, a shimmer, by the heavy, metal door leading into the warehouse that let him know a spirit was nearby.

The door had been secured with a chain and padlock, but the lock swung from the end of the chain now, its shackle neatly severed, presumably by the police. Standing on his tiptoes, Harlan peered through the grilled window in the door, his heart already racing in anticipation of a jump-scare—ghosts, once they realized someone could see them after so long being ignored by the living, had a tendency to act out, like bored, lonely toddlers. The glass was coated in grime that wouldn't come away, even when he wiped it with a corner of his T-shirt.

The tip of Harlan's thumbnail was between his front teeth before he realized it—not biting, not yet, just holding it, pensively. He jerked it away before he started chewing in earnest, hoping Officer Definitely-Not-Partners hadn't seen his moment of weakness. A glance at the car showed that his attention was in his lap—hopefully on a phone.

Sighing, Harlan pulled the door open. It moved smoothly and quietly, without the shriek of rusty hinges he'd expected. It was a little disappointing, honestly. It didn't fit with the spooky atmosphere.

The interior was large, cool and dimly lit by filthy glass-block windows set high in the walls. Stepping inside, Harlan automatically closed the door behind himself. It was, he reflected, probably a stupid thing to do. If the ghost were dangerous, not only would he have something between him and escape, but the policeman couldn't see him and would be less likely to hear him if he screamed. Not that he expected much help from that direction, honestly, and the place didn't *feel* dangerous.

The opposite, actually.

Harlan closed his eyes, his breathing and heart rate slowing properly for the first time since the phone call that had awoken him.

The Centre had a small, non-denominational chapel, for kids with a spiritual or religious inclination or those who believed their powers came from the divine. A boy a few years younger than Harlan, Malcolm, had limited power over water, which he maintained was a gift from God. He'd been quite a little prick about it when he'd first arrived, constantly quoting the Bible and finding fault with the other kids. Most of them would have happily given up their powers and returned to their normal lives, and barring that, would've used them against Malcolm, if the punishment for misusing them hadn't been so severe. None of them wanted to lose TV and Internet privileges for three months. Finally, Mr. Addison—Tom—had taken Malcolm aside one day and explained that he should, perhaps, keep his religion to himself.

Harlan hadn't pointed out that, powers from God or not, Malcolm's parents had ditched him at the Centre, just like the rest of them.

It was a bit of a point of contention, actually, between Harlan and the religious kids. He believed in an afterlife, obviously—what else could ghosts be, if not proof of its existence? Still, no ghost he'd ever spoken with had told him any kind of grand, overarching, unifying, all-encompassing revelation of God, nature or the universe.

Harlan had rarely visited the chapel. While he barely remembered his parents, he was firmly in the group who would have given up his powers for a nickel, and he felt that any divinity who'd inflict this on him wasn't worthy of shining his shoes, never mind worship. He'd never sensed the peace, the deep sense of connection that others had described when visiting a holy place—at least not in the Centre's chapel. He'd sometimes snuck out of his dorm at night, moving cautiously so he wouldn't wake Leon, who'd want to follow him because Harlan was older. Leon was always begging Harlan to show him ghosts, no matter how many times Harlan told him there weren't any just wandering the buildings.

With a stolen flashlight—Harlan hadn't stolen it himself. He'd traded a baseball he'd found just inside the Centre's fence for it and thought he'd definitely gotten the better end of the deal—he'd go to the Centre's gym. He'd plopped in the middle of the floor, the flashlight safely wedged between his feet so it wouldn't roll away, leaving him with vertigo in a dark, windowless room, helpless until the lights were turned on in the morning and he was caught, his flashlight confiscated.

He'd simply sat in the vast, empty space, stretching away and above him in all directions, imagining that the same depth was below him, that he was suspended in the middle, with nothing but his own breath to anchor him to anything. Then, for a moment or two, he thought could feel the touch of the divine.

This warehouse had the same quiet softness, the tranquil emptiness, as the darkened gym. Calm come over him after a few slow, steady breaths and Harlan was the most relaxed he'd been since before the phone call — since he'd been ejected from the Centre three days before, including while he slept. His dreams had been troubled, even before the rain, since Tom had told him he had to leave.

Reluctantly, Harlan opened his eyes again. He had a job to do...apparently. Though he could see dust in the air, motes shivering in the faint light the cracked, grimy windows allowed in, the concrete floor was surprisingly clean. It showed signs of having been swept recently, and he doubted the police had bothered. *A neat-freak ghost?*

There was a light switch beside the door, and he flicked it on automatically. Nothing happened, which he'd expected, and he switched it off again, just as automatically. The building probably didn't have power, so it wouldn't matter what position he left the switch in, but he couldn't bring himself to leave it 'on'.

"Hello?" he called, his voice echoing in the dim, cavernous space.

He heard a sudden, frantic sound from the far end of the building — familiar, but not quite identifiable. He cautiously made his way through the warehouse, feeling a bit foolish going towards a disturbance rather than away. He dodged a few old-fashioned wooden desks with all their drawers pulled out, a few lying beside them like bureaucratic entrails. A few overturned chairs. Machinery. The detritus of production, though Harlan couldn't tell what the building had produced or stored.

In the corner farthest from the door was a makeshift cage, cobbled together mostly from pallets and wire. Inside were several pigeons, still fluttering and darting in small, frantic, futile bursts around their home.

The hairs on the back of Harlan's neck prickled, but he didn't turn around, addressing the birds instead. "I'm sorry I startled you. You've probably been through a lot in the past few days."

Slowly, one feather, one beady, watchful eye at a time, the pigeons settled back onto their two-by-four perches, cooing amongst themselves.

Harlan cooed back as best he could, which, admittedly, was not very well.

"They're beautiful," he said aloud. And they were. No two birds were alike. The feathers on their necks gleamed purple and green, catching the faint, dusty light. Their body feathers were all uniquely patterned in grey, black and white. A few were white and cream or fawn, rather than grey. Harlan had always liked pigeons, left crumbs for them in the Centre's courtyard so he could watch them eat from his bedroom window. He'd found an injured one once and had tried to keep it in his chest of drawers, to nurse it back to health, but it had been discovered — or, more likely, ratted out by one of his roommates — and taken away. He still wondered what had happened to the bird.

There was a gruff sound of acknowledgment behind him, and Harlan allowed himself to turn.

A woman stood there, tall and proud and daring him to judge her too-big overcoat, her stained, ripped sweatpants and her unwashed hair.

Well, what was left of a woman. If she'd been physically present, Harlan suspected she would have smelled of sweat and food and probably bird shit, but ghosts, when they had a scent, never smelled the way they necessarily *should*. This one smelled like a pigeon—dust, breadcrumbs and feathers. The way she glared at him out of the corner of her eyes, her gaze darting away when he looked directly at her, reminded him of a pigeon, too.

"My name is Harlan," he said, softly, once he was reasonably sure she wouldn't bolt or attack him.

"Millie," the ghost replied. The pigeons cooed in response to her voice and she smiled at them. She was missing one of her lower incisors but was no less beautiful for it. "I'd offer to shake your hand, but..." She laughed, a harsh sound that ended in a cough, a memory of lungs she no longer had.

"It's nice to meet you, Millie." And he meant it. Strangely, the discomfort he felt talking to people— living people—and the strangeness they saw in him never seemed to arise when he spoke to ghosts. Even though they were, after all, the remnants of people.

"Do you know what happened to you?" Based on her words, he suspected she knew she was dead, but this was his first time out on his own, and it was natural to fall back on the ghost communication script that had been drilled into his head. He wished the officer had given him a little more information than...none. Knowing the date of Millie's death, something about the circumstances, anything, would have been useful.

"Yep."

Harlan hoped she didn't notice his sigh of relief. "You know that you're…?" *Fuck.* Out on his own and he still couldn't just come out and say the 'D' word. 'Dead' had been treated almost like a swear during his training. The textbooks never used the word 'death'. It was always a softer euphemism — deceased, departed, passed on…

"I know I'm dead." She narrowed her eyes at him. "You think, just because I'm here like this, with only my birds for company, that I'm slow?"

He shook his head. "No, ma'am." *Ma'am?* He'd never called someone 'ma'am' in his life. *Where did that come from?*

Millie snorted. "Don't 'ma'am' me."

She knew she was dead. That was half his work done right there. He could skip step one in the Grief Counseling textbook — 'when the client isn't aware that they are deceased'. 'Ghost' had been nearly as much of an anathema as 'dead'. Harlan had been taught to think of them as clients, instead.

"What's keeping you from moving on? No, wait, that's not what I'm supposed to… Uh, do you want to talk about it?" *Step Two — once you've gotten a client to acknowledge their passing, calmly help them move past the trauma of the event. Do not become emotional, no matter how tragic the circumstances.*

Millie gave him a cagey look. "New on the job, huh?"

He nodded, blushing, wishing he could take back the gesture. The Three Cs — Calm, Cool and Collected. He wasn't making a very good impression.

"I'll make it easy for you. I don't need to sing 'Kumbaya' and tell you what those assholes" — Millie's eyes literally sparked, the industrial lighting above them glowing for an instant before dimming again. She cleared her spectral throat—"what they did to me. It's over. It's finished. I'm going to my rest, right?" She laughed, the sound ending in a cough again. "I'm done. But these guys"—she pointed to the pigeons—"they're still here. They need somewhere to go. You promise...? You promise me that you'll do well by them?" Another brief flash of light, gone in a blink.

Harlan nodded. He wouldn't have just left them here anyway, to die of thirst. "I promise."

Millie stared at him, a long, hard look, then she nodded, once. "Good. I'll hold you to that. You break your promise, and I swear I'll come back and haunt your ass." The clatter of wings and she was gone, not even the sparkle remaining to show that she was still there, invisible.

The pigeons stirred. One took brief flight, moving restlessly around the cage, before settling again.

Harlan watched the birds peck and scratch and preen, content in their tiny corner of the world, enjoying the peaceful feeling of the place. With a regretful sigh, he traipsed back to the door he'd entered from.

The officer had hardly moved, barely looked up when Harlan opened the passenger door and slid inside.

"Did you do it? Five more minutes and I would've come in after you."

"...Pigeons."

That made the man look up. "What?"

Harlan bit his lower lip hard, forcing himself to repeat, more emphatically, "Pigeons. The old lady, the client, the—the ghost, she kept pigeons. She wanted them to be safe. That's why she stayed."

"Those flying rats?" The man grimaced. "So, what? Is she gone or not?"

"She's gone."

"Good. Maybe you're some fucking use after all. Let's go. We've got lots more places to hit."

"No. Not until we call the SPCA or...something." Harlan wasn't sure who to call to take in a flock of pigeons.

"For some fucking pigeons?" He waved a dismissive hand. "Forget 'em. The crazy pigeon lady's gone. We're finished here. The fewer of those things around, the better."

Harlan wasn't sure if he meant the pigeons or the homeless woman. He didn't think he wanted to know.

"No!" The volume of Harlan's voice startled him, uncomfortably loud in the enclosed car, and the cop shot him a look of utter disbelief.

"Whoa! All right, *fuck*, we'll save the pigeons. But you're making the call."

Harlan insisted they wait while the pigeons were caught and loaded into carriers for transportation. He even got out of the car and anxiously informed the animal control officers that they all had to stay together as a flock, that he'd be checking up on them. Working with the police had to carry some clout, even if he was at the bottom of this particular cop's hierarchy. These pigeons were going to be loved and cared for. He'd promised, and he'd make sure of that.

He'd finally caught a glimpse of the cop's nametag. *C. Hamilton*. He'd been amusing himself while waiting for the pigeons to be picked up by thinking of what the C could stand for — *Clod. Confused. Claptrap.* Hamilton's rank was probably indicated by his badge or epaulettes, but Harlan had no idea what they meant.

Watching the last pigeon being loaded, Harlan asked, "How did they find her body, anyway?"

C is for Coronary.

"What?"

"M — the homeless woman. The ghost — " The word came more easily now. "I just..."

"Oh, that old broad. The city's tearing the building down. They sent some guys in to inspect the place and found her body."

That was a shame. The warehouse had good, quiet energy. He wondered what would be built in its place, how long it would have taken for Millie's body to be discovered otherwise.

"There, the fucking birds are safe. Can we fucking go now?" Hamilton was already turning the ignition.

Harlan nodded, then froze, his neck stiff. "Wait. There's something..." He frowned. There was a prickling at the edge of his senses — the ones that detected ghosts, not the ordinary sort. Something dark.

Ignoring him, Hamilton drove away before Harlan could home in on the feeling, and soon he'd forgotten about it, washed away by the wailing country music, the smells of the city and the flood of ghosts they passed.

Hamilton dropped Harlan off in front of his apartment building. "Half an hour late. Only one ghost down. Fucking pitiful." He reached past Harlan and opened the passenger side door. "We'll do better tomorrow, *right*?" he asked, the inflection in his voice making it clear that 'we' meant '*you*'. The cop had done little enough to help dispatch the ghost. Harlan might be a glorified janitor, but that made the cop a glorified chauffer.

Harlan shrugged and unsnapped his seatbelt. *C is for Cataclysm*. One that would swallow this guy up, or maybe just Harlan. Either way was fine with him. "Sure."

"Nine a.m. Tomorrow. Here."

Biting back a sarcastic, "Yes, sir!" Harlan just nodded, opened the car door wider and slid out.

Great, more of this to look forward to tomorrow. At least the ghost part had been mercifully easy. It was the human part that had sucked. Harlan wondered how long he had to do this before he could retire and collect a pension, tried not to think about the statistics — police mediums tended to die young, killed either by ghosts or the toll of years of expending psychic energy.

At least then he wouldn't have to work with C. Hamilton for long.

C is for Cranky. No, that one was too obvious.

Chapter Five

Harlan came to an abrupt halt, almost falling down the narrow concrete stairs. Luckily, there was no one behind him or they would have bumped into him. With his luck, they'd both fall and break their necks — or at least *he* would.

The upstairs area was a fairly normal bar — tables, chairs, tastefully lit drinks on display — but down here…

Officer Hamilton smirked up at him from the bottom of the steps, and two things were immediately obvious to Harlan — the man had known what kind of place the next ghost was haunting and he'd let Harlan walk into it blind, just to laugh at his reaction.

Take a picture. It lasts longer, asshole, Harlan thought, mouthing the last word silently when Hamilton turned away in response to someone's question. *Asshole.* The word felt good on his lips, sculpting his tongue, even if he couldn't give it volume.

"Hurry the fuck up!"

Part of Harlan, a very large part, wanted to turn and run back through the heavy, non-descript door at the top of the stairs, but he also didn't want to give Officer Fuckface the satisfaction. As slowly and with as much dignity as he could manage, considering that he probably looked like he'd just seen a fucking yeti shamble past him, Harlan descended the rest of the stairs.

The room was deceptively spacious, stretching back almost the full length of the building, though its contents distracted him from looking very far ahead. It was broken up into little areas, marked out with white lines on the black-tiled floor. In each area was a…device, for lack of a better word. No two areas had the same contraption, but they all bristled with straps, chains and shiny hardware, clearly designed to keep people in place.

The place looked like a bizarre mishmash of a medieval torture dungeon and a trendy gym. It was spotlessly clean, with a spray bottle next to each piece of equipment. There were no screams resounding off the matte-black walls, though that might simply have been because the equipment wasn't currently in use. The room was lit by overhead fluorescents, and Harlan could see smaller pot lights above each station, presumably for mood lighting when the room was used for its intended purpose, rather than dispelling ghosts. What that purpose might be—or if he even wanted to find out—Harlan wasn't certain.

It smelled like a combination dungeon-gym, as well—sweat, leather and metal, overlaid with the scent of cleaner. It also, unlike either of those locations, smelled like sex.

Before he could think too deeply about why his dick was getting hard at the same time as his balls tried to crawl back up into his abdomen for safety, Hamilton waved him over, sharply.

"Do your thing. Let's get out of this freak show." He laughed. "Unless you like it here."

Part of him...did, and he wasn't going to think about that. At least not right now.

Harlan's face grew hot. *Is Hamilton telepathic? Does he know what I was just thinking?* Or maybe, Occam's Razor, he'd simply noticed Harlan's growing erection. *Fuck.*

He didn't see any ghosts from where he stood, meaning he had to go deeper into the room. He occasionally had to turn sideways to avoid brushing the bizarre equipment. Cleaning spray or not, he didn't want to touch any of it.

"Nothing here will bite. Well, unless you ask real nice."

Harlan jumped, startled by the voice. His eyes had been mostly closed, hands in front of him as he sought the elusive ghost. There had to be one here, somewhere. There had to be, or he wouldn't have been called here. He didn't think even Officer Hamilton was quite enough of an asshole to bring him here just for shock value, but maybe that was just wishful thinking on his part.

"Sorry?" he managed, once his heart had slowed enough for speech.

"Sorry I scared you! I'm Charles. Charles Moore." The stranger looked to be in his late twenties or early thirties, with rich brown eyes and short black hair with a few hints of silver. His skin was a few shades darker than Harlan's. He was quite a bit shorter than Harlan was, but wider, and his presence made him seem to take up more room. His arms were muscular and well-defined. He was wearing a full-length apron over a black T-shirt and jeans, and holding a clipboard. He was probably the bartender from upstairs, called down to let the police in.

Harlan took a moment to reply, having to mentally shift from dealing with the dead to dealing with the living. "Harlan," he said, softly, taking the man's hand, glancing down and to the side rather than meeting Charles' eyes while they shook, pulling away as soon as he could.

"It's nice to meet you, Harlan. You looked kind of nervous, which is why I came over to talk to you. I hope you don't mind. I hope I'm not distracting you! I'm not sure how...this" — he waved his hands at the empty air between Harlan and Officer Hamilton — "works. Nobody's ever died here before. And I know what you must be thinking, but the guy who died — whose ghost is haunting the place — wasn't playing. He was from the delivery company, dropping off a new St. Andrew's cross." He pointed with one thumb over his shoulder, indicating one of the pieces of equipment — two planks forming an X, covered in black leather padding, and, of course, the ubiquitous chains, straps and other assorted hardware.

"He died of a heart attack. He'd never even been here before. Everything that happens here is between consenting adults. No one is ever forced into doing something against their will." Charles laughed, softly. "Sorry. I tend to get a little carried away, talking about safety. I just wanted you to know that this wasn't some kind of grisly sex-dungeon murder." Charles scanned

Harlan's face, then nodded. "I'll let you finish. Out of curiosity—have you seen anything…interesting…yet?"

Lots. It took Harlan a moment to realize that, while the bondage gear was interesting to him, Charles saw it every day. "A ghost?"

Charles nodded.

Harlan shook his head. "No, nothing." Not even the sparkle that meant a ghost was present but not currently visible.

Charles shrugged. "Well, someone dies in a place like this and rumours get started. Someone sees a shadow they can't explain, hears something during the day when the place is empty…and you've got a ghost. Right?"

Now it was Harlan's turn to shrug. "I guess," he replied, not sure what else to say, what he was *expected* to say.

Charles laughed. "I hope that's all this is, anyways. All these days I've been shut down are killing me."

That caught Harlan's attention. "You own this…place?" He wasn't sure what to call it—a dungeon, a house of ill repute? If it had a name, Charles hadn't said it, and Harlan hadn't seen it outside. There had been nothing to indicate that the building was anything but an old, brick residence, with nothing on or over the door but the building's number.

"Yep. It's all mine. Everything the light touches." Grinning, Charles spread his arms, taking in the room and all the unsettling—and unsettlingly arousing—furniture.

"That's…nice." *'That's nice?' What the fuck?*

Hamilton whistled for him, like he was a dog, clapping his hands a moment later. "We're not fucking paying you to flirt. Find the ghost, get rid of it and let's go." He tapped his wrist with a meaningful look at Harlan, though he wasn't wearing a watch.

Harlan opened his mouth to protest, to say he hadn't been flirting — probably — but decided there was no point. He continued scanning the room, looking for any sign of a ghost or even a sparkle.

Not, however, before he noticed Charles frowning at Hamilton.

A few minutes later, Harlan shook his head, shoulders drawing together when both men's attention fell on him. "There's no ghost," he said, barely above a whisper.

"What?"

Clearing his throat, Harlan repeated, "There's no ghost here. Never has been, as far as I can tell."

Hamilton had been lounging against the wall next to the stairs...as far from the dungeon equipment as he could be, letting Harlan brave the labyrinth of metal and leather on his own. Now he looked up, scowling. "Well, look again. We got a call about this place, and one of the coroner's guys says she saw a ghost, and I trust her word a hell of a lot more than I trust yours."

Harlan's breathing sped up, dangerously fast. He needed get out of here, now, caught between Hamilton's glare and Charles' look of concern. He brushed past Officer Hamilton and stumbled up the stairs, past the bar, through the grey-steel door, out into the fresh air. Well, as fresh as it could be in an alley lined with Dumpsters and grease bins. Even the smell of rancid fat was preferable to the stink of leather, sex and sweat right now, and there were no people here, looking at him expectantly or otherwise. Not yet, anyway. He doubted he'd be left alone for long.

Right on cue, the door banged open behind him. "You did *not* just walk out on me!" Officer Hamilton growled, his voice mere decibels away from shouting.

Guiltily pulling his thumbnail from his mouth, Harlan hunched his shoulders, kept his head down and started walking back to the parked police cruiser. Hamilton could shoot him or handcuff him if he wanted, but Harlan wasn't going back down there of his own free will, especially when there was no ghost for him to deal with.

A pause, an exasperated sigh, then the sound of Hamilton's heavy boots behind him, the beep-click of the car being unlocked.

Indulging himself in a brief, triumphant smile, Harlan climbed into the passenger seat and buckled his seatbelt with a satisfying click.

* * * *

Harlan was greeted by a surly, "What the fuck?" when he got into the police cruiser the next morning at exactly eight-fifty-eight and four seconds.

A thousand snarky comments that would never be spoken aloud crossed Harlan's mind. *Was Tim Horton's out of your favorite donut? Did you break your handcuffs?* He stayed silent, hoping 'the fuck' had nothing to do with him.

"Dispatch got a call last night."

Okay. That seemed like a normal occurrence.

"Someone saw a ghost."

Again, not that unusual, not to mention their combined jobs. No matter how quickly Harlan and other police mediums worked, there were too few of them to keep up with the rate of people dying.

"At the place where, yesterday, *you* told me there was *no* fucking ghost."

Fuck. It *was* about him. Harlan gulped, his breathing ragged, feeling the blood rush away from his head. He felt faint and nauseous. "I... I..."

"'I, I,'" Hamilton mocked, sneering. "I got torn a new one about this, and shit flows downstream, so I'm passing it on to you." He reached out, his blunt-tipped finger stopping just short of touching Harlan's chest.

Hamilton had never actually touched him, Harlan realized. *Huh.* He wondered if the cop was a little afraid of him — not that he had any reason to be, but fear was anything but reasonable. Lots of people had been afraid of Harlan's abilities, including his own parents. He was used to it.

He was still trying to decide if what Hamilton had said was a mixed metaphor or just a horrible mental image when Hamilton pulled away from the curb, tires squealing. Then all of Harlan's concentration was devoted to holding down his breakfast.

They drove in uncomfortable silence, Harlan's mind racing. There hadn't been a ghost in that...dungeon. There *hadn't*. There was no way anyone had seen a ghost there unless one had arrived in the last twenty-four hours, which was extremely unlikely. Contrary to popular belief, ghosts could roam from where they'd died or been buried, but they did tend to be homebodies. If a second person had died there in as many days, that was troubling.

Fuck. Harlan forced himself to slow his breathing.

In... This wasn't his fuck-up.

Out... It was like Charles had said, a shadow. A mouse. Whatever.

In... Not a ghost.

Out... He'd done nothing wrong. There was nothing wrong with him. He'd seen the lobby ghost this morning on his way out.

In... Hadn't he?

Out... Yes, he had. Someone had walked right through her.

In, slow.

Out, slower.

Hamilton lunged at him and Harlan cowered in his seat, afraid the cop was going to hit him, but the man only flung his door open, violently.

Glad to get away from Hamilton, Harlan undid his seatbelt and slid out of the car.

There was a blank, metal security door leading into the bar slash dungeon. Its name was Rattling Chains. He'd looked it up online, only so he knew what to call it. That, and for no other reason.

The door was locked. He knocked, tentatively at first, then harder when no one answered.

Charles opened the door, holding it wide for Harlan with a grin. "C'mon in. The others are downstairs already."

Others? Oh God. What am I about to walk in to? He followed Charles down the stairs reluctantly. He wasn't sure if he was relieved or disturbed to see a woman in a tan trench coat wearing a police badge. Did that mean something official was going on, or something *really* kinky? Both her and the woman beside her were still dressed, at least.

The woman wearing the badge frowned at them when they entered, pressing a finger to her lips. Both Charles and Harlan nodded, silently watching. Harlan still didn't know *what* they were watching. Both women were just standing there. Maybe they hadn't quite started yet?

He heard the sound of heavy boots on the stairs and did his best not to roll his eyes or groan when Hamilton stepped into view. He stopped close to Harlan, closer than Harlan would've liked. "They had to call in another team over this," he hiss-whispered. "A more *experienced* team that's got better things to do than fuck around with beginner-level ghosts like this!"

"Quiet, please," the woman in the trench coat murmured, shooting a disapproving look at both of them before turning back to the shorter woman in front of her and giving her an encouraging nod.

Oh! The willowy woman staring into space must be a medium, the plainclothes officer her escort.

Harlan frowned. Why couldn't he have gotten paired up with someone helpful and supportive, a partner, like those two women? The officer had done the speaking for the duo, dealing with the mundane while letting her partner concentrate on the otherworldly.

Instead, he'd gotten stuck with Officer Sourpuss.

The other psychic's eyes unfocused. Her expression was somehow both dreamy and direct at the same time. She looked ridiculous, and Harlan wondered if that was how he looked when communing with the dead. He hoped not.

Her arms drifted up and out, trailing through the air as though it were water. "He's here," she said, the first words Harlan had heard her speak. She pointed very deliberately into an alcove in one of the corners closest to the door. There were curtains that could be drawn across it, but they were currently open. It had a small table, two chairs and piles of soft cushions and neatly folded blankets. It looked...cozy. If Harlan had to be a ghost—and he sincerely hoped he never became one—it looked like a nice place to haunt.

The alcove was empty. Harlan couldn't see so much as the slightest distortion, any hint of the sparkle that usually let him know a ghost was nearby. He wanted to believe the police medium was lying for some inexplicable reason, but that explanation made less sense than the obvious. Occam's Razor. Harlan, for whatever reason and however temporarily, could no longer sense ghosts.

The woman began quietly questioning the ghost, while her partner stayed close and supervised, occasionally taking notes. Harlan kept his distance.

Hamilton rounded on Harlan, so angry his words burned where they hit, as though he were spitting sparks on Harlan's skin. "What. The. Fuck."

Harlan recoiled, glancing around the room for help, support. He briefly considered approaching the other officer, but all her attention was on the woman speaking to the ghost. The capable psychic, the one who could see and speak to ghosts all the time. When she was supposed to—*required* to—not just at the worst possible moments. Someone who wasn't fucking useless. For all the mental name-calling Harlan had thrown Hamilton's way, the cop had been right about him from the beginning.

Charles frowned, looking like he might speak up, but Hamilton cut him off with a curt motion of his hand.

Hamilton grabbed Harlan's arm and hauled him out of the dungeon, past the empty, darkened bar and into the alley, the smell of leather and sex changing into alcohol and sweat, then to rotting garbage.

Harlan didn't resist, blinking in the sudden glare of sunlight that hit him directly in the eyes.

"Go home. Take a fucking... I don't know! Eat a mushroom. Drink some tea. Cool your...chakras! Do whatever the fuck it takes." Throwing his hands up in disgust, Hamilton stalked off down the alley toward the police cruiser, kicking anything small and loose he encountered and muttering under his breath.

Halfway to the street he turned, shooting Harlan an exasperated look when he saw he hadn't moved. "Well? You coming?"

That interaction had been almost...friendly. Harlan did an awkward half-trot to catch up, smiling just a little once Hamilton had turned his back. Even the too-loud country music and the nostril-assailing air freshener scent couldn't wipe it off his face.

Chapter Six

Hamilton dropped Harlan off at his apartment building, then peeled out, tires squealing, almost before the car door had closed. Reaching into his pocket, Harlan felt the familiar, sharp-edged bulk of the broken keychain he still hadn't replaced. Running a thumb over the cracked side, he felt the edges beginning to wear smooth. Maybe he'd keep it.

He hadn't complained about the tricky lock, either. It was almost a way of keeping his apartment a little more secure from the outside world — except, of course, from the neighbour who'd shown him the trick in the first place.

Still buoyed up by Hamilton's unexpected show of affection — or at least that was how Harlan chose to interpret it — Harlan nodded a friendly acknowledgment to the lobby repeater, even though she wasn't aware of him. He ignored the bewildered look thrown his way by a woman leaving the building, when Harlan greeted the apparently empty air but not her.

Harlan decided to think of a name for the repeater. Libby, maybe. He snorted, groaning at his own terrible idea. *Libby from the Lobby. Lobby Libby. Right.*

He should feel like shit, and he knew it. He'd failed so spectacularly that the police had brought in another team to do his fucking job, and the other medium had been less powerful than him. He'd been able to feel *that*, but not to see the fucking ghost the first time. What was wrong with him? He wished the solution was as simple as the one Hamilton had suggested — drink some tea. Balance his aura. *Fuck.*

It wasn't until he reached his apartment, key in hand, that he realized what had just happened. He ran back downstairs, fortunately not encountering anyone — the advantage to taking the stairs rather than the elevator — praying that Libby would still be there. Apparently, the stupid name had stuck.

There she was — pace, nervous nail biting, step, step, flicker. Repeat.

He could see her.

He could *see* her!

Waiting until she was clear of the door so he could pass without walking through her, he ran outside. For the first time in his life, he went in search of ghosts. They were everywhere, just the way they always were — a sparkle here, a crushed skull there, but he could *see* all of them.

He forced himself to stop, to breathe, to look at this logically. What was the same, and what was different? He was alone. Hamilton wasn't with him, but he'd seen ghosts when Hamilton was around before, of course, so that was unlikely to be the problem.

The policewoman and her medium? Again, he had no reason to believe the psychic had been lying. What did that leave? The location? Ghosts being spread unevenly, it was hard to test, but Harlan couldn't think of an unwarded building where he'd never been able to see a ghost before.

His shoulders slumped, and he started trudging back to the apartment. He'd felt so close to an answer, but he couldn't think of any other...

Charles.

Of course. That was the only other variable. Charles had been there both times, and Harlan hadn't been able to see a ghost on either occasion. He didn't know why Charles would affect only him and not the other medium. Hell, he didn't even know why, if he was correct, Charles *had* an effect on him in the first place, but it was the only other variable he could think of.

Wildly relieved that he at least had something to go on, he flagged down a passing taxi, which miraculously stopped. His luck was holding. He couldn't remember the address of the dungeon, and he didn't want to describe the place he was looking for, but he remembered the name of a street it was close to. The cabby was happy to accommodate his uncertainty. If they had to circle the block a few times, it meant a larger fare for him. Finally, Harlan spotted the alley and directed the cab driver to turn.

He hopped out of the car, completely forgetting he had to pay, then he realized he didn't have any money on him, anyway. He didn't have time for this, and the cab driver was shouting at him...

The door to the dungeon opened and there was Charles.

He looked surprised to see Harlan, naturally. The other medium had almost certainly cleared the ghost, and what would a fuck-up psychic be doing here again, but he only raised an eyebrow and took a quick assessment of the situation. Shooting Harlan a brief smile that brought him back from the brink of hyperventilating, Charles dug his worn, brown-leather wallet out of the back pocket of his equally worn jeans, pulled out twenty dollars and handed it to the red-faced cabby, who promptly drove off.

"Hey," Charles said, tucking away his wallet.

Harlan squeaked in response, cleared his throat, tried again. "Hey." *Brilliant. Fuck.*

"I'm guessing you're here for one of two reasons. Either you're wondering why you couldn't see the ghost when the other psychic could, or" — he grinned — "you liked what you saw down there and you couldn't stop thinking about it." Looking Harlan up and down in a hungry way that Harlan had witnessed directed at other people, read about, but never personally experienced, Charles said, "Personally, I'm hoping it's the second option."

The words, that look, went straight to Harlan's dick. He blushed, shaking his head. "N-no, nothing like that. I mean, yes. The first." *Just* the first. *Right.*

There was a look of disappointment so brief that Harlan might have imagined it, then Charles nodded. "C'mon downstairs, then." He propped the door open for Harlan, who did his best to ignore the ominous sound of the heavy door clicking back into place behind them.

Trying to hurry without looking like he was fleeing, Harlan walked the now-familiar route through the bar, down the stairs and into the dungeon.

"I'll be right down," Charles called. "I was in the middle of taking out the trash when you got here." That made it sound like Harlan had been expected, invited, hadn't simply shown up unannounced and unwelcomed.

A little nervous to be down there alone, Harlan took a tentative step into the dungeon proper. Only a few lights were on, making the hulking shapes of the...equipment...look like prehistoric monsters lurking in the darkness.

Sparkle.

There, movement out of the corner of his eye. He whirled, came face-to-face with a bewildered-looking, uniformed ghost. It made no move to harm or even approach Harlan, but its sudden appearance startled a scream out of him.

Rapid footsteps coming down the stairs, then Charles was there and the ghost was *gone*. Not even the sparkle remained.

"What. The. Fuck," Harlan whispered, echoing Hamilton's earlier words. He stood there, blinking, while Charles asked what was wrong.

"Wait, wait, just...go back upstairs."

"Are you sure you're all right?" Charles asked.

"I'm fine, please, just..." Harlan made a shooing motion, his mind racing.

Casting him a final, doubtful look, Charles turned and went up the stairs.

Still nothing.

"Farther!" Harlan called, the mad rush of inspiration that had struck him making him bold. He heard the floorboards creak above him. "More! Go outside!" he demanded. As soon as the steel door clicked shut behind Charles...*sparkle.*

Ghost.

Harlan ran upstairs after Charles, throwing open the door and almost hitting the poor man with it. He grabbed Charles' shoulders, shaking him a little—not that it did much. Charles was shorter but far outweighed him. "It's you!"

Charles carefully peeled Harlan's hands off his arms one at a time, frowning. "You're scaring me a little. Let's get you inside, give you some water..."

Harlan waved a hand dismissively, pacing in tiny circles between Charles and the door. "It's you. It's something about *you*."

"Look... If you aren't going to explain what's going on, I'm going to have to ask you to leave, okay?" Charles spoke in the calm, slow manner people used with the mentally unstable, and that snapped Harlan out of his reverie.

Breathe in, slow. Breathe out, slower.

Of course Charles thought he was crazy, and if he ever wanted him to think otherwise, he had to calm down and explain himself now. "The ghost is still down there."

Charles nodded. "Yeah. The woman they brought in said she needed...I don't know, something...before she could get rid of it. She's coming back tomorrow—another night I have to be closed." He shrugged. "At least I'm getting lots of cleaning done."

Harlan shook his head, wildly. "No. No, I can get rid of him right here, right *now*. I just need you to stay here." He hoped. None of this made sense, and he was running off instinct, but it felt right. "Stay here. I'll come back up when I'm done."

Charles blinked. "Well. I guess it can't hurt to try. I'd still have to wait until tomorrow to open, when the place has been officially cleared, but..."

Barely acknowledging that Charles had spoken, Harlan slipped inside and hurried down the stairs.

The ghost was still standing in the same spot Harlan had first seen him, looking forlorn. "Hey. I was hoping you'd come back. You can see me, right?" He waved.

"I can see you."

"You were here yesterday too, but you couldn't see me then."

"That's right. Sorry."

"That's okay. I just thought it was kinda odd, because" — he frowned — "it *felt* like you should've been able to see me. Does that make sense?"

"It does, actually." Harlan was in too much of a rush to explain the supernatural semantics, what he thought was going on here. "Do you know you're — Do you know what happened to you?" Still, impatience was no excuse to be rude.

The ghost nodded. "I died. Right over there." He pointed to the floor a few feet away, and Harlan automatically turned. It looked just like the rest of the floor. It had always bothered Harlan a little that no one could just *tell*, by looking, where a human had died. That the deaths didn't leave a trace on their surroundings. On the other hand, the world would have gotten pretty full of traces.

"I'm sorry."

The man tried to look nonchalant, but his expression was miserable.

"Do you know why you're still here?"

He stared down at his translucent, ergonomic shoes. "I'm worried people will think I'm a freak because I died here."

"You... They won't. I'm sure..." Harlan wasn't sure he believed himself. "Is that what's keeping you here?"

He nodded. "I don't want my kids finding out about this when they're older, being teased at school..."

Ugh. Harlan could see — sort of — where the man was coming from, though he found it a little odd that the man seemed more concerned about *how* he'd died than the fact that he was dead. He also wasn't sure how to deal with this, how to prove to the man that wasn't how he'd be remembered.

"Wait here a second. I'll be right back. I promise."

The man stepped forward, looking for an instant like he might try and stop Harlan, but he just nodded.

Harlan hurried up the stairs, through the bar and out into the alley, but the door wouldn't open all the way. He pushed again, harder, almost falling on his face when it swung freely.

"Ow," Charles said wryly, rubbing his arm.

"Sorry!"

Charles laughed. "Well, I probably shouldn't have been standing right in front of it. What's up?"

"Do you have today's newspaper?"

"You're joking, right? I mean, I guess I could look it up on my phone."

Harlan shook his head. "I think it has to be a real — physical — one."

Charles' eyes narrowed for a moment while he studied Harlan's face. "There's a store just up the street that I think sells papers. You want me to go get one?"

"Please? It's important, and I promise I'll explain after." He had to restrain himself from giving Charles a little push to send him on his way, but he didn't want to leave the ghost alone long enough that he might think Harlan had abandoned him.

Charles sighed. "All right. I'm taking a lot on faith here."

Harlan nodded vigorously. "I know, and I really appreciate it."

"I'll be right back." Charles jogged slowly up the alley, seeming to have picked up on some of Harlan's urgency.

Harlan returned to the dungeon, feeling oddly ashamed by the open look of relief on the ghost's face. "What's your name?" He was only slightly fonder of—and better at—small talk with the dead than the living.

"Chris. Chris Kijeck." He held out a hand, then frowned at it. "Can you...? Can I?"

"I *can* shake hands with you, because I'm a medium, but it's...uncomfortable for me."

"Sorry." Chris withdrew his hand.

"No problem." A few moments of semi-uncomfortable silence. What was taking Charles so long?

No.

It had only been a few minutes since Charles had left. It just *felt* like forever.

"No offense, but that cop who was with you, your partner, seems like kind of an ass."

That startled a laugh out of Harlan. "Yes, yes, he does."

Chris elbowed Harlan in the side, his arm sinking in a few inches. Harlan did his best not to flinch or gasp at the icy cold filling his chest. "You shouldn't put up with that. You deserve better, man."

"Thanks."

Luckily, he was spared having to talk more about Hamilton by the outer door opening and Chris vanishing as soon as Charles stepped inside. He came downstairs and handed over the newspaper with a snap. "Need anything else?"

Harlan shook his head, eager to get this over with.

"Do mediums usually need newspapers for this kind of thing? Is that what the other medium was missing?"

Harlan laughed again. "No, not really." He stared at Charles as pointedly as he could without being rude, especially because he was standing in a building Charles owned.

"You need me to go back outside?" Charles guessed, looking resigned.

"Yes, please. I'll come up and get you when I'm done."

"All right. It's a good thing you're cute."

Harlan hoped his blush would fade before Charles made it into the alley and Chris snapped back into view—although, from what Chris had said earlier, it sounded like he'd *always* been able to see Harlan, even when Harlan couldn't see him. *Shit.*

Still... Charles thought he was cute?

As soon as he heard the door shut above them, Chris reappeared.

"You have a sudden craving for news?" He sounded a little peeved.

Ignoring him for the moment, Harlan flipped through the newspaper. He got to the end without seeing what he was looking for, but it had to be there, didn't it? *Aha—obituaries.* He ran a finger down the page. There. "Christopher William Kijeck?"

"Yeah?"

He read through the block of text quickly, then shook his head. "Nothing about where or how you died. Just 'beloved husband' and 'loving father of two'."

"Let me see." Chris held out his hand for the paper and Harlan automatically handed it to him, both of them laughing when it drifted to the floor.

Harlan bent and picked it up, holding it so Chris could read.

Chris nodded, apparently satisfied. "Okay. Thanks so much for doing this for me."

"It's my job. I mean, you're welcome."

"Can you see that?" Chris asked, staring at something behind Harlan.

"Yeah." Harlan didn't have to turn to know what Chris was talking about. A rend in the veil between life and...whatever came after. He knew it wouldn't look the same to him as it did to Chris. "Go on."

"It's good?"

"It's good," Harlan agreed. He watched Chris go through the portal to 'the other side', then walked back upstairs.

Flushed with success, Harlan pushed the door open again—more carefully this time. Charles was still standing in the alley, waiting for him.

"He's gone. The ghost is gone." Instead of stopping there, Harlan blurted, "Come home with me."

Charles laughed. "Look... I'm grateful that you sent the ghost packing, but I'm not..."

Now Harlan was blushing again. "No. No, it's not like that! I just need you to... I have a theory that..."

After a long, assessing glance, Charles said, "Fine. Where do you live?"

"I, uh, don't have a car..." Harlan scuffed at a large stone embedded in the alley pavement. He didn't even have a driver's license.

"Ah. All right, well, I should've figured that out when you showed up in a taxi. I guess I'll get my car...if you trust me to drive you."

Harlan's internal response was an immediate, visceral *Yes!* He wasn't sure why. He hardly knew Charles, and he wasn't usually this trusting of anyone, even people he'd known for years. For all he knew,

Charles had killed the deliveryman who'd died in the dungeon and was planning to kill Harlan next. But Harlan's body trusted Charles, even if his mind had doubts.

He forced himself to pause, to look as though he were considering the offer.

He'd opened his mouth to agree when something else occurred to him. Something strange and unprecedented was going on with his power, something that had never happened outside a ghost-warded room, something he'd never read or even heard about, and by all appearances, it centred around this man. If he spent too much time with Charles, would he lose his powers permanently?

Charles didn't feel at all threatening, but Harlan was suddenly leery of being alone in a car with him.

On the other hand, he'd been alone with the man in a literal dungeon. Charles could easily have grabbed him, strapped him down to one of those mysterious, bulky contraptions, and…and…Harlan didn't even know, really. He scowled at his sudden, unwelcome erection.

Charles laughed, sounding uncertain for the first time. "Sorry… I didn't mean to scare you. I understand if you don't want a ride from a guy you just met." He reached out and lightly touched Harlan's hand — the first time they'd come into physical contact.

Harlan half-expected to feel something like an electric shock, a tingle at least, but there was nothing. Well, nothing but warm, rough skin on his own much paler, softer hand, and that was almost more extraordinary. He imagined he could feel Charles' pulse everywhere their hands touched, an answering beat throbbing through his groin.

"You're not really afraid of me, are you?" Charles asked. "That sounds like something someone scary would say, doesn't it?"

That startled a laugh out of Harlan, and they shared a fleeting smile.

He needed to figure out to what extent this man was affecting his powers. The quickest, easiest, least awkward solution was to get a ride with him. Harlan shook his head. "Let's go." Not waiting for Charles, he strode off down the alley, head down, shoulders slightly hunched.

"The car is this way. And I need to know where you live."

Chapter Seven

"Stay here. Please," Harlan added, as an afterthought. He was so excited, so tense, that he could barely hold still long enough to undo his seatbelt. He hated being so obvious with his emotional state. It made him feel vulnerable, but he knew he was on the edge — or maybe the *precipice* — of a major discovery.

Still wearing the same bemused expression he'd had, more or less, since Harlan's arrival in the alley, Charles nodded.

Niceties out of the way, Harlan let himself out of the car and hurried to the apartment building, moving as fast as he could without looking like he was hurrying. Fumbling the front door open, he frantically searched the lobby for Libby.

For a long, desperate moment he didn't see her — maybe this had nothing to do with Charles after all. Maybe his powers were just fading on their own, and what would he do then? He was useless. Without them, he had no skills, nothing. The Centre wouldn't take him back. He'd no longer be psychic. Maybe he could work there as a janitor or something.

Fuck.

She had to be there. She had—

There. Step, step, flicker. Right where she should be.

Okay.

Harlan ran outside, too exhilarated to care how stupid he looked. After hurrying around to the driver's side, Harlan yanked the door handle. It was locked.

A moment of hesitation, then Charles turned the car on and rolled down the window.

Bent nearly double—Harlan was built like a scarecrow, all height and knobbly joints—he fought to keep his voice calm and steady. "Come inside with me. Please." He could see the doubt in Charles' eyes, see him considering simply rolling up the window and driving away, but then he nodded. Turning off the car and rolling the window back up without ever looking away from Harlan, Charles stepped out.

As relieved as Harlan was, he had no idea why. If their positions were reversed, he'd be at the end of the block by now.

He barely came up to Harlan's nipples, a thought that Harlan immediately regretted. He felt himself blushing, and he hoped Charles wouldn't notice. He walked away quickly and opened the front door, holding it for Charles. He almost turned around to make sure Charles was actually following him, and he was relieved when he heard footsteps behind him.

"What—?" Charles began, but Harlan silenced him with a gesture, too excited to explain now, emboldened by his excitement.

Harlan's eyes darted around the lobby. No sign of Libby. So far, his theory was right. "Okay. Go back outside."

Harlan could see a protest forming behind Charles' lips, creasing the corners of his rich brown eyes, but there was no time for that. Harlan had to know. *Now*.

"Please. Just one more time, then I'll explain everything. Promise." Harlan clenched his hands into fists with the effort of not pushing Charles outside.

Charles turned around without a word, and Harlan watched him retreat to the sidewalk. He found himself pacing Libby's usual route as he watched, wondering if Charles would keep walking, get back in his car, leave. Maybe that would be for the best, actually. Whatever effect Charles had on his powers, all Harlan had to do was stay away from him and he'd be fine. Hopefully. If the damage hadn't already been done.

The effects on his libido were an entirely different matter, one Harlan didn't want to consider, especially right now.

Charles stopped before he reached his car, watching Harlan as intently as Harlan was watching him through the lobby window.

No sparkle.

Harlan waved his hands, motioning for Charles to go farther.

One step back, three. He was on the boulevard, almost into the street, and how much farther could he reasonably ask the man to go, then...*sparkle*.

Harlan gave Charles a quick thumbs-up, beaming. He curled his toes inside his canvas sneakers, a silent, hidden display of his delight. After a quick visual confirmation — there was Libby, right where she belonged, again — he waved Charles back.

Charles glanced over his shoulder at his car, clearly considering whether it wouldn't be better to simply get in and drive away. But he came back.

Harlan unlocked the door for him, held it open, still grinning. "Thank you," he said, half whispering.

Charles nodded. He looked hesitant, but he stepped inside.

Just like that, Libby — and her sparkle — vanished.

Harlan let out a deep, deep breath. One he'd been holding since the car had picked him up at the Centre, it felt like. "I was right."

"Right about...? You said you'd explain everything," Charles prompted.

"Yes. Right. But not here."

Charles' expression soured.

"J-Just upstairs. Please. In my apartment. Just to talk," he rushed to add, seeing Charles' expression change again, the shift in his shoulders as he prepared to turn, to leave.

Charles laughed, shaking his head. "One of us is crazy, but damned if I know which. All right, let's go." He walked towards the elevator.

Of course. That was what normal people did.

Swallowing hard, hoping Charles wouldn't notice how pale he was, how badly he was shaking, Harlan followed Charles to the claustrophobic box. He caught a glimpse of himself in the elevator's shiny, brass doors before they slid open. His golden reflection looked terrified.

He closed his eyes, just for a moment. Opened them for a tentative peek around the elevator compartment. Empty, aside from Charles, who looked ready to step out again.

One big step, and Harlan was inside. He hadn't been in an elevator since he was five, just before his parents dumped him at the Centre.

"Which floor?" Charles asked.

Jaw so tight with fear he couldn't open his mouth to respond, Harlan reached past Charles and pressed the 'four' button. The elevator lurched into motion. Was that normal? Barely containing a squeak, Harlan grabbed the brass railing that ran around three sides of the elevator car. He clutched it like a lifeline, his eyes squeezed tightly shut, too afraid even to worry about what Charles thought of him. He shouldn't have gotten in. He should've taken the stairs, made some excuse — he needed the exercise, he had claustrophobia… Fuck, he'd made a mistake.

He realized he was holding his breath and forced himself to breathe, but it was too loud. Charles had probably heard.

Harlan did cry out when something touched him, shrinking away from the presence.

"Are you all right?" Charles' voice, and now Harlan realized it was Charles' hand he'd felt on his own.

Stiff with fear and with every muscle tensed, Harlan managed a jerky nod.

"No, you're not." Charles sighed. "Claustrophobic?"

An easy out. Harlan nodded again. "S-Something like that."

Strong, comforting — living — arms wrapped around his middle, drawing him close to a warm, solid body. Charles was shorter, but far sturdier and more muscular. "Hey. I'm sorry. We'll take the stairs down, okay?"

Fuck. If Charles hadn't thought he was completely fucking nuts before...

Charles moved his hand in slow, sure circles on Harlan's back. Normally, Harlan didn't like being touched, even by accident, but Charles was surprisingly comforting. Harlan relaxed, ever so slightly, just enough that his heart didn't stop during the short elevator ride. *Fuck.* Good thing he didn't live on the twenty-fifth floor, though the prospect of walking up and down all those stairs every day might have forced him to overcome his fear.

He opened his eyes a crack, glancing around the elevator car. Still just the two of them. Maybe he could do this on his own eventually.

The elevator dinged, stopped, and the doors slid open.

Charles gave Harlan's hand a quick, firm squeeze, then stepped into the hall.

The elevator door started closing and Harlan still hadn't moved. Charles waved a hand in front of the doors' sensor, and they parted to reveal him still huddled in a corner with his hands in a death grip on the railing. Finger by finger, he forced himself to let go. Then it was easy. He wanted out of there. Two quick steps and he was safe. He could see his door from here.

As quickly and forcefully as he could without being rude, Harlan brushed past Charles, fumbling the key out of his pocket. He forgot about the tricky lock in his hurry and shot Charles an apologetic grin when the key didn't turn.

Charles looked more sympathetic—and perhaps pitying—than annoyed now, but Harlan wasn't sure that was an improvement.

He pressed the doorframe this time, and the door swung open. As always, when he crossed the threshold into his ghost-warded apartment, Harlan felt an avalanche of tension pour off him. "Come in," he invited, carelessly kicking off his shoes and leaving them where they landed. If Charles could deal with Harlan having a full-blown panic attack over an elevator, he could tolerate a little clutter.

There were obligations, things he was expected to do when entertaining guests, things he was supposed to say... "Would you...like some water?"

Charles grinned and kicked off his own shoes — just as haphazardly, Harlan was pleased to see.

"Yes, please. I hope I don't sound like your dad or anything, but you could probably use some too, after..."

He didn't sound anything like Harlan's dad. Harlan's father had been ashamed of him. Still was, as far as Harlan knew, though he'd grown tired of receiving letters he'd sent with 'Return to sender' written on them and he hadn't contacted his family in years.

Rather than telling him to drink water after a fright like that, he'd probably have grabbed Harlan by the arm, shaken him a little and hissed at him to stop being such a baby.

"You don't," Harlan reassured him. He nodded vaguely, then headed for the kitchen. "Make yourself at home," he called back, hoping that was the right thing to say. He'd never really understood the phrase.

He filled two glasses with tap water, offered one to Charles, then sat as far from the other man as possible, on one of the armchairs rather than on the couch beside the guy. He set his own glass, untouched, on the end table beside him.

The armchair looked nice, but it was stiff and unyielding when he sat on it, without the give or comfort of a properly broken-in piece of furniture, and he was glad Charles had chosen the couch instead. He knew it was marginally more comfortable.

Charles took a long swallow of his water—Harlan had to force himself to look away, not watch his throat working and think of—then set it on the coffee table.

"Well," Charles began. He leaned forward, hands between his knees, palms together.

"Well," Harlan repeated, his voice rising at the end, turning it into more of a question than the statement he'd intended it to be.

"I think you offered to explain...everything?" Charles prompted.

Harlan opened his mouth a few times, reconsidered, closed it, then it all tumbled out in a rush. "The other day when I first went to your dun—*club*—I didn't see a ghost, but there *was* one. Obviously. You know that part. And when I went back, I could see it—but only if you weren't in the room with me." He paused, panting a little with the sheer volume of words, the joy of sharing this with someone else, of proving he wasn't just a useless fucking failure. That something was *happening* to him.

None of his lessons at the Centre had even hinted at anything remotely like a...human ghost ward.

Unless... He frowned. How disappointing if it was that simple, after all.

"Do you have any tattoos?" Harlan asked.

Charles raised an eyebrow. "Yeah."

Of course he did. He was the owner of a dungeon slash sex club, and he had several piercings in his ears alone. Harlan's cheeks got hot.

Normally, Harlan couldn't flirt to save his life—not that he'd had much practice. The group of people who were close to his age at the Centre had remained more or less the same, and the one boy he'd had a crush on for years hadn't been interested in Harlan beyond a few furtive blow and hand jobs. Receiving them, of course.

With Charles, he felt like every word he said sounded like a come-on, even though he didn't mean it that way. Not really. Yes, he found Charles attractive, but he wasn't trying to flirt, just to explain...

Harlan shook his head. His mouth was dry, but even the motion of reaching out for his glass of water seemed like it would leave him too vulnerable. This was Harlan's space—it hadn't been for long, but it was his all the same—and Charles had taken it over just by being there, sitting still on the couch. Harlan was so fucked. So, so fucked, but he had to know. He cleared his throat.

"Could I see them?" His voice barely squeaked, and he was unreasonably proud of that.

Charles rolled up his left sleeve, showing a bird—a swallow, maybe—in plain black ink.

Frowning, Harlan decided to just ask, tempting as it was to have Charles undress for him piece by piece. "Are you ghost-warded?"

"Am I what?" Charles rolled down his sleeve again and glanced at the door.

"I can see ghosts..."

Charles snorted. "So I've heard."

"*Except* in places that've been specially warded against them...like this apartment." Some mediums had the ability to create wards, and some non-gifted people were able to copy them precisely enough that they worked, but Harlan couldn't do either. His designs never worked.

Ghost-wards were time-consuming to draw and had to be reapplied every few years — less, if a ghost had attacked them — so it wasn't feasible to have them everywhere.

"I'll be right back." Harlan grabbed a pen and a piece of paper and, squinting at the glowing symbols he could only see in his peripheral vision, he drew a few of them, shoving the paper in Charles' face in his excitement. "They'd look something like this. Maybe you didn't know, or..."

Charles took a long, slow breath, leaning back on his armrest. "No, nothing like that." He paused. "It's me. You can't see ghosts around me. That's what you meant earlier."

Harlan nodded. That had been much easier than he'd expected. He both wanted to stay as close to this man as possible for the rest of his life, so he'd never have to see another burned, mutilated, dismembered ghost — and to put thousands of miles between them. The man's ability — or perhaps *lack* of ability — was dangerous to Harlan.

"Hmm." Resting his left elbow on the couch's armrest, Charles cradled his stubbly jaw in his hands. "I'm guessing, by your reaction, that this doesn't happen all the time."

Harlan shook his head. "Never."

"Never." Charles laughed. "If I were a scientist, I'd want to experiment, see if I could find out more about it. Hell, I'm not much more than a trumped-up bartender and I still do!" He slapped his thigh with his right hand, the sudden sound startling Harlan.

"Sorry," they both said at the same time. Charles laughed again, while Harlan looked away, suddenly engrossed in picking out minute details of the rug.

Harlan's brain finally caught up to his frenzied, erratic thoughts. "I have to make a phone call," he said, leaving before Charles could respond. He knew it was rude, leaving a guest on his own like that. Even though Harlan had very few personal effects and most of them were in the bedroom, it felt strange to have a...*stranger* in his living space unattended. But this couldn't wait.

Hamilton answered with only his last name, on the fifth ring, right before Harlan decided to hang up. He added a barked, "Hello?" when Harlan didn't answer immediately.

"It's me," Harlan murmured, cowed by the ferocity and volume of Hamilton's voice.

"Who is this?" Hamilton asked, sounding peeved. Then again, he always sounded peeved.

"Harlan."

"Oh." Slightly lower volume, slightly less hostile, but not followed by anything else.

"I, um, I figured out what—"

"Speak up. I can't hear you!"

Now that Hamilton had mentioned it, Harlan could hear a sort of background rumble, punctuated by high-pitched, intermittent beeping. "Are you at a construction site?"

"No shit, Sherlock. Now, will you hurry the fuck up? This body's not getting any less squashed."

Ugh. Trying to suppress the mental image—unfortunately, having seen so many ghosts, Harlan had an extensive mental library of almost every kind of death—Harlan was profoundly glad he wasn't at the scene. And hoped he wouldn't be delivered there tomorrow. "Was it a murder?"

"Why? You think you can crack the case with your ghost pals? No, it was a fucking accident, and unless you can summon a giant spatula, get off the phone."

"I can see ghosts again! Well, I always could. It's just...I figured out why. Why I couldn't. Before. But it's fixed now."

"Nine a.m. tomorrow." *Click.*

Setting his phone down on the bedside table—there were two identical tables, one on either side of the bed, even though it was just him—Harlan gave a sigh of relief. One problem solved. Now he just had to get rid of the man in his living room.

Or he could ask him to stay…

No. Bad idea.

Charles was already standing when Harlan returned to the living room. "Well. If you're okay…"

"Yeah."

"I should probably…"

"Yeah."

"So…" After a moment, Charles offered his hand.

Harlan took it, wondering if he was misreading the subtle way Charles shifted his stance, almost like he was inviting Harlan to step in closer for a hug, if he wanted to. He probably was. Almost certainly.

After Charles left, Harlan felt a bit conflicted. Nothing made him happier than having a decision made for him, but now he couldn't help regretting that he hadn't tried to make Charles stay.

Chapter Eight

Harlan liked routine. Some of the other residents at the Centre had rebelled against it, complaining loudly and bitterly that they needed their freedom, but Harlan had never felt that way. Leaving his predictable schedule, having his whole world shaken to pieces, had in some ways been the worst part of being forced to leave the Centre. Rather than having structure provided for him, he had to come up with it on his own, and he quickly found he wasn't very good at it.

Grating as Hamilton was, their work together took up a solid chunk of most of Harlan's days, and it always began promptly at nine a.m. The duration might only be a few hours — or more than twelve, depending on how many problem ghosts they were assigned.

Harlan didn't honestly mind the longer days. Not only did they fill his time, but he also felt like Hamilton opened up to him towards the end of long shifts, becoming a little friendlier and more personable. He was usually back to his curt self by the next day —

sometimes a few days. Harlan was usually given a day to rest if he dispelled more than two or three ghosts.

Most hauntings were easy, quickly becoming almost routine. Harlan found the spirit, talked to it and sent it on its way. A few required a little more force, but none frightened him or were more than he could handle. For the most part, once he'd convinced them they were dead — if they didn't already know — they were as eager to leave as Harlan was to see them disappear.

When he was home, Harlan watched TV and found he didn't care for most of it. He liked nature documentaries. He saw an ad for Netflix while he was online and signed up for a free trial membership. He liked it much more than regular TV, but he didn't have a credit card and wasn't sure how to get one, so he didn't renew his subscription.

He emailed the SPCA, managed to track down the flock of pigeons he'd helped rescue and been assured they were all safe, happy and together.

He thought about Charles a lot — vague fantasies of how he imagined Charles would look, naked and sweaty and stroking Harlan all over or tying him down to one of the mysterious pieces of furniture in his dungeon, grabbing a fistful of his hair and holding a paddle over his naked ass...

Tom emailed him regularly, to check in and remind him of various support groups he could join. There were several that were for psychics of any type, both social and supportive, and two that were medium-specific — one for civilians, one for police. Mediums were rare enough that neither group was very large, but Harlan had never been a joiner, and he was quite content limiting himself to contact with Hamilton, ghosts and cashiers.

He'd originally used the grocery delivery service Tom had mentioned, but he'd found that was actually more stressful. They only took cash, so he had to withdraw some from his account, make sure he had enough and calculate a tip. And now that he was accustomed to thinking of the apartment as *his*, he didn't like letting strangers in, even for a few brief minutes.

There was a small, fairly quiet grocery store only a few minutes' walk from his apartment, and he discovered that he preferred wandering the aisles to checking off boxes online. It encouraged him to try food he normally wouldn't have, enjoying more of his experiments than he'd expected. He started getting at least one box of Pocky every time he bought groceries.

Harlan barely hesitated when he entered the lobby of his apartment building, heading straight for the elevator, exercise be damned. He was *tired*. He'd spent the whole day walking, going from haunted crime scene to haunted crime scene. The ghosts didn't stay neatly in place where they'd died. They drifted off in random directions, forcing Harlan to play a frustratingly cerebral version of *warmer, colder* with his power until he found them. He just wanted to get upstairs to his safely warded apartment and tune out the outside world—living *and* dead.

He stepped into the elevator and pressed the 'four' button. He couldn't help tensing as he watched the brass doors slide shut, so he closed his eyes and quietly hummed an old Billie Holiday tune to keep himself from clutching the railing.

The elevator jerked, startling Harlan to attention. The temperature plummeted and goosebumps raised on Harlan's arms, prickling up the back of his neck. He could see his breath, trailing up and away from him in its hurry to escape. He wished he could follow it out of the small ventilation grate in the elevator's roof. An elevator shaft might be preferable to being stuck in the car with a ghost.

A smell filled the elevator, heavy and unpleasant. It was familiar, but he couldn't quite place it.

Now, he reached behind him, grabbing at the safety railing. It was slippery with condensation and his hand slid off on his first panicked attempt. He didn't dare turn around, take his gaze or his concentration away from the malevolent energy brewing in the middle of the car. His hand met metal, but he pulled away with a cry. The rail was so cold that his hand froze to it and he had to painfully tear it loose. It hurt, but he wanted his hands free. Not that they'd be much help, but he could at least use them to shield his face—although a ghost could simply pass through them. He hated the thought of helplessly facing down an angry ghost with his hands pinioned neatly behind his back.

He was trapped in a haunted elevator...again. He wasn't sure how it was possible. He'd taken the elevator almost every day since he'd first ridden it with Charles. Cautiously at first, in case Charles' dampening ability was the only thing keeping ghosts away, but no spirits had ever materialized here.

Until now.

"No...no, fuck, fuck, fuck," Harlan moaned, watching the spirit slowly coalesce.

It shifted from a bitterly cold shimmer in the air to a heavy, purposeful mist, to a large, vaguely human form, trailing an ectoplasmic shroud.

Not all of Harlan's training had been with docile, harmless ghosts who'd just needed a bit of a nudge to shuffle off the mortal coil.

He'd been as curious as the other kids the first time a massive, unmarked black shipping crate had arrived at the Centre and been unloaded from the back of an equally unmarked black truck.

It had been delivered during one of the regular, academic classes, which were divided by age rather than ability. There had only been two other mediums at the Centre, both much older than Harlan.

He'd sat at his desk while his classmates had pressed their faces to the grille-covered windows, speculating wildly about what might be inside. *I bet it's a lion! Don't be stupid. Why would they give us a* lion? — until the teacher had herded them back into their assigned seats.

Harlan had sat in the middle of the room. He was quiet and non-disruptive, so the teacher didn't need to watch him closely, but he also had a tendency to daydream, sometimes zoning out completely for minutes at a time, tuning out everything happening around him, so he wasn't allowed to sit in the back of the room anymore.

He still hadn't lived down an incident about a year before, when he'd been twelve. While the rest of the class was filing outside for recess, he'd suddenly been overcome by a feeling of complete and utter terror. It hadn't been caused by a ghost — the whole Centre was carefully warded, the wards updated even more frequently than was technically required. This was a formless, sourceless, all-encompassing fear that left him, huddled and shaking, beneath his desk, with no idea what was happening to him or why.

Within a few days, his teacher had referred him to the Centre's psychologist, who'd prescribed him antidepressants. Within hours, Harlan had felt the difference. It was as though he'd been living beneath a grey shroud, so light and thin that he hadn't noticed it until it was gone and he could see and breathe freely. He still had bouts of depression, but it had been reasonably well-managed for years.

Harlan still awoke from nightmares of the warped, twisted spirits inside those black crates—at least half a dozen, from the first until he'd left—but those tests, horrible as they'd been, might be the only way he could save himself now. There was no one else coming for him.

At least, when he'd been in a black crate, he'd known there was an instructor nearby, monitoring his heart rate and breathing, ready to lower a ghost-warded, opaque plastic dome over Harlan if his vitals spiked too high, ending the test. Temporarily.

Here, there was only him. *Fuck.*
Breathe in. Breathe out.
In, slow.
Out, slower.

He visualized a barrier, a shield of energy between himself and the ghost. He was huddled on the floor in the farthest corner of the elevator, making himself as small as possible. The ghost was between him and the door.

Couldn't think about that. *Shield. Barrier. Protection.* A flimsy layer of imaginary light that was the only defense between him and a furious, powerful spirit.

Trailing tendrils of ectoplasm drifted away from the main mass of the ghost, cautiously brushing his barrier, testing its strength.

Knowing what to expect, Harlan braced himself, but it *hurt*. His pitiful shield shattered, disintegrating into tiny shards of ice that crackled beneath the heel of his shoe as he shifted his weight to evade the tendrils now seeking him. *Well, fuck.* That had been useless. The Centre's instructors, like drill sergeants, had stressed the importance of practice, of repeating a lesson until it became automatic — second nature, even in dangerous, frightening situations. They wanted their students to respond properly, even when their bodies shut down with terror. Noble, if unpleasant during training.

Now, the only thing Harlan could picture was *Chapter Thirteen — Malevolent Spirits*. This was the only time ghosts were called anything other than 'clients' — to differentiate malevolent 'spirits' from the befuddled, harmless 'clients'.

Nothing else. Only the Chapter title. None of the text that followed, none of the exercises, nothing actually fucking *useful*.

Sensing his complete lack of defense, the centre of the swirling ectoplasm thickened, forming a howling face. The familiar smell intensified, and suddenly Harlan could place it. He recognized the face — the man on the third floor on the day Harlan had moved in, who'd opened the door when Harlan was searching for his apartment. The one who'd broken the stupid keychain. The smell was his offensive, overpowering cologne or body spray. For the briefest instant, an irrational part of Harlan was convinced he'd somehow been responsible for the man's death. He'd met Harlan then he'd died. The keychain's vengeance.

But that was absurd. He *knew* it was, despite his lingering, needling doubts.

Fuck.

The man had been intimidating enough while he was alive. Now that he was a ghost — and an unusually powerful one — Harlan was terrified. He had to be fresh too, for Harlan not to have felt him before, making it even more unusual for him to be this strong. They'd only met once, but he wasn't surprised by the spirit's targeted attack. They tended to be drawn to mediums, and his only previous experience with Harlan had been antagonistic.

The ghost swirled closer, its spectral teeth bared. Harlan flinched, closing his eyes and curling into an even tighter ball, as though his physical size would make any difference to a being that could pass through solid objects. The ability that allowed Harlan to see and interact with ghosts also made him more vulnerable and open to their attacks.

He felt a whiplash. He looked up and saw a spear of ice at the end of an ectoplasmic tentacle cut his forearm a second time. The pain and bone-biting cold were so intense that he screamed. He could feel that deadly coldness creeping up his arm, moving slowly but inexorably. Nothing could stop it. Maybe it was even taking its time intentionally, savouring his pain and fear. Maybe he didn't *want* it to stop. Maybe he just wanted to close his eyes...

The cold was past his elbow now. The lash was wrapped around his arm, keeping him frozen in place and drawing his energy, the very life from his body.

The icy feeling reached his shoulder, closing on his heart. If it reached that vital organ, he'd die. He knew that more surely than he knew his own name. He'd be so completely drained that he'd simply lose the will to live. He'd just stop breathing, and the ghost would drink every drop of life from his corpse until all that remained was a frozen husk.

Harlan felt a renewed surge of energy through his connection to the ghost. It was getting greedy, trying to drain him more quickly. Harlan grinned unpleasantly, baring his own teeth. The ghost had made a mistake and fed him some of its anger, its rage. It held him by his left arm, leaving his right free. Carefully keeping his expression blank, his jaw slack, he slowly, slowly slid his right hand into the pocket of his jeans, barely containing a triumphant grin when his fingers brushed the familiar edges of the broken keychain. Moving quickly now, praying it wouldn't catch in his pocket as he pulled it out, Harlan yanked the keychain free and hurled it at the ghost.

"You broke my keychain!" he screamed. His keys hit the far wall of the car and clattered to the floor. He was suddenly alone in the elevator. The temperature returned to normal so quickly that he gasped, his throat and lungs feeling almost burned by the rush of warm air.

The doors slid open, revealing his helpful neighbour—Jim? Jordan? It didn't matter right now—standing in the hallway, looking frantic.

"What happened? I heard yelling...God, you look... Here." J-whatever-it-was offered Harlan a hand, which Harlan ignored.

He was still breathing too fast, too hard, gulping down the blessedly warm air as fast as his lungs could handle. He hauled himself to his feet, using the railing behind him. The cold and fear had locked his muscles in place. He brushed past the man, stumbling in the direction of his apartment.

"You forgot your—" he began, but Harlan had already turned.

He snatched the keys out of his neighbour's hand, whirled and unlocked his door on the first try.

He was *never* replacing that stupid keychain.

Chapter Nine

The ghost had been dispelled temporarily, but Harlan knew it would be back. It was powerful enough that Harlan could *just* feel it through the ghost-wards, lurking on the other side, waiting for him to come out. Still, for now, he was safe. He didn't have to deal with it yet. He had time to come up with a plan—in the morning, after he'd slept. If he had to, he could run down the stairs and hopefully get out of the building before the ghost could fully manifest. He could get help from other mediums. Of course, it would have been easier and safer if the ghost had been stopped before draining so much energy from Harlan, energy it could now use to attack, but it was too late for regrets. He'd deal with it, the way it was, in the morning.

For now... Barely able to keep his eyes open, Harlan collapsed on the couch, not even taking his shoes off. He opened his eyes, briefly, when he heard a soft knock on his door, but didn't even bother lifting his head.

It was dark when he woke with a start. He'd been having a strange dream, and it took him a moment to realize that the sound he was hearing was real, not just in his dream. Someone—no, Harlan realized, *something*—was pounding on his door, a staccato, irregular beat that set his teeth on edge.

He rolled off the couch, landing awkwardly on all fours. His body still felt stiff and uncoordinated, and he grunted with pain when he landed. The fall was farther than he'd expected, but the impact jarred him fully awake. His head pounded a counterpoint to the assault on his door. He'd never had a headache like this, and he was torn between investigating the sound, finding some water and a painkiller and staggering to the toilet. He blinked, swiping a hand across his eyes to clear the sleep grit from them. He was so weak he almost toppled over, unbalanced on only three limbs. He lowered his forehead to the floor to brace himself and immediately regretted it as a sharp spike of pain shot through his head, almost making him throw up.

How long had the banging on his door been going on? Why hadn't anyone come to investigate the sound?

Forcing himself to breathe slowly and carefully, swallowing frequently, Harlan managed to keep himself from vomiting. A wave of smell reached him, the overpowering stink of the ghost's aftershave filling his nostrils. *What a terrible fate—reeking of cheap cologne into the afterlife.*

Harlan gagged and burped unpleasantly but kept the bile down. He decided the smell and banging were more urgent than his headache—and contributing to it. Hopefully, getting rid of the ghost would also help his head, at least a little.

As he crawled towards the door, the pounding intensified. The door actually shook on its hinges, banging against the lock. It wasn't until he was within a few feet that he saw the cause, how the ghost was able to penetrate the wards even this far. There was a piece of paper shoved under the door, half in the hallway, half in Harlan's living room. Apparently that was enough for the ghost to break the wards, at least a fraction.

His neighbour must have left the paper, and it had been him Harlan had heard knocking while he'd fallen asleep. It had taken the ghost this long to regroup after its initial attack, but now it had launched another volley at Harlan.

Harlan reached out, tried to shove the paper back into the hall. He wished, not for the first time, that he was telekinetic rather than a medium. He pulled his hand back with a startled cry. The paper was frozen to the floor.

"You sly motherfucker." Biting his lip, increasingly frightened as the door banged harder and harder, Harlan mentally ran through a list of options. He was on the fourth floor, so he couldn't escape out of a window. He briefly considered knotting bed sheets together but...he'd never been very good at rope climbing. He'd probably just fall, break his neck and become bunkmates with the ghost he was currently trying to avoid.

Maybe, if he poured hot water on the paper, he could push it out into the hallway before it turned to mush. More likely, he'd burn himself, ruin his floor *and* the ghost would just use the water to enter the apartment more easily.

He could burn the paper, but again, he'd probably set the door on fire and trap himself in the apartment until the door burned and the ghost could come through at its leisure, if he didn't die of smoke inhalation first. *Fuck.*

Harlan crept away from the door, back onto the bland area rug the living room furniture sat on. He winced every time he heard a floorboard creak. He drew his legs up to his chest, wrapped his arms around them and rested his chin on his knees, rocking back and forth a little, hoping the movement would shake loose an idea.

The banging had gone on long enough that, if anyone were coming to investigate the sound, they would have by now. Either the ghost was somehow keeping everyone else asleep or only Harlan could hear it. Either way, he was on his own.

He let out a long, slow breath, speeding up when he realized he could see it—the temperature in the apartment was dropping. Fast.

Fuck. Fuck.

Bang.

Bang!

The rhythm slowed down even more, each thud harder, louder than the last.

Harlan covered his ears, whimpering, "Go away, go away, go away," over and over under his breath, after each blow to the door.

He could see dust raining down all around the doorframe. The ghost might not be able to break the door in half or pass through the wards, but if it could smash the door out of its frame…

He didn't have any exorcism supplies in the apartment. The ones he'd used at the Centre hadn't belonged to him. He hadn't bought any of his own. Even if he had the supplies, exorcisms required *conviction*, a presence of mind he didn't currently possess. He wished popular beliefs were true, that he could simply fling table salt at the spirit and make it disappear.

There was nothing that worked like—

Harlan had to uncurl in order to reach into his pocket, which made him feel vulnerable, even though he knew, intellectually, that a few inches of skin, muscle and bone weren't going to affect the ghost one way or the other.

He closed his fingers on his phone and pulled it out. He'd charged it during the night, and the ghost couldn't drain the battery with the door between them. Good start.

Shit. He didn't have Charles' number. He couldn't remember the name of the club. He kneaded his temples, trying to physically press the memory out, but it was so hard to think with the assault on his door— *bang. Bang…bang-bang!* The irregular rhythm broke his thoughts, scattering them to the far corners of his mind, striking again before he could gather them into any sort of helpful order.

Thin curlicues and tendrils of ice were sweeping into the apartment, spreading from the piece of paper under the door, slowly working their way farther into the room, gaining ground centimetre by centimetre. He couldn't quite see the ice moving, but if he looked away and back again, he could tell it had spread.

He was shivering, his teeth chattering as the temperature continued to drop. Much longer, and his fingers would be too cold and stiff to type or hold the phone.

Another *bang!* This one was the loudest yet, followed by the sound of splintering wood.

Harlan looked up. The ice had leeched deep into the door and split it. It now had a jagged crack. It wasn't the entire thickness of the door, so the ghost couldn't enter, but the door wouldn't remain a barrier for much longer.

Frantic, his breath pluming in front of him as he barely held himself back from hyperventilating, he googled *'dungeon Toronto'*. He had to re-enter it a few times, his hands were trembling so badly — *dibhein yofiyo, sygeib tieoyi*.

There were only three results. 'Rattling Chains'. That sounded familiar. No picture, and Harlan wasn't sure about the address, but… There was a long, tormented squeal of protesting wood, a groan from the door, as though the spirit of the tree it had been made from cried out against the further torture it was forced to endure.

Harlan clicked the phone number, hit *call*. Waited. Bit his lower lip.

Ring.

Ring.

Fuck. It was the middle of the afternoon. No one was going to be there. Why couldn't ghosts only come out at night, like in the movies?

Ring.

The door creaked again, followed by a thud. Harlan squeezed his eyes shut.

"Hello?"

Harlan could hear fast-paced, up-beat music playing.

"Charles?" Oh, thank God, he'd reached someone. Even if it wasn't Charles, they'd have his number. He could tell them he was in danger, and they could send help. He didn't care if he looked like a crazy idiot, as long as someone came.

It hadn't occurred to him until that moment to call 9-1-1, Hamilton or even the Centre. That was interesting, but currently irrelevant.

"He's not here right now. Can I say who's—" A muffled thump, like the phone being put down.

No, no, *no*...

Voices in the background, another thump, then...

"Hello?" A different voice. This one was familiar—or so Harlan hoped.

"Charles?" The word was barely a squeak.

"Who is... Harlan?"

Harlan was amazed that Charles had been able to recognize his voice from one word. *Oh God.* Had Charles been thinking about him as much as he'd been thinking about Charles? A fraction as much?

"Hello? Are you still there?"

He'd taken too long to respond, distracted by Charles' voice and the beautiful, deadly fractals creeping towards him. The ice was all around the doorframe now, not just the beneath it. "I, uh... Yes. Fuck."

A few moments, and the music faded. "Are you okay? You sound—"

"No, I'm really not." Cutting someone off, someone whose help he needed, frightened Harlan, but not nearly as much as the slow-motion destruction of his door, the unnatural cold that was making his hand so stiff and clumsy that he was afraid he'd drop the phone. "I'm... I need...help. I need help."

"Are you on something?" Charles sounded more sympathetic than accusatory, which Harlan appreciated.

"N-no, I'm not. Just...please..." The phone went silent. "Hello? Charles?" Nothing. Harlan glanced at it.

The screen was dark, and it didn't respond to any buttons he pressed.

Oh, shit. The ghost was getting very close to breaking through, if it had drained the battery. *Closer, and more powerful.* Even if it hadn't actually killed the phone, ghosts made electronics erratic.

Dropping the useless hunk of plastic, Harlan pulled himself up onto the couch. It would give him a few more moments of protection from the encroaching ice — unless the door broke before it reached him.

Chapter Ten

Harlan hardly opened his eyes when he heard a crash, even though it was only a few feet away. He realized he *couldn't*. His eyelashes were frozen together, the condensation from his breath gathering there and turning to ice. He tried to reach up, to clear his eyes, but his muscles were sluggish and unresponsive with cold. He saw a dark shape loom over him, and the only thing he could do was defiantly squeeze his eyes shut. If he couldn't open them fully, he could at least control how closed they were while he waited for an icy spike of ghostly energy to penetrate him and steal his last remaining breath of warmth.

"Not my fault... The keys..."

"You're not making sense." Warm hands on his shoulders, pulling him up. Resistance, as his clothes stuck to the ice beneath him.

He struggled, briefly, futilely, against a much stronger force. He could feel heat blooming, spreading through his skin. He blinked, trying to clear the ice from his lashes, still unable to lift his arms. Warm fingers spread across his cheeks, hot thumbs pressed to his eyelids, smoothing the ice away.

Harlan opened his eyes, blinking away the last of the melted water. Charles knelt in front of him, his big, warm hands cradling his face, keeping his head up.

He tried to pull away, but Charles held him fast. He settled for dropping his gaze, but that brought his line of sight to Charles' chest. That wasn't much of an improvement. Charles' shirt was tight enough that Harlan could see his nipples. At least one of them was pierced. He wasn't sure about the other from this angle—and a swirl of chest hair peeked over his collar. Even the slight swell of his stomach was enticing. Harlan could too easily imagine following that curl of chest hair down, teasing Charles' nipples with lips, tongue, fingers, his head pillowed on Charles' stomach while he…

If he got an erection now, he'd probably die. Literally. Not just because, kneeling between Charles' legs, Charles was sure to notice, but if all his blood—all his *warmth*—congregated in one place right now, there wouldn't be enough for the rest of him. There barely was now.

"What happened? Was it a ghost?" Charles' thumb traced a long, slow path of heat down Harlan's cheek, to his jaw, before starting again from the top.

"I'm not high."

"Uh-huh. What you are is freezing."

All he wanted was to get warm—for *Charles* to warm him. His head was so heavy, and Charles' hands were so steady and sure, supporting it… His eyes slowly, slowly…

"Hey! Don't fall asleep. You might have hypothermia."

Harlan laughed. In his present state, the word sounded silly and made up. "Hypothermia isn't real."

Frowning, Charles withdrew, just a little. "I know some basic first aid. It's a good skill to have, running a BDSM club," he clarified, seeing Harlan's blank look.

"So...are you actually into that?" The words were out before Harlan could take them back, so he did his best to look as though they'd at least been intentional. His jaw clenched, hard, as another wave of shivering struck, then he couldn't say anything else.

"No," Charles said, with a quirked grin. "I'm the co-owner of a BDSM club, but I'm totally vanilla."

"Really?" As soon as he'd said it, Harlan blushed. He'd picked up on Charles' teasing tone a fraction too late.

"I really think I should call an ambulance," Charles told him, mercifully changing the subject.

Not that this one was much better. More people in his apartment, seeing him like this? Harlan shook his head.

Charles laughed wryly, shaking his own head. "Yeah, I thought you might say that. Let's get you out of those clothes. They're cold and wet and probably not helping you any. But if you don't start improving soon—ambulance." He started peeling off Harlan's T-shirt.

Harlan's blush intensified. He felt like he was living out a cheesy porno, but he also didn't want it to stop. "I—" His protests were cut off by Charles pulling his shirt over his head. "Now I feel *colder*," he complained.

"I know. I'm sorry. Gotta get them off, though. They're just trapping cold air against your skin at this point." Charles lowered his gaze—and his hands—to Harlan's groin, quickly and efficiently undoing his fly and button.

Harlan wondered how many men he'd undressed like this. He leaned forward, his body shaking with effort, barely containing a whimpered plea for Charles to touch his bare skin again, with the warmth and safety he offered. Even though Harlan was almost certain ghosts wouldn't appear even much farther away from Charles, right now only Charles' hands on him seemed like enough protection.

"Can you sit up?"

Harlan lifted his hips as far as he could, so Charles could slide his jeans down.

"Blankets?"

"B-Bedroom." Harlan pointed, his teeth still chattering.

Charles left, returning with an assortment of bedding.

"Don't slip!" There was still a small patch of ice on the floor, directly in Charles' path, and he couldn't see it with his arms full.

Charles stopped, pressing the blankets to his chest so he could see over them. "On what?"

"The ice!"

Brow furrowed, Charles slowly shook his head. "There's no ice. Not on the floor, anyway. Might be some on *you*."

Harlan leaned forward, peering down at the pale, faux-wood laminate as though something might leap at his face.

No ice.

He leaned back, still shivering.

"Here." Charles tucked him in carefully, making sure all his extremities were covered in several layers of thick blankets. "Do you have tea? Soup?"

Harlan paused. He hadn't bought either of those things, but there had been a lot of cans in the cupboards, and he hadn't looked through all of them thoroughly. He considered explaining he'd only purchased some of the groceries himself, that the apartment had come pre-stocked, but decided that just made him sound pathetic.

More pathetic.

"Maybe?" Hopefully Charles would chalk his uncertainty up to shock or something.

"Right." Giving Harlan one last concerned look, Charles disappeared into the kitchen.

Harlan heard cupboards opening and closing, some clattering, water running, then Charles was back.

"Earl Grey okay?"

Harlan shrugged. He didn't really like tea of any kind, or really know the difference between teas, to be honest, but he was so cold...

Charles laughed. "I think that was a shrug, but it's hard to tell." He set the steaming mug on the coffee table in front of Harlan, where a ring of condensation immediately appeared on the glass. "I'll take that as a yes."

For some reason, Charles was blushing. It was the first time Harlan had seen him look so...vulnerable.

"Ah...I don't know how much you know about hypothermia... I looked it up on my phone while I was making tea."

No. Oh, no. Harlan thought he saw where this was going. He tried to open his mouth, to protest, to insist he was fine, that Charles should leave, now, but another shiver locked his muscles. At least he couldn't get an erection. *Probably.*

"But, well, it's not safe to put you in hot water. Not yet. The best way to warm you up is to, uh…" Charles' fingers danced over his simple metal belt buckle, then away. He was still blushing. "I'm not coming on to you!" he insisted, raising his hands.

Harlan couldn't decide if that was a good thing or not. These were pretty terrible circumstances for flirting, and Harlan was a trembling mess, but maybe that wasn't what Charles had been referring to. Maybe he didn't want Harlan at all, and the only reason he'd get naked with him was to save his life.

It was—almost—worth it.

Charles stared down at Harlan for a few seconds, fully dressed. Harlan slowly realized he was waiting for a response, for permission.

"Oh! Uh, yeah." Harlan nodded, sinking farther into the blankets. He'd almost vanished completely by the time Charles took off his shirt. He stopped, peeping his eyes out of his nest. He *needed* to feel that skin against his own, couldn't believe he had the perfect opportunity to do just that. He almost felt grateful to the ghost for being his wingman.

Charles undressed quickly, methodically, without looking at Harlan. This wasn't a striptease, wasn't even a wild, passionate, desperate rush to get naked. He was just taking off his clothes, the way he might at the end of a long day. So he could hold Harlan. Naked.

Charles undid his jeans and stepped out of them, leaving him in just his underwear and socks, the same as Harlan. "Scoot over," he said softly, waving his hands in a shooing motion.

Taking his heap of blankets with him, Harlan slid to the far side of the couch, giving Charles as much room as possible, much more than Charles needed if he intended to hold Harlan.

Almost reluctantly, Charles sat beside him. Sliding over, he groped through the thick layers of blankets, laughing. "I know you're in there somewhere. Let me in." Finally, a warm hand found Harlan's cold, bare thigh. He gasped, and it withdrew for a moment. "Fuck, you're cold!"

He managed to separate the blankets from Harlan, and then they were both under the covers. Together. Naked...or close enough.

Both of them took a long, slow breath, almost together. Paused. There was still a small gap between their bodies.

Harlan was the first to move, for purely practical reasons. Even beneath all the blankets, he was shivering, every muscle tensed. He could feel the heat of Charles' body bridging the air dividing them, and his body moved before he could reconsider.

Charles hissed when he felt Harlan's cold skin against his, paused for just a moment, then wrapped an arm around Harlan's shoulders, drawing him close. "Brr! I should've made a cup of tea for myself. You're eventually going to explain why I just rescued you from a blizzard in the middle of your apartment, right?"

Harlan nodded, distracted, hoping that was the correct response. He would've agreed to almost anything in that moment, provided it meant Charles would stay. He could feel warmth soaking deep into his skin wherever their bodies touched, and he was barely aware of Charles' words as anything but sound. His head was still so heavy that he let it fall to rest on Charles' shoulder. Charles tensed for just an instant, then his fingers were in Harlan's hair.

"Mmm. We should get some of this tea into you before you fall asleep. It should be cool enough by now," Charles murmured, still stroking Harlan's soft, brown curls.

Harlan made a small sound of protest. Charles' voice rumbled in his chest, the sound deep and soothing. Charles' heartbeat was a slow, even rhythm that steadied his own too-fast pulse in response. All he could smell was Charles—a faint tang of leather, sweat, his understated aftershave and beneath it all, the soft, simple scent of Charles' skin. He buried his nose in the crook of Charles' arm, closing his eyes. He smelled warm and alive, completely different from the chemical reek of the ghost. He didn't want to move, didn't want to take his arm out of the tangle of limbs and blankets, especially not for *tea*.

Charles wiggled his shoulder, gently jostling Harlan's head. "Mm-mm. Nope. You've warmed up a lot already, but I still don't think it's safe for you to fall asleep. I'll give you some tea—me, too, if you don't mind sharing—then I'll sit on your other side, to warm it up. Maybe put on a movie?"

Harlan groaned, but he knew Charles was right—despite how comfortable he felt now, he knew he'd come close to dying. He sat up with a sigh, releasing Charles' shoulder, shivering anew as cold air touched his skin.

Charles leaned forward and grabbed the mug, careful to uncover as little of Harlan as possible. He started to pass the tea to Harlan, paused, gave Harlan a questioning look. "Mind if I…?"

Harlan nodded.

Charles took a sip. "Mmm, thanks."

"Are *you* okay?" Harlan asked.

Charles nodded. "I'm fine, though I might take a hot shower when I feel safe leaving you alone for a bit."

"You can now, if you want." How long did Charles plan on staying? The thought of Charles, naked, in *his* shower, maybe both of them together... It was a heady image. It *would* warm him up, after all...

He squirmed uncomfortably, leaning forward so quickly that he almost spilled the tea all over both of them.

"Sorry," they said at the same time.

"Here." Charles handed over the mug, holding it from beneath until he was sure Harlan had a firm grip on the handle.

Their fingers brushed, lingered and they both pulled away.

Harlan took a long gulp of tea and swallowed as quickly as possible, making a face at the taste.

"Yeah, yeah. Drink up. It's good for you. Hopefully the caffeine will help keep you awake a little longer."

The mug was comfortably warm in his stiff hands, and the steam felt good on his face. He didn't drink tea often, so he always forgot that it had caffeine. He always thought of it as a soothing bedtime drink, at least for other people.

Swallowing the bitter liquid, he decided it was worth it as its warmth coated his insides.

They shared the tea, passing the mug back and forth, Charles making sure Harlan drank most of it, while Harlan tried to do the same thing. He settled on Harlan's right side, warming him again.

It felt so right, so natural and familiar, to lay his head on Charles' shoulder, with Charles' arm around him. Harlan had never especially liked being touched—not that there had been many volunteers—but this... Lying here with Charles, neither of them speaking, bare skin to bare skin… He felt as though he'd been here before, like he'd *always* been here, like he never wanted to leave.

That last thought, terrifying in its intensity, made him recoil and sit forward on the couch. "Um…"

Charles cleared his throat, pulled his arm back and leaned away just a little. What had felt simple and easy a moment ago was suddenly awkward.

"How do you feel?" Charles asked, already sliding out from beneath the blankets. "Your skin feels warmer." He laughed. "Though it'd be hard for it to feel *colder*."

Harlan nodded. His teeth had mostly stopped chattering, and his shivering wasn't constant anymore.

"I, uh, think I'll take that shower now, if it's still on the table. You don't mind?" Charles was standing now, clad only in his boxers. "I think you're warm enough that we can safely give you a shower. Is your stall big enough for two?"

Harlan blinked at him, stupidly.

"I'm not an expert, but I think the most dangerous part is past and the hot water'll do you some good."

Harlan wasn't sure how much of his sudden enthusiasm was due to the thought of warmth and how much was from the thought of being naked in a shower with Charles. It took him a humiliatingly long time to untangle himself from the blankets. Finally, Charles had to help dig him out, like a St. Bernard. *No cask of brandy, unfortunately.*

As soon as his bare skin came into contact with the open air, he started trembling again.

Charles frowned at him, thoughtfully. "Maybe I should…"

"I'm *f-fine*," Harlan insisted, matching Charles' frown with a scowl.

Sliding one arm beneath Harlan's, with the other braced on the opposite shoulder, Charles helped him to his feet.

On reflection, it was a good thing Harlan *hadn't* tried to stand on his own—even with Charles' support, his legs wobbled, and he fell heavily against him. He appeared to have expected it and had already braced himself.

Harlan allowed himself to be steered through the apartment. It was small enough that the bathroom was easy for Charles to find, even without directions. Harlan was too cold to move away from contact with Charles' skin, so he tried to ignore how good Charles' naked body felt against his own—comfortably padded, with an ample amount of muscle beneath. Curves and hair and his *smell*...

He was relieved when they reached the bathroom.

"Can you stand by yourself for a moment?"

Harlan opened his mouth to protest, felt one of his calves spasm, shut it again and shook his head.

There was only one towel hanging on the bar. Charles grabbed it, put the toilet seat down and closed the lid, then covered the plastic seat with the towel. "Sit." He pointed, his expression playful, but he clearly meant it.

Harlan sat before his legs gave out completely. He set his jaw so his teeth couldn't chatter. He was *so cold*, deep down where nothing could reach it, that nothing could ever melt.

"Stay." Now Charles was grinning. "Where can I find more towels?"

"The linen c-closet. In the hall." Harlan counted only stuttering once as an achievement.

With a final, firm glance—wasted, because Harlan wasn't sure he could've stood, even if he'd wanted to—Charles left. He returned a moment later with two fluffy blue towels and one of the blankets from the couch. After hanging the towels on the empty bar, he carefully tucked Harlan in, covering him and draping a layer of blanket behind him so he could lean back without touching the cold toilet tank.

Harlan cuddled into the blanket. It still smelled like Charles, and he hoped Charles would assume he was sniffing because his nose was running.

It took Charles a few moments to figure out Harlan's shower, but soon the small, white-tiled room filled with steam. Once he'd gotten the water to a temperature that satisfied him, Charles gently untucked Harlan and helped him to his feet. He very impersonally stripped off Harlan's socks and briefs—Harlan supposed he saw a lot of naked people, what with owning a…dungeon? Sex club? He still wasn't sure how to think of it, and he didn't want to ask and give away that he'd been thinking about it.

Chapter Eleven

Charles guided him into the shower, and Harlan was relieved it was a proper stall rather than a tub, or he would've been afraid of slipping, breaking his neck and adding yet another ghost to the building. If he did fall, the walls would keep him from going far—unless the glass shattered—then he'd not only be hurt when he hit the floor, he'd be sliced up, too...

Charles stepped into the shower behind him. He was completely naked. Harlan could feel it. The shower stall was small enough that it forced their bodies into constant contact, at least a few inches of skin, wherever they stood.

Harlan balked for the first time, feeling...*all* of Charles behind him.

"Hey. I'm sorry." Charles took a step back, as much as he could, leaving his hands on Harlan's middle to steady him.

"It's o-okay," Harlan murmured, jaw tight, teeth chattering. The water was hot—he could see the steam, how pink his skin was—but he still felt cold. "It's just..." *Just what? Been a long time? You startled me?* It was too much, too many things. Harlan couldn't pin any single thought down long enough to say it out loud, so he said nothing.

"I'll get out if—"

"No!" Harlan interjected, more forcefully than he'd intended. "No," he repeated, softening his voice, "stay. Please."

"All right. If you're sure."

Harlan nodded. Charles was cold, too. He could feel the chill of skin against his back. Without speaking, they arranged themselves so they were both under the spray of warm water, Charles' arm wrapped around Harlan's shoulders, holding him close, with Harlan pressed against him. It wasn't sexual, though only by the space of a wiggle and a squirm from either of them, but neither of them wiggled...or squirmed.

Finally, *finally*, Harlan's core began to feel warm again. He shifted his feet slightly, careful not to step on Charles' toes.

Charles moved his thumb slightly, tracing a short arc that terminated right above Harlan's left nipple. He cleared his throat. "We should, uh, probably get out soon, before we run out of hot water and kill you."

Harlan nodded. He agreed—if cold water hit him right now, he'd die. He leaned forward just a little, separating their bodies. He shivered as cool air touched his skin where they parted, but it was quickly replaced by the water's warmth. He hoped he hadn't imagined the regret in Charles' voice.

"Right." Charles reached past him and turned off the water. "You seem steady enough on your feet for the moment. Wait here, and I'll hand a towel in for you. You'll stay warmer that way."

That made sense. Even the brief draft from Charles leaving, though he'd quickly shut the door behind himself, had raised goosebumps on Harlan's naked skin.

Charles opened the shower door just enough to pass one of the towels through before shutting it again.

Harlan dried himself, his hands already trembling again as he wrapped himself in the towel and stepped out of the stall.

He wasn't sure if Charles approached him or he approached Charles, but a moment later they were pressed together, body to body.

"The towel's cold," Charles said, laughing.

"Sorry." Harlan tried to pull away, embarrassed, but Charles' strong hands caught the hem and kept him in place.

"I wasn't complaining," Charles clarified. "I'm just worried about you being wrapped in something cold and wet, after all that trouble to warm you up." He tugged at the towel, then quirked a smile, as though he'd only just realized Harlan wasn't wearing anything underneath. "Do you have a bathrobe?"

Harlan didn't know the answer and he felt absurd, being babied like this. "I can—" he began, taking a step off the bathmat. He recoiled when his toes touched frigid tile.

"Stay." Charles pointed at him, a smile softening the command. "Bathrobe?"

Harlan had seen one, now that he thought about it, though he'd never used it. "Closet," he replied, amused that he'd started answering Charles in single words as well.

"Stay," Charles repeated, backing out of the bathroom. He kept his eyes on Harlan, hands up, as though Harlan were a velociraptor he was training. He was back in a moment, holding a dark blue terrycloth robe. With clinical detachment, he whisked the towel off Harlan, tossed it onto the floor and wrapped the robe around him. He grabbed the third towel, the dry one that had been folded on the toilet, and laid it on the floor in front of Harlan, covering the floor to the doorway. "So you don't have to walk on the cold tile," he explained, offering Harlan a hand.

Besides the man's miraculous ability to make ghosts vanish, that one gesture tipped Harlan over the edge. He was smitten.

He carefully cupped his hand in Charles' larger one as he led him across the towel. He felt like a princess being escorted to the ball.

Charles held Harlan's hand all the way to the bed, getting Harlan safely seated before releasing his grip. The moment turned awkward, both of them suddenly aware of Harlan, naked except for a robe, in bed. Charles smoothed a piece of lint off the duvet, watching it fall with exaggerated focus. "Do you have pyjamas? They'd probably be more comfortable than the robe for sleeping, especially because it's a little damp now."

Harlan usually slept naked, but he pointed wordlessly to a drawer where he remembered seeing pyjamas during his explorations.

The set Charles offered was flannel — pastel blue, a pattern of cartoony sheep with *zzzs* coming out of their mouths as they jumped over fences. To his credit, Charles didn't laugh, but Harlan still felt compelled to explain. "I didn't buy them." That just sounded worse, he decided, like he was so helpless that he didn't even buy his own clothes — which, while technically true, wasn't something he wanted Charles to know.

"Here." Charles set the pyjamas, still neatly folded, on the corner of the bed. "I'll, ah, let you change." He closed the bedroom door softly behind him.

Harlan froze, listening, wondering if Charles had stayed in the living room or kept going — leaving the apartment entirely. He didn't hear the front door open, and he let out a breath that he hadn't realized he'd been holding. He had the brief, absurd idea of pressing the ridiculous pyjamas to his nose and inhaling Charles' lingering scent. Telling himself not to be ridiculous, he slid off the bed, removed the robe and pulled on the pyjamas. The fake wood floor was much warmer than the tile, but he still wished he had slippers.

He kept his hair short enough — and had mostly kept it out of the spray of water — that it was almost dry already. He was hardly shivering anymore, so rather than climbing into bed again, he slowly opened the door. He'd been hoping to catch a glimpse of Charles before the other man finished dressing, but he was too late.

Charles looked up from examining Harlan's bookshelf — more things he hadn't chosen. If Charles wanted to gain any insight about Harlan, he wouldn't find it there. The books, like everything else in the apartment, had already been there when he'd moved in. He'd hardly glanced at the titles, never mind added to the collection. He had books he actually liked on his phone.

Charles smiled. Harlan smiled back.

"Feeling better?" It was more of a statement than a question.

Harlan nodded.

"Come sit down before you fall over." Charles sat on the couch, patting the seat beside him.

Harlan sat, pressing himself against the far armrest and keeping his distance from Charles.

"So…" Charles fiddled with the empty mug, sliding it back and forth between his hands. "What happened? Or can you not tell me? It's okay if you can't, if you're not ready to talk about it or…anything."

Harlan shook his head. "I don't mind." He didn't really want to talk about it — not now, maybe not ever — but he also wanted Charles to know why he'd ended up in need of rescue. "My apartment is ghost-warded. I think I told you that."

Charles nodded.

"This angry guy, he lives — *lived* — in the building. He must've died. We only met once but he, uh, didn't like me. He trapped me in the elevator, but I threw my keys at him. Metal can sometimes interrupt ghosts, briefly.

"I got off the elevator and into my apartment and I *should* have been safe, but my other neighbour left a note under my door, and it must've — I don't know — bridged the gap between the apartment and the hall, and he…" Harlan shivered, knees drawn up to his chest. "He used it to get in, and he was so angry, so cold…" He looked at Charles, more directly than normal. "Thank you for coming. I'm pretty sure you saved my life."

"Oof. That's a lot. No wonder you were so messed up." Charles reached over and it looked like he might touch Harlan's hand, but he patted his shoulder instead. "I'm glad I was around when you called." He glanced around the apartment, his eyes narrowed. "So, is he still here, but he can't do anything more because I am?"

"I don't know. Maybe. I think you just make it so I can't sense them. I don't think he can hurt me as long as you're here."

"I mean, I'm glad about that, and obviously I'm happy to stay as long as you need me, but that's just a short-term solution. How do we fix this?"

Harlan couldn't help feeling a little internal glow at Charles' use of 'we'.

"You'll need a new door, for starters."

Harlan followed Charles' gaze, widening his eyes when he saw the ruin of his door. The ice had thoroughly cracked it, and Charles had finished it off when he'd broken through to save Harlan. Most of the middle section lay on the floor, with only some wood remaining on the hinge and lock sides.

"Holy shit."

"Do you have the building manager's number?"

Harlan shook his head.

"What's the name of this building?"

"Parkview."

Charles pulled out his phone and typed for a moment before lifting it to his ear. He paced into the kitchen, and Harlan was happy not to listen to the conversation. He let his eyes drift shut, basking in the peace Charles' presence gave him.

Charles returned a few minutes later. "They'll send someone out right away. I told them you were with the police. That should speed things up a bit."

They shared a grin.

"He sounded a little grumpy. Apparently, these are the original doors. Your new one might not be so pretty."

"It was a nice door." Great, now Harlan felt guilty about the stupid wooden closure.

Charles gave his hand a quick squeeze. "But you're safe. That's what matters. Okay. That'll take care of the physical part of your safety. What about the ghost?"

Harlan's breathing sped up, his heart racing, just at the thought of his downstairs neighbour's malevolent remains.

Remains.

"What if they haven't found his body yet?"

"What?"

Harlan sat up, shaking his head. "It had to have been really recent, and something tells me this guy didn't have a lot of visitors. His body might still be..." He pointed down, and they exchanged horrified looks.

"I'll call the police. Is that right? Is that...the thing to do?"

"I think so?" Harlan sighed. He didn't really want Hamilton finding out about this situation, but they would need the police anyway, to get rid of the body, the ghost and to ward Harlan's new door. He was sure they'd have a ghost-warder on call.

"You want me to call?"

Harlan nodded, grateful.

"I don't think I need to call 9-1-1, just the non-emergency number."

"I agree."

Charles perched on the arm of one of the chairs, quickly explaining the situation and what they needed before hanging up.

"They'll be here in about an hour. Would you like me to stay with you?"

"Please." The word came out more pitiful than he liked, but he'd meant it. He didn't want to be left alone, not until he was *sure* the ghost was gone.

The building maintenance man arrived first, carrying a door. It was metal, not solid wood like the old one and not nearly as attractive. Not that Harlan spent a lot of time contemplating his front door.

Leaning the new door against the wall in the hallway, the man whistled at the remains of the old one. "Holy shit. Must've been a hell of a ghost!"

Both men looked to Harlan to respond, but he didn't know what to say.

"It was," Charles answered for him. "Thank you for coming so quickly. I know it's late."

Within a few minutes, he'd removed the hinge pins and taken down the splintered wood that still hung from the hinges. He unlocked it — he had his own set of keys, which was good, because Harlan found himself reluctant to let anyone else handle his — and lowered the rest of the door to the ground.

"You got lucky." He tapped the wooden doorframe. "Good, solid old building like this, the frame stood up to the beating. Doesn't even need to be replaced." He gathered up all the shattered pieces in the hallway, then stood the new door up in its place.

The hinges didn't quite line up, so he moved the ones in the doorframe, using a small tool Harlan couldn't identify to dig grooves into the wood so the hinges wouldn't stick out. He had to do the same on the lock side.

The man caught Harlan watching and laughed. "It won't be the prettiest with the old grooves still there, but it'll do."

He finished up and handed Harlan a key.

"What's this for?"

"Different lock, different key. The old lock didn't fit in this door, but I brought one with me, just in case."

Harlan hoped his irrational disappointment didn't show — after using it to fight off the ghost, he'd grown attached to his old key. He decided to keep it on his key ring.

The repairman locked and unlocked the door a few times, swinging it to make sure everything worked smoothly. He had Harlan unlock it from the hall, laughing when Harlan automatically pressed on the doorframe.

"Right, I forgot about that! Shouldn't need to do that anymore."

The door unlocked easily on the first try. Again, Harlan couldn't help feeling a tiny bit disappointed that the door had lost even more of its character.

The police arrived just as the man finished gathering his tools and the shattered door. A uniformed officer murmured something to the repairman, who went white, nodded and set down his burden before leading her to the elevator. Probably looking for the man's body, Harlan reasoned.

That left three more—another uniformed officer and two in plain clothes. The woman wore a badge, and the man had no identification.

Charles patted his thigh. "Well, I should probably..." He glanced at the door. "Just...promise you'll call me. If you start feeling bad again," he added, quickly. "Any time, day or night, I mean it. If I don't hear from you, I'm calling tomorrow, and if you don't answer, I'm coming over. And if you *still* don't answer, I'll break the door down. Again. Deal?"

"Deal," Harlan agreed.

Charles nodded at the others on his way out, looking back at Harlan several times until the elevator doors closed behind him.

Harlan assumed the man was the medium, until he reached into his bag and pulled out a paintbrush and a jar of clear fluid. Harlan recognized the scent as soon as he opened it—the oil used for painting ghost-wards.

Everyone had their own recipe, but the basic ingredients were similar enough for Harlan's nose.

Ignoring the others, he knelt in front of the door and started painting.

Charles must have gotten out of range. The ghost snapped into existence, howling and diving at Harlan, clearly determined to continue where it had left off.

The woman's nose wrinkled, as though she'd smelled something odd, besides the oil. "Wow! You really managed to piss off this ghost! It's weird, though. It was totally ignoring you until just now." Standing firm, she grabbed the ghost by the throat, her face twisting in pain.

Harlan grimaced sympathetically. He knew the bitter-cold agony of touching a ghost—which was worse with an aggressive one.

"Get. Out!" she growled, physically throwing the ghost at the nearest wall. If he'd still been in his body, it would have been impossible—he'd been much larger than her—and Harlan could see her straining, but it worked. A hole appeared behind the ghost, black and empty. With a final howl, the ghost disappeared. His fingertips tried to find purchase on the edges, but the medium stomped them with her booted foot and they let go. The hole closed behind him.

"Whew. That was a nasty one."

Harlan wasn't proud of himself for it, but he was a little glad to see beads of sweat dotting her forehead and that she was breathing heavily. She'd made it look so *easy*, and he was relieved it had actually been a struggle for her.

Her partner, who had stayed still and quiet throughout, gave her a questioning glance.

"I'm fine, Phillip." She laughed, turning to Harlan. "What did you do to this guy?"

"I tried to unlock his door. Once. By accident." He shrugged.

"Weird. Well, he's gone now. Do you want us to stay until he's done painting?" She inclined her head at the warder, who'd finished the door and was now reinforcing the damaged lines on either side of it.

Harlan shook his head. Now that the worst of his fear had passed and he felt safe again, he wanted to be as alone as possible, as soon as possible. One man who hadn't said a word was infinitely preferable to three people.

She clapped a hand on his shoulder. "Happens to the best of us. Some of the stories I could tell... Phew, they would give you nightmares. But you don't need that right now. I'm Beth. I've heard good things about you."

Harlan squirmed, uncomfortable with the praise. Also, who would have been talking about him, never mind positively? Certainly not Hamilton.

Beth handed him her card. "If you ever need anything or just want to talk, call me."

He took it and tucked it into his pocket, beside Charles'.

"It'd be nice to see more of you, when we're not dealing with ghosts. The three of us—there are four police mediums in Toronto now, including you—like to get together every few weeks. You're welcome to join us. You've already met Leo—and Benjamin's nice."

Leo must have been the woman he'd seen at Charles' dungeon.

"Anyway. Let me know if you have any more trouble." She twirled her forefinger and left, careful not to smudge the fresh oil on the door. Her partner followed her, giving Harlan a little nod of acknowledgment.

Half an hour later, the warder stood, stretched and capped his jar of oil. "Should be good to go now," he said, the first words he'd spoken. "I'd like to come by next week and make sure everything's holding up the way it should be."

Harlan nodded. He'd agree to anything if it meant everyone would get out of his apartment and leave him alone.

He closed his new door behind the warder and locked it. He desperately wanted to call Charles. That desperation made him more determined not to. He'd answer Charles' call tomorrow, thank him and reassure him he was okay.

Then he'd be done with him.

* * * *

Charles didn't call until late afternoon, late enough that Harlan was tempted to call him first to get it over with. He didn't.

When it finally did ring, Harlan stared at his phone like it might attack him if he touched it or even got too close. He didn't want to answer it and he desperately wanted to answer. He finally snatched it up, almost dropped it, then pressed the talk button. "Hello?" *Hello? Who actually says, 'hello'?*

"Hey! It's Charles."

"Hi." Slightly better.

"How are you? No heart palpitations or anything?"

"No, nothing like that." Had Charles googled 'hypothermia aftereffects'? Harlan hadn't been aware that was something he should have been worried about. Now he was. He couldn't be sure if his heart was racing because he was talking to Charles or because it was about to explode because he'd almost frozen to death the night before. He was relieved when Charles continued.

"Your new door got installed okay? No ghost troubles?"

"Yes. No—I'm fine. Thanks for checking in." He tried to sound as crisp and businesslike as possible. He was cutting Charles off after this conversation, after all. There was no point in getting too friendly.

"I said I would."

"Yeah. And...thanks. For helping me. Again. Thanks again for helping me, *and* thanks for helping me, *again*." *So much for businesslike.*

"Of course. Any— You're sure you're all right?"

"Yeah. Look... I...I gotta go. Thanks."

"Take care. Call—"

"I will." He hung up. It was too bad that his last words to Charles were a lie.

Chapter Twelve

An unfamiliar police code crackled over the radio in Hamilton's squad car. It wasn't one Harlan recognized. Hamilton had never taken the time to tell him what each one meant, but Harlan was slowly learning them by context and repetition.

And Google.

Hamilton cursed as he pulled the car around into oncoming traffic, barely turning on the lights and siren before starting the manoeuvre.

Harlan stiffened in his seat. Usually, their 'missions' weren't at all urgent, except from the perspective of the people whose property was haunted and wanted the ghost removed as quickly as possible so they could reopen for business.

He glanced at Hamilton. The officer's mouth was tight and grim, and the frown lines beside his mouth and the crows' feet around his eyes—well, the one eye Harlan could see from this angle—were etched even deeper than usual. Whatever was happening, Hamilton didn't bother explaining, weaving in between cars and taking turns so sharply that Harlan squeaked, digging his nails into his palms. Harlan didn't ask. Hamilton rarely said more than the bare minimum to Harlan, and Harlan was happy to return the favour.

They drove in silence, Hamilton gripping the steering wheel so hard that the black imitation leather creaked.

They passed an alley, blocked by blue police sawhorses and uniformed officers whose pinched expressions were eerily similar to Hamilton's, as though they'd all attended the same seminar — *How to Scowl* — during their training. There were three cruisers parked on either side of the alley's entrance, lights on and sirens off, and one unmarked car with its dashboard light on.

Hamilton muttered under his breath when he couldn't find a parking spot. The alley was barred at the other end of the block too.

As they passed for the third time, Hamilton stopped the cruiser so abruptly that they were almost rear-ended. The driver behind them had probably been trying to see past the police barricade, not paying attention to the road.

"Get out."

Harlan shot Hamilton a brief, worried look.

Hamilton sighed but softened his voice a fraction. "Get out here. I'll find a place to park farther out — if you think you can go three minutes without me holding your hand."

That was a relief, actually. Hamilton's surliness, combined with the unexplained urgency, was putting Harlan on edge, and that was never a good mindset when dealing with spirits.

With such a large police presence, it must be an especially aggressive ghost. Possibly more than one. *Great.*

Harlan opened the door with a tiny nod at Hamilton, who barely waited until Harlan had both feet on the pavement to take off.

With the cruiser out of the way, the man in the car that had almost hit them pulled even with the alley, waving frantically at Harlan.

Puzzled, Harlan approached.

The man rolled down the passenger side window, leaning over as far as his seatbelt would allow. "Hey! What happened?" He jerked his head in the direction of the barricades.

Harlan opened his mouth to say he had no idea, that he'd just gotten there, but... While he wasn't a cop, he was at least associated with the police now. Deciding he needed to sound slightly more official, he settled on, "I'm not at liberty to say," and walked away before the man could reply.

A uniformed officer stopped him at the barrier. His mind went blank for a moment, then he reached into his pocket.

Shifting his stance, the officer dropped his hand to his holster and unsnapped it, not drawing it yet.

When he realised how close he'd come to getting himself shot, Harlan's eyes widened and his voice was barely a squeak. "I'm just... ID!" He pulled out the laminated card with a metal clip that Hamilton had given him. He'd never had to use it before. Hamilton had always led the way. Everything about Hamilton screamed 'cop' so loudly that Harlan suspected he could get through even out of his uniform — in a city where no one knew him.

The cop took the badge from Harlan, frowning at it, then at Harlan.

"I haven't gotten my photo ID yet," Harlan apologized, feeling like he needed to justify his entire existence.

Still without speaking, the man handed Harlan's badge back and stepped aside.

"Thank—"

His mouth was full of blood. He coughed, retched, trying to spit it out, but more flowed in to take its place. He fell to all fours, felt a crunch as one of the delicate bones in his face shattered, screamed as a sudden, invisible blow struck his ribs. He curled in a tight, protective ball in the dirty alley, drowning in his own blood as something unseen continued to batter him.

"Hey."

A hand on his shoulder, gentle, but he flinched away from it.

"You're not the first person this has happened to. That's why you're here. Get up."

Hamilton. Not who—or *what*—had attacked him.

Harlan swallowed, tasting only his own saliva, without a hint of blood. He could breathe. He wasn't choking. Nothing had hit him.

He wanted to leave, now, before the spirit he could feel circling came howling back into him. He was shaking badly, his teeth chattering, covered in rapidly cooling sweat.

"Can I—?"

He had to stop, clear his throat, swallow again before he could continue. "Can I see the body?" He didn't want to, didn't want anything but to leave and never come back, but he *needed* to see it.

Hamilton gave him a look he couldn't read, and for a moment Harlan flashed back to school at the Centre. He doubted Hamilton cared that he'd said 'can' rather than 'may,' the way certain teachers had insisted.

Was he not allowed to view the victim's body?

A pause, and Hamilton shrugged. "Sure." He inclined his head in the direction of the pathetically small form in a body bag off to one side. "She's been moved," he warned. "I'm not sure if that makes a difference to you either way."

Oh, please, not a child. The spirit hadn't felt like it was that young, but ghosts didn't always manifest the way they'd appeared in life, including chronological age. Though Harlan had never heard of a ghost appearing older than the person when they'd died.

As he approached the body, the uniformed officer standing beside it gave Harlan a quizzical look but didn't stop him. She must have assumed he belonged there, and he frantically wanted to tell her he didn't, but he forced himself to keep walking.

He knelt, hovering his fingers over the zipper, his hand trembling. He touched the metal tab, jerking his hand back as though it had burned him. Taking a deep breath, almost a sob, he grabbed the zipper firmly and pulled, exposing the corpse's face.

Pain. Pain pain pain pain fear. Rage. Helpless Nothing.

"Hey. Hey!"

Pain, but different. His face stung. He tried to open his eyes, realized they were already open, but all he could see was black. Panicked, he sat up, blinking, trying to clear the darkness from his vision. A pale blur, a shaky outline, then a face. Hamilton. Again. Harlan smiled, found moving even that much hurt. *You do care,* he thought, distantly. One of his eyes still wasn't tracking or focusing properly, making Hamilton's face look flat and distorted.

There was a murmur of voices around them, but Hamilton used his body as a shield. Harlan's smile widened before he could stop himself. *Ow.*

"What the fuck are you smiling about?" Hamilton leaned down, snapped his fingers in front of Harlan's face. "Hey. You still in there?"

Harlan nodded. Slowly. Every muscle felt raw and stiff. Even though he knew Hamilton was speaking normally, his words sounded too fast, slippery, darting away like minnows when he tried to grasp them.

"Good. You scared the sh— What happened? You hardly looked at the body, then you fell down and started twitching like you were having a fucking seizure. An ambulance is on the way." He leaned down farther. "Your eye's all fucked up."

That didn't surprise Harlan. He felt like he'd fallen at least a few feet—and been slammed into the pavement a few times.

There was something physically wrong with his eye. He could start from there.

"Show me," Harlan said, impressed by how even his voice sounded.

Hamilton held up his cell. Harlan nodded, opening his eye as wide as possible, even though it hurt. Hamilton passed him the phone with the camera app already open and reversed for taking a selfie, and Harlan winced. It looked pretty bad. His sclera was red and bloodshot, like a vessel had burst when the ghost had slammed in or out of him.

"No."

"What?"

"No ambulance." With a monumental force of will he hadn't known he possessed — perhaps a poor choice of words, given the circumstances — Harlan managed to stand. "No ambulance. No people. Get everyone out of here."

"You still possessed?"

Harlan hoped he was imagining the twitch of Hamilton's hand toward his holster. He shook his head, his chin abruptly falling onto his chest when his neck stopped supporting his head. "Making her stronger. Need..." He blinked, realized what it was. "No men. Women can stay, but *back*."

"All right." Giving Harlan a long, searching look, Hamilton started wrangling the other police officers. Once the men had left and the women were out of the barricaded area, Hamilton returned.

"Go... I'm fine," Harlan protested, not at all convincingly. He didn't honestly want to be alone behind the barriers with the ghost, but he also knew she would either attack Hamilton or not appear.

"Uh-huh." Crossing his arms, Hamilton raised an eyebrow.

"No men."

"You're a man."

"But I'm —" Harlan pushed at Hamilton, weakly. "Go. She hurt me because she's scared, and she's scared because of you. Because you're a man."

Another thought Harlan couldn't read flashed across Hamilton's face, but he nodded and backed away. He didn't turn, didn't move farther than ten feet until Harlan started waving at him in frustration. He stopped the instant Harlan nodded, and stood guard, arms crossed.

Harlan closed his eyes, wincing. Even his eyelid hurt when it slid over his damaged eye. It had never occurred to him that his *eyelid* could hurt, and it was an unwelcome discovery.

He couldn't tell where his fear stopped and the ghost's began. He was afraid of her attacking him again, and she was afraid of him, but she also knew he was the only one who could communicate with her.

He held out his hands, parallel to the ground at the level of his hips, trying to make himself as nonthreatening as possible. "They're gone. I won't hurt you."

She lashed out, her agony and fear coalescing into a bright, hot point of pain that seared Harlan's forearm. He'd barely covered his face in time.

"*Get out!*" she screamed in his face, her breath cold as deepest winter. "*Get out, get out, get* out!"

"I can't do that. I'm sorry. You're hurting people, scaring people—and it's not good for you to be here, either." He could feel tears streaming down his face, unsure if they were hers or his own—not that it mattered either way. "You don't need to hurt anymore. You can go someplace…safe."

She wavered, her indecision making her outline shimmer and disappear before flashing nearly solid again, over and over. "You can do that?" she asked finally, going still. Her spectral arms were wrapped around her too-thin torso, and she shivered in a wind she could no longer feel.

Harlan shook his head. Enough had been done *to* her in her life. He could feel it as clearly as he felt his heartbeat. He didn't want to be yet another in a lifetime of men who had taken her agency and turned it against her. "*We* can do that. *You* can do that. I'm just here to show you, but you're the one who can help yourself." He couldn't believe how easily the words were flowing out of him, how confident and competent he sounded.

She nodded, sniffling audibly, even though she no longer had mucus. "Okay. What do I gotta do?"

"First, you have to let go—"

"*No!*"

Flickering madly again, she slammed him against a filthy Dumpster hard enough to knock the wind out of him, and he could feel something wet soaking through his jeans. He hoped he hadn't pissed himself. He didn't think so, but the thought of garbage juice in his underwear wasn't much better.

"*No, no, no, never!*"

Coughing, Harlan shook his head. "Don't forgive. Don't forget." His words were tight with pain and the heaviness that surrounded her, making it hard to catch his breath. "It happened. It happened, and it shouldn't have, but now it's over. It's over, and you're more than what was done to you. You can go."

"Go?" She stroked his shoulder, almost apologetically. Frost spread across Harlan's jacket.

He nodded, trying not to show how badly he hurt. It wouldn't help either of them right now if he made her feel guilty on top of everything else.

"There's so much..." She shook her head wildly, her bleached hair slapping her cheeks. "I want to *kill* him. I want to do to him what he did to me. I want—"

Hating himself for it, Harlan cut her off before he lost her completely. "I know. I can't say I know what you're feeling, because I haven't... But I think I would want to, too. And I'm not saying he doesn't deserve it. But..." Something clicked in his mind. "But *you* don't deserve it. Hurting him would feel good, but it would hurt you too, because you're a good person."

She shrugged one pale, bony shoulder. "You don't know me. I'm not."

"It's true. You don't have to become like him. You can go," he repeated.

"Will I go to Hell?" She was sniffling harder now. "'Cause, I haven't exactly…"

Harlan shook his head. He was almost sure the tears were his own, now. "You won't go to Hell."

She narrowed her eyes at him.

"I don't know where you'll go, that's the truth, but I promise it won't be Hell."

"It'll be good? Better?"

Harlan didn't want to lie to her, but he also wanted to comfort her. "I think so. It'll be…different."

She nodded, wiping her face on her skimpy shirt. "Okay. What do I do?"

Harlan closed his eyes again. He could feel her wavering, just on the edge, felt the moment she released what was holding her there.

"Oh my God," she breathed. "It's…it's beautiful."

Harlan didn't turn around, just smiled at her and extended a hand to show her the way. "It's all for you."

Chapter Thirteen

Harlan was so shaken when he got home that he took the stairs rather than the elevator. After being attacked by his dead neighbour, he'd briefly avoided the elevator again, but that had only lasted a few days and one shopping trip worth of carrying groceries up the stairs. Today, though, he'd rather walk than take any chances.

Even behind his locked door and warded walls, protected from both humans and spirits, he still didn't feel safe. He turned on every light in the apartment, even though it was well before sunset. His neighbours were all at work, and the building was eerily silent. He stripped out of his dirty clothes. Hamilton had made him sit on a plastic bag before he'd drive Harlan home. The dampness on his pants and underwear was drying, and he didn't want to know what it was. He tossed both in the garbage.

He turned on the TV for a bit of sound and distraction, curled up on the couch and stared at the screen without noticing what he was watching. He had to keep muting it, convinced he'd heard something in the apartment.

He played a game on his phone. Maybe, now that he had a job with the police, he'd be able to buy a new phone that could actually run Pokémon Go without crashing—but got frustrated when he kept losing, making a wrong move because he thought he saw movement out of the corner of his eye.

He tried doing his Booster Buddy for the day, but the app's guided relaxation exercise didn't do anything for his nervous energy, and he eventually gave up on it.

Out of ideas, he scrolled through his very short list of contacts—two. He could call Hamilton, but the man had seemed pretty freaked out watching Harlan work, and Harlan suspected he wouldn't be much comfort, anyway. He'd been silent during the drive from the crime scene to Harlan's apartment. Finally, just as Harlan had opened the car door, Hamilton had told him not to come in the next day, to just keep in touch if he needed more time.

Tom had told him to call if he needed anything, and he definitely needed *something* right now. He just didn't think Tom could give it to him.

That left Charles. Charles might actually come over, comfort him, hold him in his strong, warm, safe arms, and the rush of excitement he felt at that thought almost made him put the phone down again.

Ghosts couldn't appear around Charles.

He'd sworn to himself that he'd never bother Charles again, though he'd taken the number out of his wallet enough times that the paper was starting to turn translucent and tear along the folds, the numbers smudging a little, but he didn't want to save it in his phone. That would have been too much of a temptation.

His longing and his desire made him stubborn, and he dialled the Centre's number instead. He let it ring twice, then hung up and punched in Charles' number, barely letting it ring before ending the call. He considered turning his phone off, crawling into bed and hiding under the covers, hoping he'd eventually just fall asleep once the adrenaline was out of his system.

His phone rang. Startled, Harlan almost dropped it—almost threw it across the room when he saw it was Charles calling—but he forced himself to answer.

"Hello?"

"Charles?"

"Speaking." His tone suggested that he didn't recognize Harlan's voice.

"It's, ah, it's Harlan…"

"Harlan! Great to hear from you."

Was he imagining the genuine enthusiasm in Charles' voice? Fuck, he hoped not—though the man was a business owner. Maybe he was feigning friendliness, hoping Harlan would return as a paying customer.

Oh. That was a sobering thought. He wished he hadn't given in and dialled Charles' number, but he couldn't quite bring himself to hang up, either.

"Hello? Are you still there?"

Fuck, he'd waited way too long to reply. "Yeah. Sorry, I'm just…"

"Everything okay?"

Harlan opened his mouth to utter the socially acceptable *Yes*, but he swallowed the word down and, "No," came out instead.

A pause, then, "I have to open the club in a few hours, but…you sound like you really need someone."

Harlan inhaled deeply. His first instinct was to try to laugh it off and insist he was fine, but he couldn't bring himself to do it. "I do. Please. Sorry."

"Don't be sorry. Are you up for meeting me here?"

"I don't think I can." Leaving his ghost-warded apartment was unthinkable.

"I'll be right over. You'll be safe until I get there?"

"Yeah."

"I'm leaving right away. I'll see you soon."

He flipped on the television, not watching it, just letting it pass the time. A few minutes later, even though he'd been expecting it — anticipating it, even — the sound of the buzzer still startled him. He pressed the call button.

"It's Charles."

Harlan pressed the button to unlock the front door and a minute later there was a knock on his suite's door. He peered through the peephole, half expecting something to jump out at him or a phantom hand to grab him and pull him through the tiny opening into a hellish netherworld.

All he saw was Charles.

He unlocked the door, stepped aside and practically slammed it behind Charles as soon as he was through.

"Sorry I took so long. I wanted to get you a sandwich, but I wasn't sure what kind you like, so I got one of everything." Grinning self-effacingly, he held up a bulging plastic bag. "I know food always helps me when I'm...well... And I noticed you don't have a lot of food here."

Harlan wondered, but didn't ask, what Charles hadn't finished saying — *having a meltdown? A psychotic break?*

"Thank you."

Charles sat on the sectional and started pulling plastic-wrapped sandwiches out of the bag and setting them on the coffee table.

Selecting a sandwich more or less at random, Harlan barely glanced at the contents before unwrapping it and taking a bite.

"Thank you."

Charles nodded, his smile crinkling his eyes. He chose his own sandwich. "You're welcome."

Harlan's phone rang, startling him again. He glanced at the call display, wide-eyed. *Tom Addison.* "Sorry... I have to take this."

Mouth already full of meat and bread, Charles nodded.

Harlan retreated to the bedroom and shut the door behind him. "Hello?"

"Harlan? It's Tom from the Centre. Did you try calling a minute ago?"

"Yeah. Yes, I did. Sorry."

"Please, no need to apologize! Is everything all right? Do you need something?"

Harlan licked his lips, staring at the door between him and Charles as though he could see through it. "I actually think I've got it under control. Sorry. Thanks. Sorry for worrying you."

"No problem. I'm always here."

Silence for a beat.

"Well, if you're sure...?"

"I'm fine. Thanks for calling back. Bye." Harlan hung up, pressing the phone against his chest. He was pretty sure he actually meant it. He *was* okay — or he would be, at least. He'd called for help and gotten it.

"Sorry about that." Harlan picked up his sandwich again then took another bite.

"No problem. Everything all right?"

Harlan grinned to himself at Charles' unwitting repetition of Tom. "Yeah. Thanks for coming over."

Charles grinned back, as though he were in on the joke. "You're welcome. I'm glad you're okay."

They ate quietly, then both tried speaking at the same time.

"I—" Harlan began, just as Charles said, "Do you—?"

"Sorry," they said, at the same time again.

"You go first," Charles prompted.

Harlan shook his head. "It's not important."

"I was just going to ask... Do you want to talk about whatever happened? It's okay if you don't. I'd understand, but...I'll listen, if you want."

Harlan shrugged. He didn't want to *talk*. He wanted... He wasn't sure. Nothing he could ask Charles for.

"Bad case?"

Harlan looked up, startled. "How did...?"

Now it was Charles' turn to shrug. "Lucky guess." He laughed. "I like to think I'm pretty good at reading people."

Harlan didn't think he was talking about cards. He swallowed, hard, wadding up his sandwich wrapper and praying Charles wouldn't notice his sudden flush.

"If you think talking about it, letting it out, will help, I'm here. If not, we'll just eat, go for a drive, whatever you need."

He reached out, slowly and deliberately, and took Harlan's wrapper. His thumb brushed the back of Harlan's hand and Harlan shivered, arching his wrist to prolong the contact.

And...

"He hurt her. So badly."

"What was that?" Charles set the crumpled plastic on the coffee table, turning so his whole body was facing Harlan, visibly giving Harlan his whole attention.

"He—*fuck*, what he did to her..." He'd stayed so calm and cool while speaking to the ghost, but now he was crying and he couldn't *stop*, and he had no business trying to help someone deal with that—*none*, and—

"Hey." Charles draped his arm over the back of the couch, giving Harlan the space to ignore the gesture or move away.

He shifted closer to Charles, tucking himself tightly against the man's side. Slowly, Charles wrapped his arm around him.

"Hey," Charles repeated, even more softly. "It's okay— It's understandable to be upset by what you see, what you do every day." He laughed, a soft puff of breath. "I'd be more worried about you if you weren't upset."

Harlan aggressively wiped away a tear with the back of his hand, furious with himself. "Sorry."

"Why are you sorry?"

"You probably think I'm a freak. A complete basket case."

"I think you're..."

Harlan winced and felt a rough, warm hand cup his cheek.

"Complicated."

"I'm pretty sure that's the polite way of saying 'a complete basket case'. It's okay," he added. "I'd probably think so, too."

Charles leaned closer, close enough that Harlan could feel his breath on his cheek. He shivered, forearms prickling as goosebumps rose.

"I kinda like complicated." He gently turned Harlan's head, eyes clearly asking a question.

Harlan didn't know what it was, but he wanted the answer to be *yes*. He nodded, closed his eyes to escape the burning intensity of Charles' gaze.

He felt lips brush his own, just for a heart-stopping instant.

The kiss ended and Charles pulled away. Harlan's eyes snapped open. Charles had retreated, blushing.

"Sorry," he murmured, looking away.

Harlan swallowed hard, struggling to catch his breath. "I-I don't mind."

"I know you're upset right now. Fuck, I shouldn't've done that. I don't want to take advantage of you when you're feeling vulnerable. I just—" Charles laughed. "I have shitty timing. Have you... You *have* kissed before?"

"Yes!"

Harlan had only kissed another person three times—the same person. Billy—or Billie, Harlan had never been sure—had been another student at the Centre. They weren't really interested in Harlan, and Harlan hadn't really been interested in them, but they'd had a crush on the same person. Kissing each other provided practice and a chance to compete, to see who could woo the object of their mutual desire. They'd been a little older than Harlan, and they'd left the Centre two years before. They hadn't kept in touch.

Harlan hadn't kissed Billy for several years before they'd left.

After letting out a small, frustrated sound, Harlan's whole body tensed and strained as though trying to tear itself in two, then he crawled over Charles, straddling his lap, his arms wrapped around Charles' neck, their faces close together.

Charles laughed again, going still as though Harlan might bolt if he moved suddenly, and Harlan couldn't say he wouldn't.

After a few deep, lingering kisses, Charles' lips weren't enough to satisfy him. He let his mouth roam Charles' jaw, stubble tickling against his teeth and lips. Down, farther, to Charles' neck, feeling his breath hitch. He fisted his hands in Charles' thick hair, and he realized he was grinding his erection against Charles' pleasantly rounded stomach.

He pulled away, mortified. "I—I'm—"

"It's all right," Charles said, his voice soft, almost breathy. "I don't mind."

Harlan leaned forward again, but Charles stopped him by gently placing a hand on his chest.

"Mm-mm. Not tonight. I want to," Charles added. "Oh, I want to, but I have to open the club soon. Tonight, is it all right if I just hold you and we'll come back to this? Promise."

Harlan nodded. He would've agreed to anything if it meant Charles would stay just a little longer.

Laughing, Charles wrapped an arm around Harlan again and pulled him tightly against his side. "If you ever call me when it isn't an emergency."

Harlan blushed, burying his face against Charles' shoulder. "Sorry." He yawned, broadly, the emotions of the day catching up with him in a rush now that sex was off the table.

"Bed? To sleep," Charles quickly clarified.

Harlan nodded, his whole body going loose and relaxed at the suggestion. Right now, he wanted nothing more than to curl up with Charles holding him tight, safe behind the double barrier of the wards and Charles' unexplained ghost-repelling properties.

Chapter Fourteen

"Hey. Sorry I had to wake you. I've got to go." Charles' hand, large and comforting, was smoothing his hair. "And I think you were having a nightmare."

Harlan blinked awake with a start. He knew he'd been dreaming, but he didn't remember any of the details. Still groggy and shaken, he felt a vicious surge of selfishness. He wanted to implore Charles to stay, tell him to fuck the club and take care of him, get him through the rest of the night.

Charles seemed to notice his hesitation. "Sorry. I'd stay if I could." He gave Harlan's hand a quick squeeze before sliding out of bed with a groan. "You work tomorrow?" he asked, pulling his jeans back on. They'd both stripped to underwear and T-shirts.

Harlan shook his head, closing his eyes to escape the glare of the lamp Charles had turned on so he could dress.

"I won't be done until at least six or seven, but after that I could come by and check on you. If you'd like."

"Six or seven in the *morning*?" Harlan made a face.

"'Fraid so."

"What time is it now?"

"Almost ten."

Still disoriented, Harlan almost asked if it was morning or night, but by cocking his head he could just see the window, confirming it was dark out.

"I'd like that. Thanks. Even if you just want to text me?"

"Of course." Charles finished dressing and clicked off the lamp. "Sorry... I guess you'll have to get up to lock the door behind me."

If he'd had a spare cut, he would've given it to Charles immediately, both so he wouldn't have to leave the bed and because he wanted, suddenly and desperately, to show Charles he trusted and cared for him — but he only had one copy.

He followed Charles to the door and locked it behind him. He leaned against his side, listening to Charles retreat down the hall.

Even though he was still exhausted after being woken from only a few hours' sleep, he didn't return to bed. He sat on the couch in the dark, staring at the TV without registering anything he saw. The coffee table was empty. Charles must have put the leftover sandwiches away, but Harlan hadn't seen him do it.

He felt as though he'd barely closed his eyes when the grating buzzer startled him awake again. He stumbled to the speaker, mounted on the wall by the door.

"'Lo?"

"It's Charles. Sorry. I texted, but you didn't reply, and..."

Harlan yawned. "'S okay. I'm... I'm glad you're here." He blushed, a little astonished that he'd just said that out loud, even if it wasn't to Charles' face. He buzzed Charles in.

Once he arrived at the suite, Charles set another take-out bag on the coffee table, even though there were still plenty of sandwiches left from the night before.

"I, uh, brought breakfast. Not sure if you're hungry or not. I always am after a shift."

Harlan wondered if he'd spent the night spanking beautiful young men, if he'd gotten off on it, if he'd thought about Harlan at all... *No.* He couldn't let himself think about that.

Charles started unpacking trays of classic breakfast foods — pancakes, bacon, eggs, toast, hash browns and sausage.

"I wasn't sure what you liked, again, so I got...everything." Charles grinned a little sheepishly.

Now that he'd smelled food, Harlan realized he was hungry. Ravenous. He quickly loaded a plate with some of everything, grabbed a plastic fork from the bag and started eating.

After several minutes of silence, broken only by chewing, Harlan felt like he should start a conversation, but he didn't know what to say. He didn't actually know much about Charles except his business.

"How was work?" That was a start, anyway.

"I'm assuming you're not talking about refilling the napkin dispensers?" Charles smirked playfully.

Blushing, Harlan shook his head.

"Y'know, you seem awfully curious about the whole thing."

"I'm just making conversation," Harlan insisted, crossing his legs.

"Mm-hmm. You've never fantasized about being spanked?" Grinning, Charles ate a mouthful of scrambled eggs.

Harlan quickly filled his own mouth with hash browns so he could have at least a few seconds to think, aware that Charles' attention was fully on him the whole time.

Swallowing hard, he shook his head, then nodded.

Charles raised an eyebrow. "Bit of a mixed message, there."

"Yes, all right? I've thought about it and watched plenty of porn along those lines, too." *Fuck. Why did I say that?*

They stared at each other for a long moment. Charles' expression was calm and considering, as Harlan felt increasingly flustered. When it became clear that Charles didn't intend to break the silence, Harlan finally felt compelled to speak.

"So...?"

Charles laughed, shaking his head. "What? You want me to put you over my knee right now?"

Harlan fought to keep his face blank. He didn't *not* want that, but at the same time, the thought was terrifying. "No? No," he repeated, more firmly.

"Good, because it's not happening." He leaned forward and patted Harlan's thigh.

"If I wanted... If that *was* going to happen, what would I need to do first?"

"Do you want that to happen?"

Oh God. Harlan swallowed, hard. He nodded, unable to meet Charles' level gaze.

"Do you want it to happen with me, or do you just want *someone* to spank you?"

Even knowing he had only himself to blame for starting this conversation—or at least continuing it—Harlan was strongly tempted to run away and hide in his bedroom. "You." He managed to force out the word.

Charles beamed. Harlan wasn't sure if his smile actually made the room brighter or if it just seemed that way to him. He reached over again and gave Harlan's hand a squeeze. "Do you *just* want me to spank you?"

This question was easier to answer, but Harlan still forced himself to hesitate. He shook his head.

"Right. Well." Charles laughed. "As...bizarre...as most of our meetings have been, I can't say I'm not interested in you, too."

Harlan managed to stop the word *Really?* from fully emerging. Barely.

"BDSM aside—and that's an entirely different conversation, for another time—maybe we could start with something simpler?"

What was simpler than spanking? That seemed pretty basic to Harlan.

"Something like...a kiss?" Charles prompted, tracing his thumb over Harlan's knuckles.

"Oh!" Harlan couldn't help laughing at himself. "Yeah. I'd like that."

"Me too." Charles slid off the armchair he'd been sitting on and sat on the couch beside Harlan—slowly, giving him time to move away.

Harlan stayed perfectly still. This moment felt fragile, like he'd only get one chance, and if he reacted badly, it would be gone forever, but at the same time he felt like, just by *thinking* all that, he was already getting it wrong.

"Hey." Charles squeezed Harlan's hand again. "Do you want to stop?"

That, again, was an easy answer. "No!"

Charles grinned, holding up his free hand in mock-surrender. "All right, I just wanted to be sure I wasn't... It works better if your face is a little closer to mine." He beckoned, keeping his hand on Harlan's but without pressure.

"Right." Harlan didn't move for a long moment, so long that he imagined he could feel waves of disappointment coming from Charles — or maybe relief that he didn't have to go through with this, after all? He leaned towards Charles, and their lips brushed for a brief instant before he pulled away again.

Slowly, Charles reached up with his free hand and slid it around to cup the back of Harlan's neck. He pulled ever so slightly, inviting but not forcing.

That brief taste hadn't been nearly enough, and Harlan eagerly allowed himself to be drawn in again. He closed his eyes — that made it easier, cutting out at least one source of overstimulation, leaving him free to concentrate on smell, taste and touch. Charles' lips were slightly dry and cracked, his stubble bristling against Harlan's chin wherever they made contact. He smelled a little bit like beer and a little bit like his dungeon, but underneath that was the scent of his sweat and his own personal fragrance. Harlan wanted to nuzzle against him like a cat, spread Charles' scent all over himself and get his smell on Charles in return.

He parted his lips, and after a moment, Charles leaned closer to explore his mouth with his tongue.

Charles pulled back with a breathy sigh, relinquishing his hold on Harlan's neck. "Do you want to keep going or is this enough?"

Harlan opened his eyes, briefly finding it difficult to focus. "I want..." Making sure he had Charles' attention, he pointedly dropped his gaze to Charles' groin, pleased to see his jeans were decidedly tented.

Charles laughed, a deep, throaty chuckle that sent a shiver down Harlan's spine. "All right. Should we...?" He cocked his head toward the bedroom.

"Yes. Right. That might be..." Harlan frowned thoughtfully. "You do like just...sex, right? Without...?"

"I'm not Christian Grey." He looked askance at Harlan.

"Who...?"

"Never mind. Yes, I like regular, non-kinky sex."

"Okay, good, because you made it sound like we wouldn't be doing anything kinky today, and if we had to stop now, I think I'd—"

Charles cut him off with another kiss, gently tugging him to his feet and leading him to the bedroom. He started undressing even before he'd crossed the threshold. "What do you want to do?"

"What *can* we do?"

He laughed, kindly. More kindly than Harlan deserved for that question.

"We can do anything you want. Anything *we* want. But I think we both want something more than kissing. I do."

Harlan swallowed hard. "Yeah. Me too."

"It's easier without clothes," Charles prompted, shedding the last of his. He dropped them in a pile on the floor, which Harlan found oddly...comforting. There was no pretense in the action, no one he was trying to impress. It also carried a sense of urgency, despite Harlan apparently doing everything he could to bring things to a grinding halt.

Harlan's body wanted this. *He* wanted this.

He pulled off his plain lime-green T-shirt—no graphic or saying or even a logo, like all the rest of his shirts—and tossed it, after a moment's hesitation, onto the floor beside Charles' clothes. He didn't know why he'd done it—the hamper was barely two feet farther—but now that he had, he was determined to play out his decision without hesitation. *Take action,* stand by *action.* He pulled off his socks and tossed them just as carelessly.

Charles sat on the bed, watching Harlan undress. He was silent, but his interest was plain in his expression.

Harlan didn't think he was really revealing anything worthy of that interest—his pale, skinny, almost-hairless torso wouldn't be gracing magazine covers any time soon—but he couldn't deny that the interest excited him.

He quickly stripped off his jeans, hesitated for a moment, then threw his underwear after them.

He wanted to dive under the blankets and cover up. It was silly, of course. Charles had seen him naked before, if under very different circumstances. They'd showered together, for fuck's sake!

It wasn't enough to get him through this moment, though. He slunk closer to the bed, to Charles, like a wild animal approaching a circle of firelight in hopes of pilfering food.

Charles held out his hand, completing the mental image, and Harlan couldn't help but smile. Charles smiled back, even though he couldn't know what Harlan was grinning about, and Harlan's tension left him. He lightly rested his hands on Charles' shoulders, slowly sliding them down to Charles' broad, well-formed pecs, dancing his thumbs across his erect nipples.

Charles hummed with pleasure, his eyes half closed. "Tease."

"I wouldn't want to tease you," Harlan assured him, his tone somewhere between apologetic and playful. Inspiration struck. He dropped to his knees, gently pushing Charles' knees apart.

Charles groaned, leaning forward so his head was almost directly above Harlan's. "Really?" He laughed. "Not what I was expecting you to pick first, but okay. I'm not going to say no. But I want it to be because you want it, not because you to feel like you have to…impress me or something."

Harlan shook his head. Well, maybe a *little*. He did want to impress Charles, especially during this, their first time together. But he also genuinely did like sucking cock. He'd missed it.

He shifted to one side, then the other, subtly adjusting Charles as well, until he was content with both of their positions. He slid one hand up each of Charles' inner thighs until they reached his groin, relishing the way Charles gasped, the bed creaking as he slid closer.

Harlan leaned forward slowly, both to savour the moment and to tease Charles a little. He breathed on Charles' damp cockhead, softly blowing warm air up and down his shaft until neither of them could wait any longer. He leaned forward again, decisively this time, and wrapped his lips around Charles' tip with a deliciously lewd *pop*. He slid deeper until his lips rested just behind the corona. His mouth was pleasantly full and he could feel the weight of Charles' cock pressing down on his lower jaw. It was everything he could have hoped for during his lonely nights of fevered desire. He closed his eyes, letting the experience ground him in his body, marking the boundary where he ended and Charles began. He felt movement on either side of him and opened his eyes to see that Charles had grabbed fistfuls of blanket. Harlan liked that, especially because he was just getting started.

He rolled his head forward, taking a little of Charles' shaft now. It was blood-hot and he could feel Charles' galloping heartbeat in one of the thick veins pressed against his tongue. He lapped at it, enjoying the way he could get it to speed up even more with every lick.

Greedy now, he took Charles deeper. His cock was thick enough to stretch Harlan's jaw, but not so long that he worried about deepthroating him. The last thing he wanted was for Hamilton to ask why his voice was raspy the next time he saw him.

"*Fuck*, that's good," Charles moaned. One of his hands left the blanket to lightly rest on top of Harlan's head.

Harlan liked that and showed it by pressing just a bit deeper before backing off to concentrate his lips and tongue on Charles' cockhead again.

"I—" Charles laughed. "I'll be honest. I didn't think you had much experience. Either I was way off base or you're a natural. Beginner's luck. Sorry, I'm babbling. Your mouth just feels so *good*."

He sounded almost giddy, and Harlan liked that too.

He couldn't help feeling relieved that his mouth was full and he didn't have to confirm or deny his experience—or lack of it. He didn't want to talk about his past, sexual or otherwise. He'd just have to let his actions speak for themselves.

He swiftly built up a rhythm, not wanting to give Charles a chance to ask any more questions — or make observations, rather. He rocked forward and back, his hands braced on Charles' thighs, enjoying the increasingly salty taste filling his mouth. Charles was already swaying in counterpoint to Harlan's movements. Harlan didn't think Charles would last long, and he liked that *very* much. He saw it as a compliment to his cock-sucking skills. Though he did find it odd that the owner of a BDSM club would ever get this pent up. Maybe he wasn't imagining 'the scene' correctly at all. Maybe that was why he was desperate enough to take up with Harlan in the first place.

Charles shook his head, his mouth opening and closing wordlessly a few times before he managed to gasp, "*Close.*"

Harlan nodded, the movement making Charles moan.

The hand on Harlan's head tightened, and Charles' other hand rested on Harlan's shoulder as he came, his hips pumping. Harlan kept his mouth loose and relaxed, letting Charles set the rhythm.

Charles pulled back with a sigh, breathing a little heavily.

Harlan licked his lips, then wiped them on the back of his hand, before grinning up at Charles.

"Sorry I, uh, didn't last… It's been a while," Charles admitted.

As Harlan had suspected. That was almost certainly why Charles was with him. But why wouldn't he be able to get someone better? More confident, more handsome, more adventurous?

Charles patted the bed beside himself, inviting Harlan up to join him.

Harlan eagerly scrambled up onto the mattress, sitting close beside Charles with their naked sides touching. Whatever the reason for Charles being here, Harlan was grateful as long as he had him.

Charles leaned over and kissed Harlan's shoulder. "What can I do for you?" he asked, his voice a low, seductive growl.

"I—" Harlan shivered, goosebumps rising on his arms. "I'd like it if we just cuddled. And you could stroke me?"

He was a little surprised by his own boldness, and relieved when Charles answered, "Of course."

Chapter Fifteen

"Hey, Harlan!"

Harlan was pleased and relieved to hear the genuine pleasure in Charles' voice when he answered the phone. "Hi, Charles."

"What's up? Is everything okay?"

Harlan laughed. "Yeah. Everything's fine. *More* than fine. I'm just calling because, uh...well, because it's not an emergency." He hoped Charles would remember saying that and he didn't just sound as weird as he usually did.

Charles answered with a soft chuckle of his own. "Well, I'm glad to hear from you."

Harlan took a deep, steadying breath. He could do this. He'd already done the hard part and called Charles. Now he just had to complete the next step in his plan. "I was wondering if you might like to..." *Fuck.* He'd practiced what he wanted to say over and over in his head, but now it felt like that practice was only making it more difficult to actually speak. "If you'd like to go for coffee?" he finally managed, turning a slight squeak at the end of the question into a cough.

"I'd like that. Well, maybe not coffee. I spend enough of my time shut away in a dark dungeon—literally—that I'd rather do something outside. And I think you could probably use some sunlight and fresh air, too."

"Oh, o-okay..." Harlan scrambled to come up with something else. *Shit.* That threw all his ideas out of the window. He wasn't really one to come up with outdoor activities. The outdoors couldn't be ghost-warded.

His eyes widened. With *Charles*, they could be. This opened up a whole new world of possibilities.

"Sure. Yeah, I'd like that!" he bubbled. "Do you have any ideas?"

"Oh, I've got plenty of ideas," Charles said, a playful growl. "But if you're asking me on a date..."

"I am," Harlan confirmed, almost confidently, glad Charles wasn't there to see him blush. God, that sound just went straight to his groin!

"How about a picnic?"

The little pessimistic voice that lived in Harlan immediately chimed in with, *Ants. Ghosts. Ghost ants*, but he pushed it aside. "That sounds lovely."

"I keep bringing you food, but nothing I've actually made myself. I'm told I'm a pretty good cook."

Shit. That probably meant that he expected... "Do you want me to bring anything?" Harlan asked reluctantly, mentally already searching, *How do I pretend I made something store bought?*

"Just you."

"I can do that."

"Great. How does Monday or Tuesday sound? Those are my days off."

Harlan bit his lip. "Lunch or dinner?"

"Whichever you prefer. Dinner Monday or lunch Tuesday are slightly better for me, so I can sleep in Monday, but I'm happy either way."

Shit again. It wasn't out of the question that he'd still be working at dinnertime, and they didn't often take a formal lunch break. Hamilton brought something from home and ate on the go, and Harlan usually just skipped the meal entirely. "Dinner Monday," he said, decisively.

"Great. It's a date. I'll pick you up? I know a great park—ducks, a pond, the whole shebang."

Harlan couldn't help grinning. "That sounds perfect." He actually held the phone to his chest for a moment after they'd said goodbye.

During the remainder of the week, Harlan mentally practiced telling Hamilton that he needed to be done by five on Monday, especially after a recalcitrant ghost kept them until almost ten at night on Friday, but Hamilton had called Monday morning and told him they didn't have any cases that day.

That meant Harlan had the whole day to get ready, but it also meant that he had *the whole day* to get ready. He was briefly tempted to call Charles and suggest meeting for lunch instead, but Charles had said he'd be sleeping in Monday morning, and Harlan didn't want to wake him.

He got out of bed with a groan and took an extra-long shower. Looking at the alarm clock when he got back to the bedroom, he groaned again—barely half an hour had passed.

He laid every single one of his shirts—the ones that had been purchased *for* him—out on the bed. There wasn't a lot of variety. Most of them were plain, without a logo or picture or anything, in colours he could grudgingly admit suited him. Shopping for new clothes would eat up some of his extra time, but would also involve…well, shopping for new clothes, so that was out of the question. But maybe…

His old phone was getting so laggy that even researching what *new* phone he should get was a chore, and that convinced him. He considered ordering a phone online and having it delivered, but he wanted it *now*, even if it meant having to interact with people.

He'd never had a contract — or a new phone — before, and he was surprised to discover he liked the feeling. It made him feel…solid. Grounded. Like maybe, just maybe, he belonged out here in the real world, not shut away in the Centre his whole life.

Plus, getting the phone had eaten almost two hours.

He spent most of the rest of the day fiddling around on his phone. He set up Pokémon Go, but quickly realized he'd need to 'Pokémon Leave' the apartment if he wanted to actually play. He read some *Cracked* articles and fell into weird Wikipedia rabbit holes and tried not to glance at the clock every five seconds. It didn't help that the clock was directly above anything he did on his phone.

Finally, after what seemed like an eternity or twelve, a text from Charles —

On my way. Ready?

Feeling a crippling sense of mingled excitement and anxiety, Harlan forced himself to simply reply —

Yes.

New phone?

Charles replied immediately, prompting Harlan to hope he wasn't texting while driving. He didn't seem like the type to do something like that.

Harlan didn't answer, just went downstairs and waited outside for Charles. He waved when he saw Charles' now-familiar car pull up in front of the building, hurrying over and getting into the front seat. Glancing in the back, he saw an honest-to-God wicker picnic basket sitting on top of a neatly folded checkered blanket. He wasn't at all surprised.

"Have you been to High Park before?" Charles asked.

Harlan shook his head. "I haven't really...been many places."

"Right. You grew up in the Centre, didn't you?"

"Yeah." Harlan sank lower in his seat, his shoulders hunched.

"Sorry. You don't have to talk about it if it's painful."

"No, I'll have to... I should tell you eventually." Harlan shrugged. "My parents left me there when I was a kid, and it's...pretty much all I've known until a few months ago. It wasn't a bad place to grow up," he added, "and I don't miss my parents."

"Fair enough." Charles reached over and gave Harlan's leg a brief squeeze, glancing away from the road just long enough to smile at him and have it acknowledged before focusing again.

Harlan slowly straightened in his seat again.

"Here we are." Charles parked and grabbed the picnic basket and blanket. Harlan followed him on a short walk to an open, grassy area with a few scattered picnic tables. Glancing between the clusters of families with small children and Harlan's feeble attempt at not looking uncomfortable at the prospect of being around so many other people, Charles led the way to the far side of the field and laid out the blanket far away from anyone else. Harlan appreciated that he just *did* it, without calling attention to Harlan's discomfort, never mind teasing him about it. His silent act of caring meant a lot.

"So," Charles announced, opening the basket with a flourish, pulling out a stack of thick sandwiches wrapped in plastic, "I know I've brought you sandwiches before, but these sandwiches are different because I made them myself rather than buying them pre-made. The only real difference is that I put the meat and cheese and veggies on them rather than someone else, but…" He shook his head, grinning wryly. "Sorry. I swear I actually am a good cook, and I had good intentions. The day just sorta got away from me. But!" He held up a hand, rummaging in the basket again. "I did bake brownies, and I brought extra so you can take some home." He laid them on the blanket like a poker player displaying a winning hand.

Harlan couldn't help grinning back at him, taking a sandwich from the stack and unwrapping it. He took a bite, only exaggerating his blissful reaction a little, playfully. "It's delicious," he assured Charles, "much better than the store-bought. Besides, I haven't really cooked anything as complicated as this"—he waved the sandwich—"and I don't think this actually counts as cooking."

Charles shrugged one shoulder, selecting a sandwich of his own. "You have other talents."

Not sure which 'talents' Charles was referring to and unwilling to ask for clarification, Harlan blushed.

Fortunately, he could think of plenty of other things to talk about—maybe being outside wasn't so bad. "It's beautiful here."

His mouth full, Charles nodded in agreement. After he'd swallowed, he pointed. "In the spring, there are cherry blossoms over there. There's also a small zoo, but I thought you might like the…quieter parts of the park, at least on the first visit."

Harlan nodded gratefully, reaching out to brush Charles' free hand with his own, trailing his fingers along the man's knuckles. Charles caught it and gave it a little squeeze before releasing. Charles' words triggered a tiny fraction of a memory. Maybe he had been here before, as a child. He didn't mention it to Charles. He was probably wrong.

He didn't have to feign any delight at the brownies. He took a bite and closed his eyes, tipping his head back. "Oh my God. This is…mmm!" He gobbled it down, then the second one Charles offered.

"I'll definitely have to cook a proper meal for you sometime," Charles promised. "I'm glad I made extra for you. I like the thought of you eating them and thinking about me when you're all alone in your apartment."

"Me too."

"I brought some chopped lettuce," Charles told him, after putting the considerably lighter picnic basket back in his car. He led Harlan past where they'd eaten to a pond.

"Okay." Harlan thought they'd eaten everything. He was pleasantly full, and he didn't really want to finish off his meal with plain raw lettuce. He wasn't overly fond of it tucked into salad and disguised with plenty of dressing, never mind on its own.

Charles laughed fondly at Harlan's expression. "To feed the ducks," he clarified.

"Oh! I thought you were supposed to feed them bread?"

"Bread isn't great for ducks, actually. Lettuce is much better." He glanced across the pond to where a mother was encouraging her young son to throw bits of bread crust into the water, where they were immediately devoured. "Obviously they're still getting plenty of bread, but I do what I can."

Harlan was skeptical that they'd be able to attract any ducks with the lettuce when bread was on offer, but a few paddled over and started snapping it out of the water. An especially bold duck waddled to shore, staring at Charles demandingly. Charles threw a few scraps of lettuce on the ground and the duck eagerly devoured them. He held a piece between two fingers and offered it. The two men shared a grin when the duck stretched out its neck to its full length to grab the snack before retreating a few steps to swallow.

When it came back for more, Charles offered Harlan some lettuce. "Want to try?"

Ducks don't have teeth, do they? Harlan wasn't sure, but the bird seemed friendly enough...for a small dinosaur. He had very little experience with animals, and none with wild—or wild-ish—ones, but he was determined to try. He was pretty sure Charles wouldn't want to date someone too scared to feed a duck.

Squatting the way Charles had, he held out the lettuce with his arm fully extended, closing his eyes as the duck approached. He felt a slight pinch on one fingertip, then felt the lettuce tugged from his grasp and heard the *plop-plop-plop* of webbed feet walking away.

They continued until Charles stood and brushed his hands together with an apologetic shrug. "Sorry, guys. We're all out of lettuce." Of course, the ducks didn't understand his words or the gesture, and they continued quacking until they'd left the pond. The intrepid duck followed them for a few meters before turning back with a sound Harlan couldn't help thinking conveyed disgust.

Charles and Harlan sat on a bench, their fingers loosely intertwined as they watched joggers and parents with children pass on the nearby path.

"It's starting to get dark," Charles pointed out at last, breaking the comfortable silence.

Harlan realized he hadn't seen any children for a while, and he nodded.

"You ready to go?"

He nodded again, a little reluctantly, and followed Charles to the car. He didn't really want to go, but he was getting chilly now that Charles had pointed out how late it was getting. He'd dressed for a sunny afternoon, not evening.

"I had a really great time today," Harlan told him when they arrived at his apartment, a little surprised to realize that, unlike most situations when he'd said something like that, he genuinely meant it.

"Me too." Charles leaned across the emergency brake to give him a kiss, which Harlan happily returned.

"Would you, uh, like to come upstairs...?" he asked, a little surprised by his own boldness.

Charles gave Harlan's hand a squeeze. "Sorry. I'd love to, but I just got a text from my cleaner that one of the toilets is backed up and I have to go see if I can fix it or if I need to call a plumber." He shook his head wryly. "'*Start your own business!*' they said. "'*It'll be fun!*' they said." He squeezed Harlan's hand again, waiting until he had his attention. "But...soon? And maybe we could try adding a little *more*, if you're still, ah, interested."

Not trusting his voice, Harlan just nodded. He hopped out of the car — keeping his back to Charles — before he tried to persuade him that the toilet could wait.

Chapter Sixteen

"I—I'm not sure what to do," Harlan admitted. He was starting to feel a little foolish, standing there naked in front of Charles, and he had to resist the urge to cover himself with his hands.

"Would you like me to tell you?" Charles asked, softly.

Not sure how else to proceed, Harlan nodded.

"Kneel on the bed, bracing yourself with your forearms," Charles said, his voice still soothing rather than commanding.

Harlan nodded. He could do that.

"Relax." Charles' hands stroked his raised buttocks, drawing back when Harlan tensed. "I'll let you know before I start, okay?"

Swallowing hard, Harlan nodded again.

Ignoring his backside for the time being, Charles petted and lightly massaged Harlan's outer thighs, his hips, as far up Harlan's back as he could reach.

Gradually, fibre by fibre, Harlan eased into the touch, no longer expecting a blow every time Charles lifted his hands.

"I just want to say, once more, that we don't have to do this. I'm happy to keep things the way they are for as long as you want."

Harlan shook his head, trying to keep his jaw from tightening. "I want this. I want to try."

A warm, comforting hand on his side... "This isn't something you have to prove to me — to anyone. It's not a rite of passage or something. It's just supposed to be fun."

"I know!" Harlan snapped, instantly regretting his tone. He forced himself to take several deep breaths, relieved that Charles hadn't pulled away. "Sorry. I am a little nervous, but I trust you, and I've been thinking about this since the first time I met you."

"Me too. Well, maybe not the *first* time. That was more like, '*Fuck, my club is haunted!*' But for a while now." Slowly, so slowly, Charles traced his way down to cup Harlan's cheeks. "Remember your safewords?"

"Yellow if I want to change something, red if I want to stop."

"Good. Ready?"

Harlan nodded.

Keeping one hand on Harlan's side, Charles lifted the other and brought it down. Not hard, at least Harlan didn't think so, but he didn't have anything to compare it to.

"Still good?"

Harlan nodded, his eyes squeezed shut, his mouth tight. He felt hot and restless, but he didn't want to use a safeword after only one smack. No matter what Charles had said, that would just be pathetic.

A second stinging blow, and Harlan squirmed forward to get away.

"Too much?"

"I—maybe? Sorry... Sorry, I didn't mean to move. I just..."

Charles sat on the end of the bed, lightly stroking Harlan's calf. "This isn't for everybody, you know. It's okay if you don't like it."

"I *want* to like it!"

"I know." Charles laughed. "I want to like opera, but I don't. That doesn't mean I don't enjoy art. Maybe you're not into impact play, but there's so much more than that."

Harlan nodded. That made sense. Something about this just felt *wrong*, like the ingredients were there, but not in the right order. His eyes widened, and he rolled over so he could look up at Charles. "Do you ever...?" He sighed. He knew it was important, but it was so difficult having to actually use his words. "I mean, do you like...*being* spanked, sometimes?"

"I do, and I think I see where you're going with this. I'd be happy to try."

"Really? Just like that? I don't exactly know what I'm doing."

"I'm not about to hand you a bullwhip and say, 'Have at 'er,' but it's pretty hard to mess up spanking—just slap my butt. I'll tell you if it's too much or if I need to stop."

"Okay. If you're sure."

Charles grabbed one of Harlan's hands, kissing the knuckles. "I am. I want to feel this"—another kiss—"here." He guided Harlan's hand beneath him.

If he'd been as hard now as when they'd started, Harlan would have come on the spot, but the interlude of talking had softened him a little. "Get on all fours," Harlan commanded, a little shocked by how forceful his voice sounded, how easily the order came.

Grinning, Charles rolled over, offering himself.

"So just...like this?" Shifting so he could reach, Harlan swatted Charles.

"That's a good start," Charles encouraged.

Once, twice more and Harlan was beginning to enjoy the way his palm stung, the way his handprints appeared on Charles' ass—first white, then pink when the displaced blood rushed back in. He tried to make a pattern, a sunflower with his palms in the centre, fingertips radiating outward like petals. Hitting harder, he could make the mark go from pink to red. He was breathing fast, hard, rocking his hips forward with each strike. He could hear Charles beneath him, making low, pleasured sounds.

Realizing he'd gotten distracted, caught up in his own sensations, Harlan forced himself to stop and check on his partner. "Is this all right?"

Charles moaned, the sound moving straight to Harlan's groin. "Definitely! Don't stop, please!"

Harlan could see the appeal of being spanked and had fantasized about it since he was old enough to have fantasies, but he'd never really understood why the person on the other end would enjoy it. Now... He'd never felt anything like it.

Harlan's cock was full and throbbing, twitching between his legs every time he struck, his pelvis canted forward to rut against Charles' thigh whenever he paused between spanks.

Charles laughed. "I hate to break it to you, but—" He was cut off by another spank.

"Mmm?" It took Harlan a moment to realize Charles had spoken, a few more for the words to make sense. He pinched and kneaded the red marks on Charles' ass while waiting for a reply. The other man's cheeks were warm, so warm...

"I think you're a top."

Harlan froze, reluctantly pulling his hands away from Charles' skin.

"Oh. Oh, God, I'm *so* sorry!"

"Hey." Charles sat up, his eyes fluttering shut when the movement tugged his freshly spanked skin. Sliding down the bed, he sat behind Harlan and wrapped his arms around him. "I'm not mad. I mean, it's not something I would've predicted, either, but it's okay. I switch."

Harlan could feel Charles' erection pressing against him, reinforcing his words.

"In fact...I don't get to bottom all that often. The way I look, people expect me to be a big, toppy bear. Which is fun—it really is—but it's nice to be on the receiving end from time to time, too."

Harlan couldn't seem to make himself move or speak, sitting still and passive in Charles' arms. He wasn't a top. His reaction alone proved that. He wanted—needed—to be told what to do...not like a top at all.

"We can stop now if you want and try again later...or not."

Another still, breathless moment, then Harlan was finally able to nod. Tears were prickling the corners of his eyes, and he bowed his head. Whatever spark had filled him while spanking Charles was gone, leaving regular, pathetic, useless Harlan in its place. "Do I have to say the safeword?"

Running a hand through Harlan's hair, Charles gave him a little hug. "No. We're both deciding to stop."

"I'm sorry," Harlan said, his voice a humiliated whisper.

"It's okay. It's a lot for your first time. You got...really into it."

Releasing Harlan, Charles lay back on the bed, one arm outstretched, patting the mattress beside himself invitingly.

Too embarrassed to even meet Charles' eyes, but too desperate for comfort to leave, he cuddled against Charles' side, facing away from him. He was relieved when Charles silently turned off the lamp. He was even more relieved when, after Charles thought he'd fallen asleep, he jerked himself off. *Good.* At least one of them had gotten off after that train wreck.

* * * *

"You might feel... Well, it hits different people differently. You might feel tired or upset for no reason, or irritable — or you might be totally fine. It's called 'top drop,' and it's important to take care of yourself and monitor how you're feeling over the next few days. I don't want you to just disappear, okay? I want to hear from you, make sure you're doing all right."

Harlan shrugged, nodding when Charles raised an eyebrow. "If I'm the top, shouldn't I be taking care of you?"

"We take care of *each other*. That's how this works. And I have more experience than you." Charles gave Harlan's hand a quick squeeze, then went back to stirring scrambled eggs.

Harlan nodded again, unconvincingly, poking at his coffee with a spoon.

"Need more cream or sugar?"

Harlan shook his head. He tried to force a smile, to stop feeling like such a failure.

"I'd do this again, if you wanted." Bringing Harlan a plate of breakfast—the eggs and some buttered toast—Charles laughed. "I know you're feeling bad, but believe me, I've had worse."

Harlan found that hard to believe, but he did feel a little better with food in his stomach. He'd felt adrift since his colossal fuck-up the night before, and now he finally felt like he was anchored in his body again.

Something occurred to Harlan, something he should have thought of much, much sooner. He felt suddenly cold. "Are you…? You said you don't get to bottom very often. Are you doing this with anyone else? Right now?" he asked, his head bowed so he wouldn't have to look at Charles.

Charles reached over and lifted his chin, making steady eye contact with Harlan before shaking his head. "No. I'm not. Are you asking because you want this to be exclusive? Just the two of us, no other partners for either of us?" he clarified, likely after seeing Harlan's obviously confused expression.

"I… Maybe? Yes. Yeah. I think… Yeah. If that's okay with you."

Luckily Charles smiled, even though Harlan had sounded like a complete idiot. "That works for me."

He was glad Charles had warned him about top drop. Over the next few days, he felt lethargic and grouchy.

Charles called, and Harlan ignored it. A few hours later, Charles texted a few links—one about top drop, another about BDSM in general. Harlan read them both, sending Charles a thumbs-up emoji to let him know he'd seen them. A lot of it was material Charles had already told him before they'd played, but it made him feel a little less like a freak, knowing there were other people out there who desired the same things he did. He texted Charles back to let him know he was okay. Charles replied with a smiley face and left him alone. Harlan got the impression that Charles was waiting for him to make the next move. If only he could figure out what he wanted his next move to *be*.

Work on Monday morning offered a pleasant distraction, and he was downstairs early enough to wait a few minutes before Hamilton pulled up.

"I have a nice, easy one for you, a nuisance ghost in a high-end apartment. They even know who it is — the former owner. Person living there now is her niece. Apparently, they didn't get along, but Auntie didn't write her out of the will. Now she's dead and still hanging around being a bitch."

Harlan blinked. Hamilton had hardly said that many words in a row before — at least in front of him — never mind giving him that much information about a case before they'd even arrived. He hoped that maybe, just maybe, Hamilton was finally starting to warm up to him.

"We're here."

There was a uniformed doorman and the lobby floor was marble. There was even an elevator attendant who made Hamilton tell him the floor number and pressed the button, rather than just letting Hamilton press it himself. The opulence made Harlan feel bristly and out of place, like he had to defend his own existence to these people. Like he was *the help*, called in to deal with an unsightly mess away from the view of the wealthy people who lived in the building.

The apartment itself was no better—all plush carpet in rich jewel tones, unfriendly oil paintings encrusting every wall and porcelain knickknacks adorning every surface.

Harlan immediately saw a problem.

"The old woman's body is gone, right?"

"Yeah, she died"—Hamilton frowned at his notebook—"eight weeks ago. She's long gone. Cremated. Why?"

"And the niece is...okay?"

"If you're asking if she's alive, I talked to her this morning. What's with the fucking third degree?"

"There are two ghosts in this apartment."

Hamilton sighed, massaging his temples. "Are you sure? You're not looking in a...I don't know...ghost-mirror or something? You've got a ghost-hangover and you're seeing double?"

Glancing between the ghosts—one a stately, older black woman, the other a white girl barely out of her teens—Harlan shook his head. "I don't think so."

"One of them couldn't have just...wandered in from somewhere else?"

Harlan shook his head again, slowly circling the ghosts. They turned to watch him, frowning but still quiet. Neither had any obvious wounds, nothing to show how they'd died—but not every ghost manifested their cause of death. The older woman looked miffed, while the girl looked frightened, but that didn't tell him anything, either.

"They usually stay pretty close to where they're buried or where they died. Sometimes where they lived, but..." Harlan searched for a polite way of saying the girl didn't exactly blend in with the expensive surroundings. It seemed rude to say it in front of her. "I don't think she lived here."

They exchanged uneasy glances.

Hamilton looked at his notebook again. "On the record, no one else has died in this building, never mind this *apartment*, since...1963. Fuck. Are you *sure* about this?"

No. There were very few things Harlan was *sure* about, but...

He nodded.

"All right. Can you question them, keep them here, whatever? I have to make some calls."

Harlan had barely thought about stepping closer to the translucent pair when the girl vanished. He could feel her nearby, in a wall where he couldn't reach her.

"Ah...hello," he addressed the other ghost, glancing over his shoulder at Hamilton, who flashed him a thumbs-up.

Hamilton had his phone pressed between his shoulder and cheek. "No, Miss Granger, we're not suggesting your aunt was a murderer. We just need—"

The aunt's ghost looked down her aristocratic nose at him. "What are you supposed to be, some kind of...janitor?"

"I... Kind of," Harlan agreed, flustered.

She made a sound that could only be transcribed as '*Hmph*.' "Are you here to get rid of that...hussy?" She whispered the last word, as though it were too vulgar to pass her lips but she couldn't think of a more accurate description.

Not sure if she meant the other ghost or her niece, Harlan nodded. "What do you—?" He decided a less interrogatory approach might work better with her.

"Do you know anything about her?" Hopefully, they were both referring to the same *her*.

"She appeared here a few weeks ago, insisting that she couldn't leave! She doesn't speak, but she screams all night long. Dreadful."

A few weeks. Well, at least Hamilton hadn't lied to the niece. It was extremely unlikely that her aunt was a killer, unless she'd murdered the girl as a ghost. Which was possible, as Harlan nearly knew from personal experience—but again, it seemed unlikely.

"Have you…seen her body?"

"Don't be disgusting!"

The ghost disappeared. Harlan groaned.

Hamilton approached. "Hey, I just got off the phone with someone who can hook us up with a cadaver-sniffing dog. You come up with anything?"

Harlan shook his head. "She wouldn't tell me anything before she disappeared."

"Ah, well."

Startled—he'd been expecting irritation at his lack of progress—Harlan glanced at Hamilton. He was grinning, actually rubbing his hands together with glee.

"I can't wait to see what these people think of a big, drooling dog in here."

Harlan couldn't help grinning back. "Maybe it won't drool."

"Trust me. They all drool."

Chapter Seventeen

At the Centre, there'd been an older girl who'd sworn she'd found a way around the internet tracking on every computer. She'd had a certain degree of authority. Her power was over electronics, and she could make a TV answer questions in an age before Siri. All the teenagers—Harlan included—had surreptitiously traded chores with her in exchange for her services. Harlan had no idea if her hacking had actually worked or if she'd just seen an easy market in a group of horny, suspicious young adults. The administrators and teachers probably had better things to do than track their charges' porn consumption. He'd always been sceptical of the oft-repeated story of the boy who'd been called to the director's office—and later expelled, put in jail, maybe—for his extreme and illegal pornography collection. No one could actually name him or even say exactly what he'd had in his possession.

Harlan's own pornographic tastes had always been fairly standard—two or more men stroking each other, fucking each other in the mouth or ass. He hadn't known or thought much about alternatives and he hadn't wanted to get caught—by teachers or other kids—watching anything *really* exotic.

Now, in what was nominally his apartment—even though it still didn't feel that way, not entirely—Harlan felt a moment of hesitation before typing the address of his favourite porn site on his phone.

He turned off Wi-Fi and opened a new, Private Mode tab. He doubted it made an actual difference, but it felt more secure, and even though he was ninety percent sure no one would be looking at his browser history, old habits died hard.

Comforted by at least the illusion of privacy, Harlan finished entering the URL and clicked on the banner asking if he was of age. He scrolled, hovering his finger over a few of his favourite videos, but none of them were quite what he wanted tonight.

He opened a new window, searched for 'gay spanking videos'. There were plenty of results, but almost all of them featured the same thing—a big, grizzled older man spanking a smaller, younger man. He wanted their positions reversed, and he wasn't finding very much.

Frustrated, he chose a video more or less at random, jerking himself to a quick, unsatisfactory climax.

All he could picture was the way Charles' ass had gone from white to pink to red beneath his hands, the way his palms had stung after each strike. The *rush* he'd felt, like nothing else in his life. He remembered how terrible he'd felt for a few days after, but hopefully that was only due to inexperience, and he could build up a tolerance or something. He wanted—*needed*—to do it again with Charles, if Charles even wanted to see him after the way he'd freaked out the first time.

After giving himself some time to recover, so he wouldn't sound like he'd just jerked off alone in his apartment, he dialled Charles' number. The call ended. Charles had hung up on him.

Groaning, Harlan threw his stupid phone towards the end of the bed, not caring if it fell on the floor and smashed, even though it was brand-new.

The phone chimed. He had a text.

It was probably just Hamilton. His shift had just ended and he was texting to check up on Harlan.

The phone chimed again.

Hamilton hated texting. He always called. He was probably the only one in the universe who felt that way.

Harlan sat up so quickly that he almost bounced himself off the bed and scrambled to reach his discarded phone.

The text was from Charles.

@ *the club. Too loud to talk. U okay?*

Harlan pressed the phone between his hands, resting his chin on it. Charles had replied, but now he wasn't sure what to say. It was a good thing Charles hadn't picked up the phone.

The phone vibrated, startling him. He dropped it on his knee. "Fuck!" It bounced off and fell under the bed. He had yet to actually find a ghost under his or any other bed, but it was still an unknown, frightening place to reach in to.

Another text from Charles—a ghost emoji with a question mark next to it.

He must have taken too long to respond and now he'd scared Charles.

I'm fine. Just wanted to say hi.

I'm glad you did. Smiley face. *Been thinking about u*

For one horrified moment, Harlan was convinced Charles somehow knew what he'd just been doing—and who he'd been *thinking* about while doing it—but reassured himself that was impossible. Well, at least highly unlikely.

Impulsively, before he could talk himself out of it, Harlan replied.

Me too

Charles sent an eggplant and a winky face.

While Harlan tried to decide how to respond to that, Charles sent another text.

Hope to see u soon. Heart emoji.

Me too

TTFN Gotta go.

Harlan held his phone long after it went silent, still feeling a warm glow.

Chapter Eighteen

It was nearly two weeks before they could secure the dog and her handler. The niece stayed in an expensive hotel rather than the haunted apartment.

Harlan and Hamilton had decided to wait before dispatching the aunt's ghost, too, in case she could be of any help in dealing with the unknown spirit.

Standing beneath the apartment's awning, Hamilton waved to the unassuming woman holding the leash of a black, brown and white Basset Hound. The dog threw herself against her leather harness when she saw Hamilton, baying.

"Hi, Moxie. Good to see you, too." After a messy, enthusiastic greeting, Hamilton held out his hand for Harlan to see. It was covered in a thick sheen of drool, and he smirked triumphantly. The handler offered him a towel, and he wiped it off.

Someone a dog liked that much couldn't be too bad, Harlan decided, declining the handler's offer to greet the dog.

Their group made it past the doorman and through the lobby easily, following in Hamilton's wake, but the elevator attendant blocked their path.

"Sir, that...animal...is not allowed on the premises! All animals must be approved by the—"

Hamilton held out his badge.

The attendant opened his mouth to continue, then jerked a thumb in the direction of a small sign beside the elevator—*No Animals Allowed*.

"Fine. We'll take the fucking stairs." Hamilton stepped around him, and the rest of them followed.

Moxie bounced onto her two hind paws, straining against her taut leash to reach the elevator attendant. Her handler, not bothering to hold back a grin, halfheartedly told Moxie to stop.

Moxie climbed one of the nine flights of stairs, then sat on a landing, panting and refusing to continue. Hamilton and the dog's handler—Carol—took turns carrying her up the other eight flights. Everyone but Harlan was panting by the time they reached the top.

After giving the hallway a brief exploration to make sure Moxie couldn't escape or get hurt, Carol shrugged and let her off her leash. "Let's see where she goes."

Moxie lowered her head and wove her way down the hall, methodically sniffing every few inches. Her huge brown ears swept the plush carpet on either side of her face. Each doorway she passed got an extra-thorough examination, her big, black nose leaving damp spots on the dark wood. She sneezed occasionally—jowls flapping, a mist of drool spraying outward—then shuffled farther.

"What will she do if she—" Harlan asked Hamilton softly, just as Moxie reached the haunted apartment's door.

After a frantic, audible snuffle, Moxie lay down in front of it.

"If she finds something? That."

Carol praised the dog, giving her a well-loved stuffed toy. Wagging exuberantly, Moxie settled down for a good chew. Soon there were spreading damp patches on the carpet on either side of Moxie's lips. Hamilton and Harlan exchanged delighted grins.

Hamilton pulled down the police tape sealing the door and unlocked it. "C'mon, girl." He stepped aside to let Moxie pass.

She stared at Carol until the handler gave her a signal. Groaning, the dog sighed dramatically, but dropped the toy and stood, leading the way inside.

Not feeling—or possibly ignoring—Harlan and Hamilton's mounting excitement, Moxie ambled leisurely from room to room, thoroughly sniffing every inch of the floor and opulent furniture. After she'd inspected the master bedroom—the room farthest from the door—Moxie looked up at Carol, wagging her tail furiously.

"Does *that* mean she found something?" Harlan asked, hopefully.

Carol shook her head, clipping Moxie's leash back onto the dog's harness. "She's not indicating."

"She sniffed the carpet for a long time."

"The aunt died in here. I'm sure they replaced it, but the floor probably still smells a little…corpse-y. Fuck, what's the range on one of these?" Hamilton jerked his head in Moxie's direction.

"If there was a corpse here, she would've smelled it."

"Ah"—Hamilton nudged Carol with his elbow—"then we have to search the *other* floors."

With plenty of encouragement, Carol and Hamilton managed to convince Moxie to go *down* the stairs, with breaks after each flight to sniff down the hallway. She didn't lie down—Harlan assumed that was what Carol meant by 'indicating'—again.

"Fuck." Hamilton had his phone in his hand, turning it over and over. "That's it? There's no body?" They'd even checked the basement, with its storage and laundry facilities. These tenants didn't wash their own clothing.

Carol looked offended on behalf of her dog. "She's found bodies in *much* more difficult terrain. If there was a body here, she'd've found it."

"Fuck," Hamilton repeated. Watching Carol load the dog into her car, he shook his head. He'd switched to tossing his phone one-handed, sending it a little higher each time he caught it. "*Fuck*. This isn't good. You said there'd be a body."

"I said there was a second ghost," Harlan protested. "I didn't say there was a body!"

"You said ghosts stay near their bodies or where they died." Hamilton gestured at the empty lobby.

Fuck. He had. "I'm sorry. I-I don't—"

"Can you at least get rid of the ghosts?"

Harlan nodded, then immediately shook his head.

Hamilton raised a warning eyebrow.

"I mean, I *can*. I just don't think…" He wilted beneath Hamilton's glower. "The aunt, no problem, but the other one, the girl, I don't think I should." He forced himself to counter Hamilton's gaze with his own feeble attempt. "She might have been murdered. We should question—"

Hamilton sighed, digging in the pocket of his crisp uniform pants. He produced a crumpled piece of paper, unfolded it and shoved it in Harlan's face. "Do you see this?" He pointed at a line of text. "This is for the removal of one ghost. *One*. The old lady's. Until—*if*—the other one causes anyone *living* any grief, she's all yours. For now…" He gestured at the elevator. "Look," he continued, his voice softer. "We've wasted enough time on this place. There are plenty of other cases waiting for us. We didn't find a body, plain and simple. Just…let it go, okay? It's easier that way."

Harlan shrugged stiffly as, dogless, they rode the elevator back to the upper floor.

In the apartment, the aunt was sitting in plain sight on a wing-backed armchair. The other ghost? He could feel her, faintly, but she was hiding from him—hiding from all three of them, living and dead. He'd have to draw her out into the open to dispel her, and there was no way Hamilton would be patient—or quiet or calm—enough for that process. "I can do that."

"Good." Hamilton clapped him on the shoulder. He sat on the sofa, inadvertently facing the aunt's ghost like they were about to have a tête-à-tête.

Harlan closed his eyes, concentrating. At the Centre, he'd been asked to describe every aspect of his ability over and over. The closest analogy he could come up with was a room, divided in the middle by a one-way mirror. On one side, the living. On the other, the dead. Most living people couldn't see through it, never mind cross it. Many ghosts didn't realize they couldn't be seen by or interact with people on the other side. Some gifted people, like Harlan, saw through it as easily as an ordinary window.

Most ghosts were easily convinced to cross that barrier. They knew they weren't where they were supposed to be and they *wanted* to leave, only they'd gotten lost. Others took some...persuasion. Harlan suspected the aunt would fall into the latter category. Forcing a ghost to move on meant that Harlan had to cross the 'mirror,' however briefly, and open a doorway.

Concentrating, Harlan could see the barrier clearly, all the places its edges touched and overlapped with the world of the living. Goosebumps prickled up and down his forearms. He hated this part, straddling the void between the two worlds. It felt like pins and needles on his whole body, but even worse was the *whispering*, like being in a dark theatre and trying to pay attention to what was happening on stage while everyone in the audience made comments he couldn't quite hear, only this audience included every human being who'd ever died.

He asked for a name. The other side answered.

Harlan drew back just a little, returning his attention to the aunt. "Violet Beaudry, please listen to me. You have passed away, and you no longer belong in this place—"

"Are you trying to tell me I'm dead?"

"Y-yes." Harlan had always thought the Centre's script for informing spirits what had happened to them was too wishy-washy and euphemistic, but her question had still thrown him off balance. "I—"

She snorted. "I know that! I'm dead, not an idiot."

"I thought you might—know you're dead, I mean, not know you are an idiot! You're not. Sorry. I have to—Look... You know you can't stay here, right?" Mentally throwing out the script, he decided a straightforward approach might work best with her.

She snorted again, shaking her head. "Of course I belong here! It's my apartment."

"Not anymore. It belongs to your niece now." He had to keep reminding himself that he didn't have to raise his voice so she could hear him. Any hearing loss she might have had in life wouldn't affect her ghost.

"*Tch*. That girl... The way she's spending my money, she'll have to sell this place within six months." She grinned, showing several gaps in her teeth. Apparently her dentures hadn't made the transition to the afterlife with her. "I'm just...speeding up the inevitable."

"It's not your money," Harlan told her, gently but firmly, "not anymore."

She flashed, glowing brighter for an instant. He wished his eyelids could protect him from spectral glare, but he knew from experience that closing his eyes wouldn't help. She wasn't glowing with something as mundane as light.

Tired of her, of this apartment, of his embarrassment when Moxie hadn't found anything, Harlan felt around for an opening to the other side and yanked it open. Still sitting on the couch, idly tapping his phone, Hamilton looked up and shivered. *Interesting.*

"I'm not going!" Violet insisted.

"I'm sorry. This isn't a choice. This is happening."

"That-that *girl* gets to stay and I don't?"

He wasn't sure which girl she meant—her niece or the other ghost—but it didn't matter. Harlan suspected Violet hadn't been told 'no' or that life wasn't fair very often in her long and wealthy life, and he had no reason to believe it would be a convincing argument now.

"It's time to go."

Violet stood, going over to Hamilton and slapping at his shoulder. "Help! You're the police, aren't you? Why aren't you helping me? I'm being thrown out of my own apartment!"

Hamilton didn't so much as twitch. Violet hadn't been a ghost long enough, exerted herself enough, to affect someone who wasn't connected to her by blood.

"He can't hear you," Harlan said, hoping she couldn't hear the quiet glee in his voice. He was beyond tired of her. "Come on." He reached out, doing a sort of mental *blink* that let him actually touch ghosts, and grabbed her wrist. Her spectral skin was so thin as it slid over tiny, delicate bones. Harlan didn't like touching ghosts. It took a lot of energy and concentration to line up his physical body with their phantom ones, and it left his skin numb and tingly, often for days. He had nerve damage in several places on his hands and arms, places that had lost sensation when a ghost had touched them and never gotten it back. So far, all of them were from the practice ghosts at the Centre, but he had a feeling that might change.

"Let *go* of me!" Violet tried to pull free, but Harlan was prepared for her struggle and held on, grimly. "Help!" She flailed at him with her free hand, leaving an icy prickling sensation everywhere she touched.

"No one but me can hear you," Harlan said through gritted teeth. He started pulling her toward the opening he'd created.

She opened her mouth impossibly wide and *screamed*, showing a gaping black void that reeked of rot and decay.

Harlan wasn't intimidated by her display. He used her moment of distraction to shove her through the hole. He felt her bony fingers close on his hand, perfectly manicured nails digging in as she tried to reverse their positions and drag him in after her. He threw himself backward, slamming the portal shut just in front of her grasping talons.

"Holy fuck."

Flat on his back, Harlan blinked up at Hamilton.

"That was... Are you okay? You're bleeding."

"Where?" Harlan's voice was hoarse, and it hurt coming out. He coughed. His mouth tasted stale and bitter.

"Your hand." Hamilton knelt beside him.

Harlan couldn't feel his left hand at all, but there was a jagged row of gouges just above his knuckles, sluggishly trickling blood.

"At least it's my left hand."

"What?"

"I'm right-handed."

"Did you hit your head or something when you fell?" Hamilton frowned, scrutinizing Harlan more closely.

Harlan shook his head, trying to clear it.

"That wasn't normal, was it? I could see you pulling against something, but there was nothing there. Scared the shit outta me. I was about to grab you when you—" He mimed falling backwards.

Harlan shook his head again. "I had to stick my hand through so I could push her. Living things...aren't meant to go there. I've got nerve damage in a few places, but mostly my left hand." He flexed his fingers. His hand was still completely numb, but he knew from experience that feeling would return—to most of it—in a few hours or days. *Hopefully.* Until it finally didn't and the numbness became permanent.

"So I always use my left hand. Better to just fuck one of them up."

Hamilton looked genuinely concerned. "You don't... It's not always like that, is it?"

Harlan shook his head. "She fought."

"Fuck." Standing, Hamilton offered Harlan a hand up. "She's gone?"

Harlan reached up with his right hand, the one he could feel. Rising unsteadily, even with Hamilton's support, he nodded. "She's gone."

"Just let me call her niece and I'll take you home. You're done for the day." It wasn't a question.

Harlan nodded meekly. Something occurred to him, and when he looked up, he could tell Hamilton had thought the same thing.

"We won't tell her about the other ghost."

Chapter Nineteen

"This is getting really fucking old," Hamilton said, actually putting a hand over his eyes for a moment.

I know that, Harlan replied, silently. *Don't you think I know* that? Matching Hamilton's frustration with his own, he said out loud, "I'm not doing this just to piss you off!" He immediately looked down and away, his cheeks heating with shame at his outburst.

Hamilton opened his mouth, closed it and gave Harlan a long, steady look that wasn't *quite* a glare. He briefly closed his eyes, moving his lips silently, as though counting down from ten in his head. "All right. I know that. There's no other explanation?"

Harlan shook his head. Not counting Violet's 'companion', this was the third tagalong ghost he'd found at a scene that was only supposed to have one. None of the secondary ghosts' bodies had been found, and they all wore recent, modern clothing. Harlan knew ghosts didn't always appear the way they had in life, so he supposed it wasn't impossible at least some of the ghosts were even a few decades old and had updated their look, but...he didn't think so. He didn't *feel* so. These were recent deaths, and each new ghost dropped another lead weight into a pit of dread gathering in his stomach. No one else seemed to share—or even understand—his apprehension, not even Hamilton.

Maybe seeing some of the tension on Harlan's face, Hamilton sighed. "Give me evidence. Give me proof, *something* I can work with! The higher-ups aren't going to let me start an investigation based on a few unidentified ghosts—whose numbers are building, I know," he continued, before Harlan could interject.

Shaking his head, Hamilton pulled out his notebook and flipped to a blank page. "Describe the ghost for me."

Harlan grinned, nodding his thanks at Hamilton before turning his attention back to the ghost that didn't belong. Well, even more than ghosts *usually* didn't belong.

Giving a description of this one wouldn't be easy. He kept winking in and out of his sight, his features distorted in pain and fear.

"About...five-nine," he began, tentatively. "Dark skin and eyes. Wavy black hair, medium long." He held up a hand to his own head to mime the ghost's hairline. "Glasses. Late thirties, maybe? Heavy-set." These ghosts had made him better at describing people, if nothing else. "Wearing a red polo shirt and black pants. Maybe East Indian or Pakistani, but I'm not sure."

Hamilton finished his notes, read over them aloud. "Any scars, tattoos or other identifying marks?"

Harlan shook his head. "Not that I can see."

"I'll run this guy by the morgue and missing persons, but I'm not holding my breath."

"I know." None of Harlan's descriptions had matched any unidentified bodies or anyone reported missing in Toronto or all of Ontario. "Thanks. For...believing me."

"It's my job," Hamilton said gruffly, but he gave Harlan a brief clap on the shoulder. "Get rid of the ghost we came here for — and the other one if you can — and let's get the fuck out of here."

Hamilton shivered, making Harlan wonder again if he might be at least a little sensitive to ghosts. The unknown spirit sent out such powerful waves of grief that Harlan had broken out into goosebumps as soon as they'd arrived at the scene, and they hadn't gone away since.

The 'original' ghost was easy enough to persuade to leave, once Harlan explained that she was dead and when and how she'd died. The interloper disappeared as soon as Harlan approached. Under Hamilton's watchful eye, he stayed for another half hour. The ghost didn't reappear, so they left.

Harlan felt restless and unsettled when he got home. He considered going for a walk, but now that he was safely behind his warded walls again, he was reluctant to leave until he absolutely had to. He dreaded seeing yet another unexplained — inexplicable — ghost, especially without Hamilton beside him.

None of them had spoken to him, barely acknowledged him except to flee, but he couldn't shake the certainty that they wanted something from him, for him to find their bodies — their killer. None of them showed any marks, any signs of violent death, but Harlan *knew*, in some way he couldn't explain, that they'd all been murdered — by the same person or people.

He opened Tumblr, half with the thought of distracting himself, half-hoping to get some kind of insight from one of the other mediums' blogs he followed.

Neither happened. A gif caught his attention as he scrolled past, and he stopped. It looked like it was from one of the many police procedural shows he'd never watched — even before he'd become a part of police procedure.

It showed a woman placing pins in a map.

Harlan almost dropped his phone in his haste to call Hamilton.

Hamilton picked up on the third ring, sounding bored as usual when he said his usual greeting. "Hamilton."

"A map, pins!"

"What? Who is this? Harlan?"

"Yes, yes, it's me. This is huge!"

Hamilton chuckled. "It must be, to get you so fired up."

"Listen. Do you have a map nearby?"

"On my phone…"

Harlan shook his head, frustrated. "No, a real map. A big, physical one that you can put pins in…or at least mark."

"What's this —? Never mind. Gimme a sec." A clatter as Hamilton put his phone down without muting it.

Harlan winced, pulling his own phone away from his ear and rubbing it. He could distantly hear Hamilton shouting, then another clatter when he returned. Harlan hoped the rustling he heard was a map.

"Where did we find the first ghost?" Harlan asked, breathlessly.

Hamilton sighed, but there was more rustling. Harlan assumed he was flipping through his notebook. "Hazelton, between Webster and Berryman."

"Mark it on the map."

"You think there's a pattern." Hamilton's voice had lost all traces of boredom and now sounded utterly focused. It was a little intimidating to be the centre of that focus.

"I-I don't know. I just thought... I saw..."

"The next was Elora Road." A pause, more flipping.

"Then Rutherford Avenue, and today's was Ava Road." No pause that time. Hamilton hadn't needed to consult his notebook. A sharp intake of breath. "Holy shit."

"What?" Now it was Harlan's turn to sound mystified.

"Where are you?" If he'd thought Hamilton's voice was focused before, now it was a laser beam.

"Home. My apartment."

"Stay there. I'll be there in twenty minutes." He hung up.

Swallowing hard, Harlan shivered. He'd heard something uncomfortably close to fear in Hamilton's normally unshakeable voice.

Twenty minutes later, almost to the second, Harlan's buzzer rang. He startled, his heart racing, and a little frightened gasp escaped him, even though he'd been expecting the sound. He touched the response button tentatively, as though afraid it might electrocute him.

"It's Hamilton. Let me up."

Harlan pressed the button, and a few minutes later he heard Hamilton's heavy tread. He waited until

Hamilton knocked before opening the door. Hamilton held a folded map tucked under his arm. He pushed past Harlan without speaking and spread it on the coffee table. He sat on the couch, hunched forward, resting his elbows on his knees.

Harlan didn't want to look at the map, didn't want to see whatever had made Hamilton rush over here with it. The weight of dread in his stomach shifted, but his feet carried him over to the map.

It wasn't much, just four dots, but... They did seem to form a rough cluster in the southwest of the Greater Toronto Area.

Harlan felt a chill when he saw that one of the marks was close to the park where he'd had his picnic with Charles.

"It doesn't mean anything," Hamilton said.

Harlan shook his head, unable to look away from those four scribbled dots.

"It's only four. It's not enough data to be a pattern. And no other mediums have reported finding any of your...wayward ghosts."

Harlan nodded. He didn't speak—and neither did Hamilton.

Chapter Twenty

Charles took another sip from the bottle of apple juice Harlan offered him. They'd just finished playing and were winding down for the night. Harlan had spanked Charles while Charles jerked himself off. He'd finished with a drawn-out moan when Harlan commanded him to come.

Harlan had gotten Charles cleaned up and tucked in, then passed him the granola bar and juice they'd stashed on the bedside table for aftercare. Charles reminded him, gently, that he needed the sugar just as much, so Harlan had eaten and drunk as well.

Harlan was hard, but not desperately so. Spanking Charles was its own form of satisfaction. For the time being, he was content to press himself against Charles' warm, sweaty bulk and just breathe in his scent.

"I think there's a serial killer in the city," Harlan blurted, unable to hold it in any longer.

Charles carefully untangled their limbs and propped himself up on one elbow so he could see Harlan's face, his other hand lightly stroking Harlan's side. He gave a soft huff of laughter. "Interesting choice of pillow talk."

"Sorry. Fuck, I don't... I didn't mean to say that."

Charles laughed. "Okay, now you *have* to tell me."

"It's just... I keep seeing ghosts."

Charles snorted, and Harlan nudged him with an elbow.

"I mean, I'll go out to a scene, and there's an extra ghost—the one I was called in for, and another one that shouldn't be there. They don't match any unidentified bodies or missing people, but I've found four now and...I just feel like something's really wrong."

Charles raised an eyebrow, shooting Harlan an uncomfortably knowing look. "Have you talked to Hamilton about this?"

"Yes! And...no."

"Mm-hmm?" Charles prompted.

"He knows about the ghosts. He's checked hospitals, morgues, missing persons, but...nothing. He wants *evidence*, and I can't give it to him. It's not that he doesn't believe me, exactly, it's just..."

"You haven't told him your theory."

Harlan shook his head. "I know it sounds crazy, I do, but I *also* know something's wrong here."

Charles laughed softly, kissing the back of Harlan's neck and making him shiver.

"Well, I'm glad you feel comfortable enough with me to risk sounding crazy."

Harlan snorted. "After some of the shit you've seen me do, *crazy* is the best I can hope for."

"True." Charles kissed him again, stroking a thumb from the crown of Harlan's head to the base of his neck. "I don't think you're crazy. You know that, right?"

Harlan nodded, burying his face against Charles' chest to hide his blush. "…There's more."

"Can you talk about an ongoing police investigation with me? I don't want either of us to get in trouble — though handcuffs could be fun. Do you have any?" Charles offered both wrists.

Harlan pushed them away, sticking out his tongue. "I'm not that kind of cop and you know it." He couldn't suppress a grin, but he soon turned serious again. "And technically, no. Hamilton knows about all of this, but he's the only one. It's not enough to convince him. Well, maybe enough to convince *him*, but not enough to start a full-on investigation. I'm just telling you about…my hobby. There's nothing wrong with that."

"Right. Well, what else?"

"Wait here." Harlan squirmed free, wincing as his Charles-warmed feet hit the chilly hardwood floor.

Charles laughed, flopping onto his back. "As if I could walk after that! It'll take me a while to get my legs back, so you don't have to worry about me going anywhere. I'm at your mercy!"

"Good." Harlan blushed, smiling softly at the compliment as he left the bedroom to get the map. He unfolded it on the bed.

Charles sat up, leaning against the headboard. "What am I looking at?"

Harlan pointed at the four dots with a sinking feeling in his gut. Hamilton was right. It didn't mean anything.

Charles leaned forward, examining the marks carefully. "These are where you saw the ghosts?"

Harlan nodded.

"I don't think they're random."

Harlan had been picking at a loose thread on his comforter, and his head snapped up at Charles' words. "You don't?"

"If they were, they'd be all over the place." Charles tapped four random points on the map. "But these seem...clustered." He paused for a moment, thinking. "It's not just because you and Hamilton only work in this area, is it? You're all over the GTA?"

Harlan shook his head, then nodded. "I mean, yes. We work everywhere. I'm so glad you see it too. I was really starting to wonder if it was just me."

"It's still not a lot to go on," Charles pointed out.

"That's what Hamilton said."

"But...I wouldn't stop marking them down, if you come across more." Charles threw an arm around Harlan's slender waist, pulling him close.

"I looked it up," Harlan continued, excited and encouraged. "And it said that serial killers have predictable patterns, right? This guy's probably based somewhere in here." He pointed to the centre of the group of dots. "And this is his comfort zone." He traced a circle with his finger that surrounded the four points.

Charles stiffened, putting a hand under Harlan's jaw and gently turning his face. "Why do I get the feeling you're planning to search that area?"

Harlan gave a guilty start, unable to meet Charles' gaze. "If they need evidence to start investigating, someone has to find evidence. These people shouldn't just be...forgotten. Lost."

"And you're going to be the one who finds that evidence? Yeah, I thought so. At least take me with you while you're out hunting a serial killer, all right?"

Harlan shook his head. "Can't. I can't see ghosts when you're around, and they'll be my best clue that I'm getting close."

Charles sighed, letting Harlan go. "I don't think I can convince you not to go, but please...just promise me that you'll be careful."

"I promise." And he meant it. His plan was strictly reconnaissance, to see if he could find more ghosts and track them to their source, definitely not to interfere with the kind of serial killer who left ghosts but no bodies. "No hunting. Just evidence."

A lighter topic occurred to Harlan. "How's this for pillow talk? Why did you text me an eggplant emoji the other day?"

Charles snorted. "That's actually even better pillow talk than you realize, I think."

"Eggplant?"

Charles' gaze drifted down to Harlan's groin and he blushed.

"Oh. *Eggplant*."

Chapter Twenty-One

Depending on need—and the availability of more experienced mediums—Harlan might work twelve hours one day, followed by three days off. There were no predictable rhythms or patterns to his work. It was entirely based on the whims of ghosts and the living people they inconvenienced. A large part of that inconvenience, for him as a living person, was simply travel time. It might take Harlan five minutes to dispatch a ghost, but it might also take him and Hamilton three hours to get to it, followed by another three hours back.

He added two more out-of-place ghosts to his map—while working, naturally, not during his off-the-clock search, because that was how Harlan's life worked. He looked for ghosts on his own and didn't find any until Hamilton was around to be annoyed by them.

Their locations fit the boundaries of the area where he'd been searching, the killer's likely comfort zone. He hoped he could find enough wayward ghosts to fill in the map and then find a void where the killer most likely lived or worked and so avoided killing—or at maybe even find the murderer he knew in his gut was stalking Toronto.

Find 'evidence' of the serial killer, he reminded himself. He knew Charles didn't approve of his search because he didn't want Harlan to get himself in danger. He suspected Hamilton knew what he was up to as well and was choosing to ignore it, but he *also* suspected Hamilton wouldn't want him doing anything dangerous either.

Harlan had done quite a bit of reading on the subject and watched a few true crime documentaries, which suggested that the best places to look would be abandoned or lightly used buildings—*not many of those in the Greater Toronto Area, at least not for long*—or single-family dwellings. It was hard to be an apartment-dwelling serial killer. Unfortunately, there *were* a lot of those in the space between the six dots on his map.

Almost every day after work—or, if he didn't work that day, as soon as he woke up—Harlan headed northwest from his apartment into his search area. Sometimes he walked, often getting much farther than he'd intended, because he was concentrating so hard on picking up on ghosts. When he felt up for it, he took the bus to explore the far side of the perimeter.

He hated taking the bus—he didn't see many ghosts while in transit, but being surrounded by miserable living people wasn't much better—but he felt he *had* to do this. He was, however nominally, a police officer, and that meant it was his duty to help where he could. And he could help these ghosts by finding out who was killing them, hopefully preventing more deaths. *If* he were right.

He searched as methodically as he could, marking off each building he could access on his big, paper map, circling the ones he couldn't get close enough to be sure. In a way, it was like playing Pokémon Go...but with actual ghosts.

He'd been chased by a dog once, and after that, he'd realized he needed to pay more attention to his psychic *and* physical surroundings.

Spending so much time with his psychic shields down, straining to feel the slightest hint of a ghost, was exhausting. Between that and continuing to play with Charles, even being careful and considering both their schedules—not that Harlan really had a schedule, aside from usually having weekends off—he was wearing himself out. He knew it, and both Hamilton and Charles had commented that he looked tired—one gruff, the other concerned—but it was almost a compulsion. No matter how tired he was, he got on the bus or just trudged through alleys between shops and houses.

He saw old ghosts—a woman in a long dress who stared at him silently until he left, a man in a severe old-fashioned suit whose nonstop crying eventually made Harlan decide he'd be better off searching elsewhere for a while, several factory workers with crushed limbs or skulls, eyes popping out of their sockets.

There were newer ghosts as well—frozen transients wearing so many layers of ill-fitting clothing that he couldn't tell if they were men or women, the occasional huddled, half-naked woman trying to hide her raw, rope-burned throat or gaping stab wounds, businesswomen whose ghostly forms were enhanced by eighties-style shoulder pads, with no obvious cause of death—maybe shame.

Harlan released the ones who were willing to go, the ones who aggressively defended their 'territories', the ones he sensed were on the edge of going rotten and causing problems in the future. Dealing with them now meant he, or another police medium, wouldn't be called out later because of them.

He left most of them alone, and most were content to offer him the same courtesy.

They all *belonged*, as much as any ghost belonged in the world of the living. None of them had the visceral, discordant resonance of the four ghosts he'd found where there shouldn't be any.

Day after day, street after street, ghost after ghost, and Harlan was no closer to proving — or *disproving* — his theory. He ended each cautious expedition with a mixture of frustration, relief and excitement.

Charles asked about his 'hobby' often. He seemed genuinely interested in hearing about the ghosts Harlan encountered and relieved that he hadn't found anything more frightening than bats swooping out of the darkness or more dangerous than rotten floorboards. He didn't tell Charles about the dog. He knew Charles would prefer he stop looking completely, but he seemed to understand that Harlan couldn't, and he offered what support he could.

Harlan was *tired*, but, overall…pleasantly tired. Too exhausted for his usual involuntary night-time ritual of revisiting the day's failings and social gaffes. He'd never slept this well or fallen asleep so easily as far back as he could remember. He started taking less of his bedtime medication, falling asleep faster and staying asleep longer, often sleeping straight through the night for the first time in his life.

Chapter Twenty-Two

"You can still change your mind, you know." Charles leaned up to plant a soft kiss on Harlan's jaw.

Harlan nodded, absently. Part of him—a *big* part, perhaps the majority—wanted to give up here and now. But...there was a heat in his blood—part curiosity, part arousal.

Charles tugged his arm, giving it a gentle shake. "You might want to try relaxing, then. You look more afraid now than you did the first time you came down here, and you knew there was a *ghost* then. Not that ghosts are exactly unusual for you, but still..."

That startled a laugh out of Harlan. He made a conscious effort to relax, feeling the tension in his body now that Charles had pointed it out. He didn't know how to explain—maybe didn't want to admit—that Charles was exactly right. He *was* more afraid now—terrified, even—than during his first visit to the dungeon, even though that had been one of the first ghosts he'd dealt with professionally, he'd still been overwhelmed by life outside the Centre in general and Hamilton in particular.

The sight of all the bondage equipment, lurking in the near-dark like prehistoric creatures hauling themselves out of a primordial swamp, made him want to turn and run, and he knew it was ridiculous. Nothing down here would hurt him unless he wanted it to be so. And the plan was for him to hurt *Charles*. Consensually.

"Do you want to sit down?" Charles chuckled. "On a chair, I mean. If this is freaking you out." He nodded at the empty dungeon. "We could even have a drink, if you're not up for playing."

Charles had stressed from their initial conversations about BDSM that — in his book — alcohol and kink never mixed.

Harlan shook his head. This had been his idea. If they were rushing things, it was at his suggestion, not Charles'.

"You're safe here," Charles rumbled, one large hand slowly kneading between Harlan's shoulder blades.

He *was* safe, Harlan realized, in a way that probably hadn't occurred to Charles. Only the two of them were in the dungeon, and Charles' presence ensured that they were *truly* alone. Or, at the very least, no lingering spirits would be able to show themselves. They could still be watching, but Harlan did his best to push that thought out of his mind.

He tried to relax again, more successfully this time. "I want to do this," he said, pleased at how steady his voice sounded.

Charles didn't say anything, but his grin spoke for him. He trailed his fingers down Harlan's arm, catching his hand and kissing each fingertip in turn. "Let's start with the spanking bench. It's something we've done before, just...more."

Harlan nodded again, not trusting his voice to sound so steady a second time. He followed Charles deeper into the dimly lit dungeon. Charles stopped beside a piece of furniture that looked like a large, wooden stepstool upholstered in black leather. Not very intimidating.

He could do this.

Watching Harlan carefully, Charles undid his jeans and let them slide to the floor, exposing his white briefs, which were already straining to contain him. Seeing that he had Harlan's complete attention, he kicked off his black boots and slipped out of his jeans before putting his boots back on.

"Underwear too," Harlan said, surprised as always to hear his own voice sounding so commanding.

"What was that?"

"I said, take off your underwear, too."

Charles' smile was like the evening sun breaking through heavy clouds as he hurried to obey. Bare from the waist down—except for his boots and socks—he climbed onto the spanking bench. He rested his shins on the lower platform, his chest on the upper, arms outstretched and hands hanging off the front edge. When Harlan didn't approach, he wiggled his rump enticingly.

Harlan laughed, stepping closer and reverently running his hands over Charles' ass cheeks. "Eager?" he teased, softly.

"Mm-hmm," Charles purred, pressing back against Harlan's touch. "Nice as this is…"

"Oh, you want more?" Harlan allowed himself to fall into character, drifting away from himself and becoming the kind of person who spanked other people.

"Please," Charles said, almost—but not quite—begging.

Harlan raised one hand, felt Charles tense in eager anticipation beneath him. He lowered it again, softly, before repeating the motion with his other hand.

Charles let out a sound that was half-laugh, half pleading moan.

With a grin of his own and pleased with how easily he could 'play' Charles and make different noises emerge, Harlan took pity and gave Charles a firm swat on his left buttock.

Charles moaned, long and full-throated. He visibly relaxed his body and splayed his legs wider on the padded bench, offering himself to Harlan.

In response, Harlan delivered a series of sharp, backhanded blows across both cheeks.

He continued in this vein for a while, until the gentle ringing noise he'd been hearing, just below his conscious perception, clicked into place. He smiled. "I don't think we're using this to its full potential."

"Oh?" His voice already a little muddled, Charles looked back over his shoulder at Harlan.

"Mm-hmm." He stepped around to the side of the bench, keeping one hand on Charles at all times, the way Charles had taught him. He lifted the leather cuff, attached by a short length of chain to the wood frame of the bench, and stroked it down Charles' forearm.

Charles shivered, his eyes visibly fluttering at the touch.

"Should I...?" Harlan offered, barely restraining himself from just wrapping it around Charles' wrist before he had a chance to respond.

"*Yes.*" Charles' answer was almost a sigh of relief.

Harlan grinned, pleased with himself.

"I didn't want to bring it up. I knew this was already a lot for you," Charles admitted, "but if you're game, I'd love to."

Harlan buckled his wrist, moving his hands in quick, sure movements that seemed alien to him — but pleasantly so. He gave first the chain, then the strap a tug. "Not too tight?"

Charles shook his head.

"Not too loose? I don't want you slipping free on me."

"No, they're good. I don't want that, either."

Harlan rewarded him with a kiss on the shoulder, enjoying Charles' happy shiver. He moved to the other side of the bench and buckled in Charles' other wrist as well. He could *see* Charles relaxing as he was strapped in, the sensation Harlan had been looking for when he'd asked Charles to spank him. He could feel that same sense of relaxation filling him, only on the other side of what he'd expected.

He repeated the same tugging check with Charles' right wrist.

Once Charles' hands were secure, Harlan returned to the back of the spanking bench. The few red marks he'd left on Charles' ass were already fading, but if anything, Charles was visibly more aroused than he'd been when they'd started. Harlan considered taking up where they'd left off, but he saw a set of ankle cuffs dangling from the bench and he couldn't resist.

"Is this all right?" he asked softly, stroking Charles' calf with the soft, supple leather.

"Mm-hmm," Charles agreed. It sounded like he was biting his lip.

Harlan liked that image. He quickly secured both of Charles' ankles, checked to make sure he was comfortable, then stepped back to admire his handiwork. "Beautiful," he murmured.

Charles laughed. "I don't know about 'beautiful'..."

"Handsome, then." Harlan leaned close and pressed a kiss to Charles' tailbone, just above the curve of his ass.

Charles moaned, squirming a little against his bonds and clearly eager for more.

Harlan happily obliged. He started off slowly again, a few strikes on one of Charles' cheeks before switching to its mate, but he quickly built up both speed and intensity.

"My hands are actually getting sore!" he laughed, resting one on Charles' hip possessively while he gave them both a chance to breathe. He mostly used his right but switched to his left occasionally to give the other a break. Striking with his left hand was a little uncomfortable because of the tingles and twinges of numb or partially numb areas—luckily, dealing with Violet's ghost hadn't added another.

"That's always a problem, yeah. There are toys over there if you want to give your palms a rest." Charles angled his head, hands bound too tightly to the bench to point.

Harlan considered the row of implements hanging on the wall—paddles, leather straps, canes, crops and floggers, a veritable kinky candy store—but shook his head. "I think that might be a bit much. Maybe at home, another time, but—"

"It's all right. You don't need to explain. Not being comfortable is enough."

Harlan sighed, letting out tension he hadn't realized he'd reacquired. "Thanks." He was used to needing to explain, to come up with excuses why he didn't want to, couldn't do something. It was a relief to be told otherwise.

"Are you done?" Charles asked.

"I think so. It was enough, for you?" Harlan answered with a question.

"Definitely."

Harlan bent to kiss the red, hand-shaped marks he'd left, enjoying the way Charles shivered and moaned beneath him. He unbuckled Charles' ankles, then his wrists, rubbing the small indentations the metal hardware had left. He noticed that there was a leather collar hanging from the front of the bench, which he hadn't noticed. *Another time, maybe.*

"Well, there is *one* more thing I want."

"Oh?"

Accepting a helping hand from Harlan, Charles slid down from the bench—and immediately dropped to his knees.

"Are you all right?" Harlan knelt, too, grabbing one of Charles' hands. He didn't *look* faint. His colour was normal, and he wasn't swaying or anything.

Charles laughed. "I'm fine. I just wanted to…" He shifted closer, running a finger up Harlan's inner thigh.

"Oh!" Harlan grinned sheepishly. "So…I should stand up again?"

"That would make this easier."

Chapter Twenty-Three

"This blows a big fucking hole in your serial killer theory, huh?" Hamilton didn't sound mocking. Almost...disappointed.

Harlan had just found a seventh out-of-place ghost, in Corso Italia—almost directly in the middle of the area on the map, the place Harlan had considered to be the killer's base of operations, where he shouldn't find any unusual ghosts. As usual, the ghost had vanished as soon as it realized Harlan had seen it—and it hadn't reappeared.

He bit his tongue to hold back a frustrated curse—all that effort, all those days of walking and worry, and there was no pattern. Just...randomness. No serial killer—and of course that was a good thing, personal disappointment and confusion aside.

"Or..." Hamilton cocked his head, thoughtfully. "Or he's spiralling. I say 'he' because, well...statistics."

"What does that mean?"

Hamilton frowned, then shrugged. "I dunno, take your pick—toxic masculinity, the decay of modern society. Fuck, video games and rock music, if you want."

Harlan shook his head, frowning back. "No, what you said about spiralling. What does that mean?" The term sounded familiar from his research, but he wanted to hear Hamilton define it.

"Means he, if there *is* a he, which is still a big 'if' in my book"—Hamilton's expression didn't match his words. He looked convinced—"he's coming undone. He's started to shit where he eats, killing too close to home. Or we might not have enough data points to see the full pattern—again, if there even is one. Sorry, kid. If it were easy, we wouldn't need cops, right?"

Harlan had started carrying the map with him to pore over whenever he had a spare moment—something both Hamilton and Charles had commented on with some concern. He unfolded it on the hood of Hamilton's squad car, ignoring the other man's groan.

"I think you're on to something..." He opened the cruiser's passenger door and rummaged in the glove compartment until he found a pencil as well as the pen he already had. He didn't want a pen for anything more than marking the most recent ghost, not yet. He wanted to be able to erase this if his idea didn't pan out.

"Brand, I didn't say that shit to get you all fired up. I—"

It was the first time Hamilton had directly referred to him by name since they'd met, even if it was just his surname—but that wasn't important now.

Harlan held up a silencing hand, surprised by his own boldness. His mind was racing, wouldn't be able to rest until he'd puzzled through this completely.

"What if the search area isn't all this?" Harlan tapped the previously blank area he'd been investigating, quickly drawing the seventh and most recent dot in pen in the middle of it. "What if there are *four* search areas, with this as the central point?" He drew two diagonal lines between the four outermost ghosts he'd found, crossing through the central one.

Hamilton squinted then shook his head. "Doesn't change anything, one way or the other."

"No, it does! Sort of." He drew four new dots—in pencil—in the centre of each quadrant he'd just created. "Instead of needing to look in this whole area"—he traced the initial circle with his forefinger—"we just have to search these four."

Hamilton raised an eyebrow, prompting Harlan to take another look at what he'd drawn on the map.

"It's exactly the same, isn't it?"

Hamilton clapped a hand on Harlan's shoulder. "Nice try, kid, but don't quit your day job." He chuckled. "Speaking of which..." He inclined his head in the direction of the ghost they'd come for, extending a hand in a showy invitation.

This spirit was an elderly white man, peering myopically at Harlan through glasses that hadn't made the transition with him. Harlan wasn't sure why ghosts always wore clothes—at least, he'd never seen a naked ghost—but were usually missing objects.

Harlan approached tentatively, even though he was fairly certain this ghost wouldn't run—perhaps *couldn't* run or even move faster than a shuffle, because of the memory of his living body.

"I'm Harlan," he introduced himself softly, in the tone he'd been taught to use at the Centre. "What's your name?"

"Charlotte? Funny name for a boy... Or are you a girl? Sorry... I don't see as well as I used to. Don't hear as well as I used to, neither." He laughed.

Harlan suspected, again, that the ghost's hearing issue was more because of what he expected rather than a problem with his ghostly ears.

There had been a deaf girl, a few years younger than Harlan, at the Centre. Harlan had liked her because she was quiet and had a wicked sense of humour. She'd missed nothing that happened around her but had continued to play innocent and allow people to assume she didn't know what was going on.

She had liked him because he didn't treat her like she was somehow damaged because she couldn't hear. She'd taught him enough sign for them to communicate without her having to constantly lip-read. It had been fun, having their own secret conversations that no one else could bother to understand.

Harlan wasn't fluent in ASL by any means, but he could usually get his point across, even if he sometimes had to resort to finger spelling.

He'd barely thought about her since leaving the Centre. He'd have to email her and see how she was doing.

"Do you sign?" he asked the ghost, using sign language.

The old man shook his head. "I'm not deaf!" he protested, his voice so loud that it was nearly a shout. "You just have to speak up 's all."

"My name is *Har-lan*," he repeated, carefully enunciating both syllables. "What is your name?"

"Peter Malloy. Pete to m' friends." He peered at Harlan owlishly. "Haven't decided about you yet."

"Do you know you're dead?" Harlan asked, blunt to the point of rudeness. Hamilton's—entirely accurate— destruction of his map theory had thrown him off balance and taken away his filter.

The old man seemed to inflate, puffing up with incredulity. "Well!" he began.

Harlan groaned internally. Dealing with—never mind sending on—an upset ghost was exponentially more difficult, and he had no one but himself to blame.

"What kinda idiot you take me for? 'Course I know I'm dead!"

Harlan hoped the ghost's difficulty hearing would apply to his sigh of relief, too. At least he wouldn't have to convince the man he was dead. That was usually half the battle by itself.

"Then you know you can't stay here," Harlan said gently, trying to make up for his earlier tactlessness.

"Don't plan to!" the ghost huffed. "I'm headed home. I just seem to keep getting…turned 'round. Is that why you're here—to help me get home?"

Harlan started nodding, then realized Peter probably meant his *literal* home—the place he'd lived, if not where he'd died.

"You can't go home," Harlan said, hoping he'd guessed right and hadn't just implied Peter couldn't go to Heaven or something.

Peter snorted, an unpleasantly wet sound, despite the fact that he had no mucus. "Who's gonna stop me—you? I was in 'Nam! I've taken shits tougher than you."

Ignoring the ghost's words, Harlan pressed on. "You don't belong here, not anymore. You have to move on."

That seemed to deflate the old man. He shifted from foot to slippered foot, looking down at the alley's gravel that was dimly visible even through his feet. "Weren't exactly the most church-goin' man," he mumbled, almost apologetically.

Harlan reached out and touched Peter's forearm with the middle three fingers of his left hand, doing the special *blink* that allowed him to physically interact with ghosts. "I don't think that matters so much." He tried to make himself look as wise and all-knowing as possible. "Were you a good man?"

Peter shot Harlan a brief, wide-eyed look, then laughed. "'Spose I was," he allowed, slowly shaking his head. "You're pretty new to bein' an angel, huh?"

"I'm not a—yes. I'm…still in training."

Harlan saw movement out of the corner of his eye—not Peter. Hamilton was looking at him with an expression of something between concern and bewilderment. He could only imagine how odd these conversations must sound from Hamilton's perspective, hearing only Harlan's side.

Peter nodded again, then offered Harlan his hand.

Surprised, Harlan took it, trying not to wince at the bone-biting cold, pins-and-needles feeling of touching bare ghost 'skin'. It didn't make sense, but their clothing was always a little warmer.

"Takes a big man to admit he's not very good at his job…yet. You'll get there. I'm sure. You can call me Pete, and…I'll go with you."

Harlan pushed aside the urge to inform Pete that he was just fine at his job—*good*, even, at least some days. Pete was cooperating. That was the important thing.

Releasing Harlan's hand, Pete asked, "What do I have to do?" His voice was quavering and uncertain now.

"Just turn around."

There was a kind of door or portal behind Pete, waiting patiently for him to enter.

Shooting Harlan a deeply suspicious look, as though he expected someone to squirt water in his face when he turned, Pete slowly shuffled around. He gasped, clutching his chest. Harlan almost jumped, ready to administer CPR—not that he knew it—or... something...when he heard Pete whisper, "It's beautiful."

Harlan closed his eyes in relief. He wouldn't have to reach through this time and risk adding even more nerve damage to his left hand. Pete would step through on his own.

"Will I...?" Pete cleared his throat, swallowed, Adam's apple bobbing. "Will my...?"

Harlan had known real, future-telling, mind-reading psychics at the Centre. He wasn't one, and he rarely, if ever, felt confident in what he said. Sometimes, though, in moments like this, he found utter conviction and clarity.

"Yes," he said, in a voice so certain he hardly recognized it as his own. "Yes, she'll be there. They *all* will."

Pete shot Harlan a brief, red-eyed look, squared his shoulders, clenched his liver-spotted fists and stepped through, disappearing into his afterlife.

"Ow," Hamilton grumbled, shaking his head like a swimmer trying to get water out of his ears. "Did you hear that? What the fuck just happened?"

"What did it sound like?" Harlan asked, suspecting he already knew.

"What are you talking about? How could you miss it? It was a huge...*pop!* or *bang!* Didn't you hear it? Was it something you did?"

Harlan nodded, then pointed out, "No one else heard it."

"Are you nuts? Everybody..." Hamilton glanced around. The few bystanders who'd wandered past and stayed to watch the 'exorcism' were just milling about—talking to one another, trying to see past

Hamilton. One was industriously picking his nose. "You mean none of them...?"

Harlan shook his head. "And *don't* call me crazy." A thin trickle of anger crept into his voice. He would tolerate a lot from Hamilton, but not that.

Ignoring Harlan's words, Hamilton's face went pale and he grabbed Harlan's arm. "Is that ghost gone?"

"Yes," Harlan replied, a little frightened by Hamilton's reaction.

"And the other one?"

"Gone. For now —"

"Good. We're leaving." Hamilton half-dragged Harlan back to the cruiser. Releasing Harlan, he stood behind him until Harlan was in the passenger seat, as though worried he'd bolt.

His whole body was tense as he climbed into the driver's side and shut the door. "What," he said, "the fuck."

Harlan swallowed hard, going still beneath Hamilton's sudden anger.

Hamilton gestured to the empty air between their heads. "Is this some kind of fucking...side effect of being near you?"

That startled a laugh out of Harlan, though he immediately regretted letting it out. "What? No!" He went quiet at the sight of Hamilton's expression. "No. I'm sorry. I thought you knew."

"Knew what?" Hamilton asked, each word clipped, almost bitten off.

"That you're..." Harlan tried to think of a tactful way of putting it, couldn't, and went with the first thing that came to mind. "...like me."

Hamilton sputtered, then his anger seemed to dissipate all at once. "It's not you?"

Still shaken, Harlan shook his head.

"I was…like this before I met you?"

Harlan nodded again. "Just a little bit. You might never have seen—you might *never* see—a ghost, but you can at least tell when they're around, especially if they're active."

Hamilton laughed. "Well, that explains a few things!" he said, not elaborating. "Let's get you home."

Chapter Twenty-Four

Charles left Harlan at the bottom of the stairs leading down from the bar. "Just give me a minute to get set up." He left the fluorescent lights off this time, leaving only the pot lights that isolated and highlighted each individual play area, the way Harlan imagined the club looked when it was open.

He wove his way between the different bondage stations and Harlan could hear him bustling around. Unsure if it was supposed to be a surprise or not, Harlan wandered over to the curtained-off area he now knew was for aftercare. He absently trailed his fingers over the soft, colourful cloth separating it from the rest of the dungeon. "You really don't mind coming here?" he called out. "I mean, I know I wouldn't want to hang out in Hamilton's car if I wasn't getting paid for it."

"I'm sure. I like being here." Charles chuckled. "Just because I'm bottoming for you doesn't mean I'm in the habit of doing things I don't want to."

"Of course not!"

"Well?"

"Ah. Right."

"C'mere. I'm ready."

Harlan followed his voice deeper into the room. He was surprised to find that Charles wasn't at the spanking bench they'd used before, but instead at the Saint Andrew's cross—the one Chris-the-delivery-ghost had died dropping off. Harlan did his best to push that thought from his mind, to concentrate on the here and now with Charles.

"I know you weren't up for it last time, but this time I thought you might want to try out some toys?"

Ducking his head to hide his blush—though the light was dim enough that he probably didn't have to—Harlan nodded.

"Don't worry," Charles quickly added. "I'll still keep it simple." He gestured to a small table sitting beside the cross that Harlan hadn't noticed until that moment. "I figured we'd just try one each of the basic kinky 'food groups,' to see what you like. There's a paddle, a flogger, a cane and a crop."

Harlan picked up each implement, one at a time. He'd never touched most of them in real life. The closest he'd gotten was during quick, frantic forays into sex stores, where he'd desperately tried to avoid making eye contact with anyone before dashing out again.

The crop was fairly standard, as far as he knew—black, with a leather-wrapped handle and a long, flexible stem topped with a folded-over strip of leather.

He swung it a few times, enjoying the authoritative way it swished through the air. He glanced sideways at Charles, trying to imagine using it on him. He wasn't quite there.

He set it down and picked up the cane instead. It looked and felt very much like the crop, but without the leather flap at the tip. Not entirely sure what Charles expected him to do with it — if anything — he snapped it in the air a few times as well, then experimentally brought it down on his forearm. He winced. Either he really wasn't a bottom, this wasn't the toy for him or it felt different — and much, much better — on an ass. Maybe all of the above. "It stings!"

Charles nodded, smiling but not in a mocking way. He just seemed to be enjoying watching Harlan explore.

Harlan glanced at his arm, where a thin red line had appeared. "Sorry. Was I not supposed to do that?"

"No, of course not. It's good to know how all these toys feel on yourself and how hard you can hit before using them on someone else."

The end of the cane drooped, almost touching the floor. Harlan's gaze followed it down.

"Hey." Charles touched his shoulder, startling him. "You're new to all this. Give yourself a break, okay?"

"Okay."

"Good." Charles stood on his tiptoes and Harlan obligingly bent down so Charles could kiss him on the forehead. "You're good to keep going?"

Harlan nodded. He set the cane down and picked up the flogger. Its handle was wrapped in black leather, and the thick cluster of suede falls alternated between black and teal. He stroked them, enjoying the way the soft, supple leather slid between his fingers. He gave it a snap, surprised by the weight of it as he swung. He wondered if his arm would get tired if he used it for a long time. Charles' probably wouldn't, but he actually had muscles.

He swung it again, extending his arm this time rather than keeping his elbow bent. The tips of the falls ended up a surprising distance away, fading into the dimness surrounding the cross.

Charles laughed. "Yeah, that's why I wanted to do this here, rather than at your apartment. Some of these toys have a long reach. Here… Try this if you're ready." When Harlan nodded, Charles took the flogger from him and passed him the paddle.

Harlan found himself strangely reluctant to part with it, but he was quickly distracted with examining this new toy. It was plain—dark brown leather, suede on one side, smooth on the other.

"Do all of these belong to the club?" he asked, stroking the suede side. This was the last one. After this he'd have to use one of these on Charles—or give up and go home.

"Nah. These are from my…personal collection." Charles waggled his eyebrows.

Harlan grinned, which he suspected was Charles' intention. He was very good at noticing when Harlan started spiraling and finding a way to bring him back down.

"Do the different sides feel…well, different?"

"Why don't you find out?" Charles asked, his voice edging on a sexy growl.

"On me or on you?"

"Either."

Harlan smacked his forearm with the paddle, smooth side down, on top of the fading line the cane had left. It didn't really do anything for him…until he imagined using it on Charles' naked ass.

"Ready to try them out?"

Setting the paddle back on the table, Harlan turned to look at the cross again. Part of him couldn't help wondering if he was purposefully *trying* to find something 'wrong' that he could use to delay or even stop the scene before it had even properly begun. Then he spotted something that actually did make him hesitate. There were clips hanging from the outermost corners of the cross on both the top and bottom, and one more at the upper junction where the two sides of the X met. "I'm not sure I'm up for..." They'd used bondage last time, but with the addition of the toys, it felt overwhelming.

Charles slid between him and the cross, partially blocking his view of it. He kissed Harlan, giving his hand a quick squeeze. "I'm happy to just try one thing at a time." After a beat, he pulled off his shirt and tossing it onto the floor beside them.

"Do I need to be naked?" Somehow that seemed like the most daunting part. He knew the club was empty except for the two of them and the door was locked, but the thought of getting undressed in such a large space made him feel very uncomfortable, borderline terrified.

"Of course not." Charles kissed him again. "Only what you're comfortable with. I don't even have to undress more if you want. I could even put my shirt back on."

Harlan shook his head—he definitely didn't want that. "No. I want you naked." He tried to recapture the character he'd assumed the first time they'd played at the club.

"Yes, sir," Charles purred, sliding both hands down his barrel chest, one resting on his thigh, the other cupping his noticeable bulge before he began undoing his belt.

Chapter Twenty-Five

Hamilton slammed on the brakes en route to a ghost assignment.

Startled, Harlan glanced across at Hamilton. The policeman's hands were clenched, white-knuckled, on the steering wheel. His nostrils flared, and he was breathing heavily. He didn't speak.

"What?" Harlan finally asked after a long moment of strained silence that stretched between them. "What's wrong?"

Hamilton released his breath in a heavy sigh. "You don't feel that?"

Frightened now, Harlan shook his head.

"Remember when you told me you thought I had...a bit of what you are?"

Harlan nodded. It had only been a month before.

Hamilton rolled up the sleeve of his uniform shirt, revealing his bare forearm. Every hair stood on end. "I get...*feelings* sometimes, and I'm getting a fuck of a strong one right now. C'mon." Barely stopping long enough to actually park the car, Hamilton opened his door and stepped out. His waist was at Harlan's eye level, and he could see that Hamilton had unsnapped his holster. The gun was still in place, but he squeezed the holster tight enough that Harlan could hear the leather creak in protest.

"I don't think—" Harlan began.

"This is more your shit than my shit. Just be glad I'm coming with you at all. Get out of the car."

The last was said in what Harlan thought of as Hamilton's 'Cop Voice'. Harlan was already unbuckling his seatbelt before he'd consciously decided to obey.

As soon as Harlan got out of the car, as though its metal and plastic—or maybe the rubber of the tires, like lightning—had insulated him from the effect, the hair on his arms and the back of his neck rose, just like Hamilton's.

They turned together, Hamilton with his mouth set in a grim line, Harlan wondering why they were walking *toward* the source of that prickling instead of *away*, like sane people. Hamilton, Harlan was certain, was doing it out of a sense of duty, and he couldn't honestly say he wasn't doing it for the same reason.

Hamilton had stopped in front of a large building surrounded by a chain link fence plastered with signs from different contractors. It must have been a Sears until recently. The letters had been taken down, but their outlines still showed, paler than the wall around them. It would no doubt be torn down or renovated soon, but for now it was empty—a rarity in Toronto.

The first ghost Harlan saw was...tattered, ragged in a way he'd never seen and couldn't explain. It wasn't dismembered so much as stretched and oddly distorted, like a Picasso painting or an image printed on paper that had gotten stuck in a printer.

There were more ghosts beyond it. Some looked disturbingly solid, but others were no more than wisps that were difficult even for Harlan to see.

"What the fuck?"

Harlan wondered how much Hamilton could actually see...or sense.

He looked to where Hamilton had stopped, a few paces behind Harlan. Hamilton stared at an unnervingly solid body part—a ghost's left arm—in a way that made Harlan suspect he could actually see it. It probably looked like a dismembered limb hanging in midair, and he could almost see Hamilton looking for the fishing wire.

"Is it—?" Hamilton swallowed hard before starting over. "Is it *always* like this?"

Harlan shook his head. The movement felt slow and difficult, like he was underwater or at a distance from himself. "No. Never."

"Fuck," Hamilton said, with feeling.

Harlan nodded.

"Let's go."

Harlan shot Hamilton a startled frown. Was Hamilton such a blowhard that he'd run the first time he was genuinely frightened? Part of Harlan, he could admit to himself, was happy to follow suit, so it was with a mixture of relief and shame that he watched Hamilton push past him, heading deeper into the oppressive miasma behind the mutilated, shredded ghosts.

Harlan fell in behind. Hamilton had drawn his gun. Even though they both knew it wouldn't affect the ghosts at all, its presence was comforting.

More and more ghosts surrounded them as they walked. Some were mangled and *wrong* — missing sections of limbs, faces or torsos but strangely solid in places. Others were more like the ghosts Harlan was familiar with — uniformly misty, but more or less intact human figures. Some of their mouths were open unnaturally wide in silent screams. Others crouched with their hands curled protectively over their heads, rocking back and forth. A few were curled in the fetal position, half-sunk in the cracked pavement where their 'bodies' didn't quite line up with the physical world.

"What the fuck?" Hamilton breathed. He laughed, the sound almost profane in these surroundings. "I think you might be right about your serial killer."

Harlan bit back a sarcastic response, overwhelmed by the sheer number — the *volume* of ghosts. If he'd felt underwater before, now he was drowning. He managed another few panting steps before he had to stop. He shook his head. The air was thick with ghosts. It felt like he was trying to walk through tightly stretched fabric, breathe through thick layers of wool pressed over his mouth and nose. He could go no farther.

Hamilton managed to stumble a few more steps, looking like a man walking against a high wind, before he noticed Harlan was no longer following him. He turned and frowned. "What?" Even the single word seemed difficult.

Harlan shook his head, gasping. "I can't. It's…" He leaned forward, his weight supported by the frantic outward press of the ghosts.

Hamilton sighed. He retreated to where Harlan stood with a look of relief, which Harlan was happy to see.

Harlan staggered back until he was free of the mass of ghosts and could breathe and move freely again. He hadn't realized just how badly it had affected him until it was gone. He doubled over, his hands braced on his knees while his whole body shook like he'd just climbed a mountain.

He shook his head again. "I can't go any farther. Neither can you."

Hamilton shot him a dark look, but Harlan could see sweat glistening on his forehead. Hamilton's nostrils flared as he tried to disguise his own heavy breathing.

"I think even a normal—a person without any mediumistic talent at all—might struggle to get through there." It was true, but he could also see Hamilton was upset by his inability to bull through as usual. He hoped his comment would help soothe Hamilton's professional pride. "We need—" Harlan cut himself off, blushing to the tips of his ears.

"We need...?" Hamilton prompted. "What? Backup? Didn't you just say it wouldn't be any use?"

Harlan sighed. He'd avoided having this conversation with Hamilton for as long as possible, with the thought always in the back of his mind that it was inevitable.

"We do need backup, but not the kind you're thinking. We need...Charles."

Hamilton snorted. "What is that, an acronym for something?"

"He's my"—a dozen words, none of them quite right, flashed through Harlan's mind. He finally settled on—"boyfriend." It seemed inadequate, but this wasn't the time to explain their relationship. Personally, he hoped that time never came.

"Your boyfriend can do what a team of trained police mediums can't?"

For their sake, Harlan hoped the other mediums' 'training' had been more thorough than his own. He nodded. "Yes. He can."

"What? Does he shoot ghost-repelling lasers from his eyes?" Hamilton caught sight of Harlan's expression and laughed.

"Not…exactly." *Shit.* He hadn't phrased that well. "I don't know what it is, but ghosts…stay away from him. We can use him to get through, to see what's past them." He waved an arm at the circling ghosts. "Then he leaves and we can take care of the ghosts, or…"

Neither of them cared to fill in the silence.

"I take it he's a civvie?" Hamilton finally asked.

Harlan nodded. "Can't you just…deputize him or something?"

Hamilton snorted. "What do I look like, a fucking sheriff?"

Harlan suppressed a smile. Now that Hamilton had mentioned it, it was surprisingly easy to imagine him wearing boots, spurs and an oversized cowboy hat with a shiny star to replace his current badge.

"What do you mean?"

Hamilton sighed. "No. I can't deputize your boyfriend."

There was a scream from inside the warehouse.

The two men exchanged looks, and Hamilton's hand dropped to the butt of his gun again. "Fuck. Okay, I don't care who this guy is. If you think he can be the help we need right now, call him."

Harlan grabbed his cell phone and started dialling when Hamilton closed his fingers around Harlan's hand. "You were out for a walk with your…Charles…

when you heard a scream. You called me, and I decided there wasn't time to wait for backup."

"But that's not..."

Hamilton sighed. "That's our story. Got it?"

Harlan frowned. He wasn't a very good liar, and his mind conjured images of interrogation rooms.

Hamilton said, "It's going to be fine. If anyone takes heat for this, it'll be me. But that's the easiest explanation that lets us both keep our jobs."

Harlan nodded, reluctantly.

"Good. You go ahead and call him, now." Hamilton glanced at the building. "Would me calling for backup—police backup—help?"

"I don't think so. This many ghosts... Even for someone without a speck of mediumistic talent, it could be dangerous."

"Won't that include Charles?"

Harlan shook his head. "It's not that he doesn't just...not have talent. He has...I don't know, anti-talent?"

"Whatever. We'll figure it out later. Call him. I'll have to radio for backup eventually, but I can try to buy us a few minutes."

Charles answered on the second ring. "Hey, everything all right? You usually text—"

"I found him."

"Found who?"

"The serial killer. I found where he's been doing it."

"Holy shit. Why are you calling *me*? Shouldn't you call Hamilton?"

"He's here with me already, but we need you. There are so many ghosts... We can't get through."

"Harlan, maybe you should—"

Harlan cut him off again. "There's no time. We just heard someone scream inside, and we need you here right now so we can get in and have any chance of saving them, never mind catching this guy."

Charles sighed, audibly. "Okay. Fuck. Okay. Just... I'll be there as soon as I can. Be careful, all right? Wait until I get there?"

Harlan could hear rustling noises, which he assumed was Charles getting dressed. He gave him the address for where they were, and they hung up.

Hamilton had been speaking to the dispatcher while Harlan was on the phone. He got out of the squad car, approached the ring of ghosts and grimaced. "I told them we found an unregistered haunting and you need radio silence to concentrate." He shrugged. "It was the best I could come up with. Fuck, I'm so going to be fired, but..." He glanced at the building again.

Harlan suspected the sentence finished, '...*but it's worth it if we save someone.*'

Charles' black Jetta pulled in beside them, parking on the wrong side of the street. Charles got out, surveying the buildings around them. "Which one is it?"

Harlan couldn't imagine not being able to tell. He suspected that even in a sensory deprivation tank, he'd still be able to sense this much spectral activity. But now that he thought about it... He pointed to the old Sears and was astonished to see Charles' presence had opened a corridor, a passage through the ghosts like Moses parting the Red Sea. They hadn't *all* vanished, but there was a clear path leading towards the building. Charles' power apparently had a radius, a defined area of affect that surrounded him.

"Take a step to the left," Harlan told him without looking away.

Looking slightly puzzled, Charles obeyed.

The area moved with him. *Perfect.*

Harlan thought it was smaller than Charles' usual radius—not that he'd explored it all that thoroughly—and he wondered if the sheer number of ghosts was affecting his non-ability.

"Charles," Charles said, extending his hand at the same moment Hamilton offered his own.

"Hamilton."

The two men shook hands, firmly but not testing each other. Neither of them were apparently insecure in their masculinity.

Right. Harlan always forgot to make introductions.

"I've heard a lot about you," Charles said. "I mean, we met once, briefly. But we didn't exactly get introduced."

Hamilton snorted. "I wish I could say the same. I'd never heard of you until a few minutes ago, but that doesn't really surprise me." Turning to Harlan, Hamilton asked, "Ready?"

Harlan nodded woodenly. Even with the path Charles had cleared, every nerve in his body was screaming at him to *run*, to get away from this place, as far as he could go—Outer Mongolia, maybe—but he'd heard that scream. He knew none—or very few—of these ghosts had died naturally. He had to keep any more from being created, if he could.

Clinging to that thought, he took a step forward. He half-expected to feel the unyielding pressure again, of so many ghosts pressed together, but he encountered no resistance. He stretched out his arm experimentally, then pulled back with a shudder. It was like submerging his hand in ice water.

Hamilton didn't shoot out the lock, as Harlan had secretly been anticipating, but watching him kick in the glass door was satisfying too. All three men froze, but they didn't hear any alarms. Hopefully no security company had been alerted to the break-in and would come to investigate.

Making sure the others were following, Harlan stepped into the abandoned store.

Chapter Twenty-Six

Harlan blinked, waiting for his eyes to adjust from the bright sunlight to the dimness of the building. There were very few windows, but every third or fourth light had been left on, leaving pools of brightness surrounded by darkness, which was also very much how Harlan felt.

Making out a huddled shape in the distance, Harlan froze. Gun un-holstered, Hamilton silently pushed him aside, covering both of them. Peering around Hamilton, Harlan saw it was just an overturned piece of shelving.

Motioning for Harlan and Charles to stay where they were, Hamilton slowly advanced. It seemed to Harlan that he was able to look in several directions at once—*very impressive*. Maybe if they all lived and neither of them got fired, Harlan would look into some actual police training.

Hamilton stopped and held up a hand to get Harlan's attention. He motioned at his eyes, then pointed.

It took Harlan a moment to see what Hamilton had observed, and even then he could barely make it out. Did he need glasses? It didn't help that there were more ghosts in the way, beyond the reach of Charles' power, making his vision swim and blur as they moved restlessly.

In a windowless corner of the former department store, farthest from the door, Harlan could just make out a table with a bulky shape on it, and what looked like a shadowy figure standing beside it.

Another scream, muffled this time.

Without looking back, Hamilton barrelled forward, gun raised. "Police, freeze!"

The figure looked up but didn't move.

Within a few paces Hamilton began to slow, and he kept swiping at the air in front of him as though attempting to clear away cobwebs. "I can't…"

"Charles, we have to help him." Harlan reached out to take Charles' hand, only to find it was already extended for him. Hand in hand, they followed Hamilton, running to match his speed once Hamilton was clear of ghostly interference.

Harlan could see the table clearly now. What he'd taken as random debris was actually a human form, covered by a filthy canvas tarp and tied down at neck, chest, wrists and ankles. Perhaps hearing them approach, the figure struggled feebly, words or screams reduced to muffled moans.

The man standing beside the table held his hand over his victim's mouth. He didn't look up but made a strange scooping motion with his free hand. Even with Charles this close, Harlan could see what he was doing — as he gestured, a fine, silvery mist rose from the victim's body, coalescing into a stream above his chest.

"What the fuck is happening?" Just for an instant, Hamilton clapped a hand to his ear, cocking his head as though trying to block out a horrible sound. Shaking his head, he resumed his shooting stance, steady and unwavering.

"I'm...not sure." Harlan opened his mouth as little as possible, not wanting to give the bile rising in his throat a way out. Whatever he was seeing, it felt unspeakably *wrong*, so foul that it made his guts revolt.

"Can I shoot him?" Hamilton's gun was already trained on the standing figure.

"I think so...?"

"Good enough." Addressing the figure—Harlan couldn't bring himself to think of this monstrosity as a fellow medium—Hamilton raised his voice. "Freeze! Drop the— Stop what you're doing, *now*, or I'll shoot."

At that, the man finally seemed to notice that he and his victim were no longer alone. His head snapped up, his mouth falling open in an *O* of surprise when he saw the three of them, Hamilton poised to shoot. The guy's hair was pure white and he was cadaverously thin, but with an unsettlingly youthful face. He wore an entirely black suit, creating the illusion that his pale head and hands were floating in the dimness.

His mouth cracked open in a twisted smile, and he made another motion with his hands—this time a gathering motion, as though collecting something and rolling it into a ball between his palms. Harlan could see the misty whiteness thickening, being drawn into the man's hands. He'd hoped that, with the man's concentration broken, the mist would return to the victim, but he only seemed to be gathering it more quickly now.

"Last warning," Hamilton barked.

With a final yank, the man tore the shimmering ball free of the misty tether connecting it to the victim, gathering it against his chest like a kitten. He turned and ran, the canvas-covered form on the table howling now that its mouth wasn't covered, writhing as much as possible with the cruelly tight ropes holding it in place.

"Fuck!" Hamilton was already running after the man, turning to look back only long enough to shout, "You two stay with him. I'm calling for backup." He tore around the blind corner where the man had already disappeared, leading toward what had probably been offices or changing rooms in the department store.

"Should I follow him?" Charles asked, frowning after Hamilton.

Harlan wanted to say '*No*,' to selfishly keep Charles there, beside him—not so much for Charles' safety as for his own—but he suspected the clot of ghosts followed the man, which meant Hamilton needed him more. "Go with him. Be careful—and stay safe."

"I will." Planting a brief kiss on the back of Harlan's hand, Charles ran after Hamilton.

Alone, Harlan shivered. There were still a few stray ghosts drifting aimlessly through the massive space, but they ignored him. As he'd suspected, the bulk of them had gone with the man, whether they wanted or were compelled to.

He stared down at the still figure beneath the tarp. Every hair on his body stood on end. Suffering victim or no, he did not want to see what the canvas covered. He didn't want to know what effect taking the white substance had on a living person.

Steeling himself with a deep breath that sounded more like a sob—barely audible over the pitched, frantic breaths that puffed the sheet out with each exhale then drew it down into the mouth with each inhale—Harlan forced himself to examine the knots.

They were pulled too tight for him to undo, at least in a hurry. He knew both Charles and Hamilton carried knives, but that didn't help him here and now. He took a step back, stumbling over an empty shoebox.

"Hello?" The sheet-draped figure spoke for the first time. It sounded like a man, high and frightened. "Are you still there? You're not him, are you? Please don't leave me."

The words startled Harlan and he barely bit back a yelp. Forcing himself to whisper, to match the victim's pitch, he said, "I'm here to help you and I'm not going anywhere. I just have to find something to cut the rope."

Turning—and watching where he stepped more closely—Harlan spotted a jagged piece of metal lying in a pile of debris nearby. It was heavier than he'd expected, and it was a bit of struggle to hold it up to the ropes and saw at them, but he didn't want to take the time to look for something better. He could hear the covered figure's short, panicked breaths every few seconds, reminding him of the need to hurry.

The first rope, around the bound man's ankles, gave way, the flying end just missing Harlan's face.

"Good, good, keep going, please!"

Harlan bit back a frustrated response—he was sure he'd have said the same thing if their positions were reversed, but what did the man *think* he was doing?—and awkwardly lifted the scrap of metal to the next rope. It slipped, bouncing off the taut rope, and cut his hand on the webbing between finger and thumb. He hissed, dropping his makeshift knife and immediately pressing the wound to his mouth, trying to catch all the blood. It was too late.

He watched a single drop fall, as if in slow motion, to spatter the bare concrete floor between his feet.

Fuck.

With blood spilled, he could feel the ghosts' attention drawn to him, and he didn't have Charles near enough to protect him.

"What's happening?" the covered man moaned, bending his legs so he could plant his feet on the table's surface and push. The ropes creaked but held.

"I cut myself. It's fine." The bleeding had mostly stopped, but the ghosts were already drawing closer. Harlan picked up the scrap of metal again and continued sawing the rope holding the man's middle.

It sprang free. Harlan, seeing the last few fibres about to snap, ducked his head this time — and the man was free from the waist down, now held only by his neck and wrists.

"Hurry, *hurry!*" the bound man gasped, fear and his imminent release making him raise his voice rather than continue whispering.

Harlan looked up, utterly convinced for a moment that he'd see the killer standing over them, drawn by his victim's voice, but they were still alone. He began cutting the rope around his neck, but now the bound man was struggling.

Harlan froze, pulling the sharp metal away — even with the canvas, he was worried about cutting the man beneath. "Stay still," he hissed. "I know you're frightened, and I'm going as fast as I can, but it won't help either of us if I cut your throat because you're squirming."

The man beneath the sheet drew a short, sobbing breath, but stopped moving.

Harlan could see damp patches spreading where his eyes must be.

This rope was slightly looser, so it wouldn't strangle the victim, but the slack actually made it more difficult to cut. Harlan tried grabbing it with one hand to tighten it, awkwardly slicing with the other, but soon the victim was gasping as Harlan cut off his airway. Sighing, Harlan went back to sawing at the semi-slack rope. When it was cut nearly through, the man beneath jerked — probably reflexively, in a blind panic to free himself. Luckily Harlan was able to pull away in time, so he didn't cut either of them. As soon as the rope broke, the man was able to pull his hands apart — apparently his wrists and neck had been connected. He was free now.

The man sat up, gasping and rubbing his throat. The effect was unsettling, that of a sheet-draped corpse returning to life. The man coughed, then ripped off the canvas tarp covering him. Harlan stepped sideways to avoid letting it touch him. The very fabric itself seemed contaminated.

As Harlan had suspected, the victim was a young man. He looked East Asian, with black hair and dark eyes, and was wearing a pair of dirty jeans and a filthy, sweat-stained T-shirt that might have once been white. His skin was very pale, and Harlan hoped it was his natural colour or from fear, rather than blood loss from an injury he hadn't seen yet. He hadn't noticed any blood on the floor or table, but he hadn't been looking for it, either.

The man on the table turned, and as the light struck it, Harlan could see that something was terribly wrong with his face.

Harlan recoiled, his eyes wide with horror. One side of the man's face was dry — desiccated — the skin pulled tight against his skull like a mummy. One of his eye sockets was empty, a gaping hole that wasn't quite covered by a thin, shrivelled eyelid, eyelashes still grotesquely in place. It clearly wasn't a natural condition, but something the killer had done to him.

"What? What is it?" the man asked. He whirled to look behind himself, thinking that whatever had frightened Harlan might be lurking there.

He didn't know. Fuck. He didn't know what had happened to him yet, what had been *done* to him. This wasn't the time.

Swallowing hard, Harlan fought to control his face. "N-nothing," he said, his voice not sounding convincing, even to his own ears. "I just...saw a shadow."

"Do you have any water?" he rasped. He seemed to take Harlan's words at face value, and Harlan was relieved.

Harlan shook his head. "Sorry." He hadn't exactly come prepared to aid living victims. He wouldn't have minded some water himself, actually. "Let's get you out of here."

"Are you the police? I thought I heard...or was I just imagining?"

"My...partner is a cop. He's the one you heard earlier. I'm a medium with the police department. You can trust me." Harlan immediately regretted adding the final comment. If their positions were reversed, 'you can trust me' would be the last thing he'd want to hear. It was usually said by untrustworthy people.

"What's your name?"

"Right. I didn't introduce myself, sorry. Harlan Brand."

"James Price." He held out his hand which, under the circumstances, Harlan found almost absurd. He shook it anyway, wincing sympathetically at the red marks the rope had left on James' wrists.

"Let's get you out of here," he repeated, when James showed no sign of moving or getting down from the table.

"Are you sure he's gone?"

Feeling very untrustworthy, Harlan nodded. "My partner and my" — *fuck* — "*other* partner went after him. They'll catch him."

James shook his head, eyes wild. "You don't understand. He can…do stuff. I mean, you hear about the shit mediums can do — talking to ghosts and stuff — but this is *different*. He's" — James lowered his voice, glancing around almost superstitiously, as though talking about him might summon his tormentor — "evil."

"He is, and I know. Which is why we have to…"

There was an angry shout from the direction the others had gone. Harlan startled, but James cried out and curled in a tight ball, shaking his head.

"No, no, no…" he moaned. "He's got them, and now he's coming back for us."

"I'm sure that's not —"

Hamilton appeared around the corner, Charles' limp body slung over his shoulders. There was a bleeding, swelling wound on Charles' temple.

"Charles!" Temporarily forgetting about James, Harlan ran over to Hamilton, reaching up to touch Charles' head. "What happened? Is he all right?"

Hamilton pushed past Harlan, carrying Charles farther into the main room. "He's fine. Well, just unconscious, anyway. Little fucker set a trap for us, knocked him out. Luckily he missed me." He shrugged, shifting Charles a little higher and getting a better grip. "Backup should be here by now. Something's wrong. We have to get the fuck out of here."

Harlan had never agreed with him more.

"Come on," Hamilton told James. "Let's get you out of here." He didn't visibly react to James' ruined face at all, which Harlan found impressive.

James showed none of the hesitation with Hamilton that he had with Harlan. He obeyed instantly, rolling off the table and standing on trembling legs.

Hoisting Charles again, Hamilton headed toward the door they'd entered from. It was still open, letting in a wedge of clear sunlight. It seemed wrong that it was still broad daylight outside, not the middle of the night.

Harlan wanted to run, had to force himself to stay close to Hamilton and not abandon Charles or James.

"What about...?"

Hamilton shook his head, grunting a little with effort. Beads of sweat dotted his forehead, but he kept going, half-carrying, half-dragging Charles. "We'll deal with him later. Right now, they're our priority."

There was a sound behind them, and all three turned to look.

Still holding the ball of energy he'd taken from James, the killer stalked them, moving slowly, not rushing.

He didn't have to.

"Oh God. No, no!" James screamed. He tried to run, screaming again as he was violently jerked back by his head—his face. The paper-thin, mummified skin tore, releasing a puff of foul brown dust and exposing James' bare skull.

The killer made a gentle, almost beckoning motion, and James was dragged back, step by step, by the decayed part of his face.

Hamilton dropped Charles, turning to face the killer. "Stop," he ordered, in his most commanding voice. He made Harlan want to stop everything—even breathing—immediately, but the killer only shook his head silently and advanced.

Hamilton threw a desperate look between the door, Charles' inert body and the oncoming murderer. Before he could come to a decision, the full impact of Charles' unconsciousness hit them.

The killer made a gathering motion again, this time with both arms sweeping in a wide, engulfing semi-circle. All around them, one after another, ghosts winked into existence—Charles' protection only worked while he was conscious. They were surrounded.

Chapter Twenty-Seven

Hamilton grabbed for James' hand, trying to pull him back, but the invisible, irresistible force was too strong. With a wild scream, James was flung deeper into the building. He landed in the gloom, his limbs splayed.

"Is he...?" Harlan asked, so frightened he could barely force even those two words out.

"I don't know. You and me — and Charles — have to get out of here *now*, while we still can." Hamilton shot a brief glance at James' prone form, shaking his head. "We'll have to come back for him."

Part of Harlan wanted to argue, to insist they take James with them or not leave at all, but it was surprisingly small. The vast majority of him was perfectly fine with that plan, because it took care of the people who mattered to him. He didn't like his acceptance, but he could understand it.

The ghosts pressed closer, but slowly, as though frightened of Harlan — or maybe simply reluctant. He wasn't sure if they planned to attack or wanted to get as far away from their killer as they could. Harlan wasn't sure how the other ghosts—the ones that had made him suspect there was a killer in the first place—had gotten free, but that didn't matter now.

Surrounded by a ring of ghosts so thick that it partially obscured him—*how could he have killed this many people*, Harlan wondered, *without anyone noticing?*—the killer stalked forward. Still silent, he pointed at Charles, that twisted smile cracking his lips again.

"Grab his feet." Hooking an arm under each of Charles' armpits, Hamilton didn't wait long enough for Harlan to obey before he started dragging Charles back toward the door they'd entered from.

Harlan scrambled to catch up, hesitating only a moment when he realized it meant he had to turn his back on the killer and his clot of ghosts. Lifting Charles' ankles, he could tell Hamilton was taking most of Charles' weight, but he still struggled to keep up. Maybe he'd have to start lifting weights, if they all survived this.

Before they'd gone more than twenty feet, Harlan heard a scream behind him, high and wordless. Dropping Charles' booted feet, Harlan clamped his hands over his ears, trying to block out the piercing sound.

With the shriek still ringing in his ears, Harlan felt something slam into him from behind. Already off-balance, he stumbled forward. His feet tangled with Charles' legs and he fell, hard. He ended up flat on his back with his legs sprawled behind him, one of Charles' feet on either side of his head. He'd landed on one of his arms, and he'd heard a thin crunch in one of his wrists. He spared an instant to cautiously flex it. It hurt, but he could move it. Before he could scramble to his feet, a howling ghost dove at him — that must have been what had hit him before. Another ghost, its edges hazy and inhuman, swooped at Hamilton.

"Fuck!" Hamilton ducked, the ghost passing just above his arms, which were curled protectively over his head.

It turned to attack again, but Harlan used its moment of distraction to stand. Forgetting his injury, Harlan used both hands to push himself to his feet. He cried out as a sharp bolt of pain shot through his wrist, but it wasn't strong enough to break his focus for long. He threw himself between the ghosts and the other men, *blinking* so he could touch the other side. The world seemed to go quiet, the only sound the hammering of his racing heartbeat in his ears, the ragged panting of his breath.

This time, when the next ghost swooped, Harlan was ready for it. He lunged, jumping a few inches off the ground with his uninjured left arm extended. He caught the ghost where its ankle would have been, if it had been more human-shaped. As it was, what he held looked more like a pseudopod than anything that had ever been human. He flinched at the bone-deep cold that instantly spread up his arm, but grimly held on. The ghost strained to pull free, its phantom 'limb' stretching and distorting, but it couldn't escape.

Sparing a brief glance at the rest of the room, Harlan saw that the other ghosts had retreated. He hoped they were afraid of what he might do to the one he'd captured, not planning to attack en masse.

Hamilton laughed triumphantly, the abrupt sound startling Harlan so badly that he almost released the ghost.

"Ha! All right, get rid of it."

Harlan's cheeks flushed. He hadn't realized Hamilton thought so highly of his skills. He reluctantly shook his head. "Can't. Not enough time, not with all this." His arm felt like it was burning now, the cold creeping up towards his shoulder. His hand was utterly numb. He was terrified that, without any feeling, his grip would loosen and the ghost would escape. He forced his fingers to tighten, trusting that they were obeying but unable to tell.

With something like a snarl, the killer swung his arm like a general calling for a charge. A single ghost peeled away from the mass, spinning in midair and looking disoriented, as though the killer's motion had swept it forward involuntarily. The others remained huddled together, wheeling and circling the killer.

Harlan gritted his teeth and braced himself. He'd never tried to control two ghosts at the same time before, but he didn't have a choice. He grabbed for a ragged pseudopod dangling below the new ghost, caught the very edge, let go and managed to catch a decent handful.

The second ghost fought to get away but gave up after a few seconds. Harlan relaxed infinitesimally and the ghost turned on him. He cried out as one of its misshapen fists hit him in the head, but he didn't let go. He could *blink* again and the ghosts wouldn't be able to touch him, at least not as easily—but it would also mean he couldn't hold them, leaving them free to turn on Hamilton and Charles, who would be completely helpless. Ghosts this strong, this angry, could easily harm them.

That deadening, relentless cold traced across both arms now, inexorably creeping closer to his heart.

Harlan's whole body spasmed—beyond shivering—as it fought to survive. He held on.

"How can I—?" Hamilton seemed to have forgotten his gun during the horror of the last few minutes, but he raised it now. The killer was distracted, watching Harlan's struggle with an unreadable expression.

Hamilton aimed.

Instantly, the clot of ghosts began to murmur and seethe, boiling like water, their movement distracting and concealing the killer's position.

The killer looked up, realization slowly dawning when he saw the gun. He didn't move, only raised his hands in front of himself and closed his eyes.

Still gripping both ghosts as tightly as his numb fingers would allow, Harlan watched as Hamilton fired. *God, let it be this easy. Let him* want *to die.*

It was a clean shot and should have caught the killer in the chest. Harlan heard the bullet hit something, but it didn't sound like flesh, and the killer didn't so much as stumble back a step.

Harlan tried to blink the haze out of his vision, then realized the problem wasn't his eyes at all. A ghost had solidified in front of the killer. It must have deflected the bullet. Somehow, he'd *forced* the ghost solid. Harlan had never seen, never heard of, a medium with that ability.

His grip slackened for a moment, and only the sudden jerk on his arm let him know a ghost was trying to escape. Both of his hands were completely numb with cold, but Harlan forced himself to hang on. He glanced down—the tips of his fingers were white. He looked away, horrified. He couldn't hold them much longer, not without potentially losing the use of his fingers, maybe needing to have them amputated. *Just a little longer.* A few more seconds, enough time for Hamilton to do...something. He had to have a plan, *had* to, even though the killer had just done something Harlan never could have predicted, never mind Hamilton.

Hamilton fired again, the bullet whining as it ricocheted off a ghost and disappeared sideways into the darkness. He jammed his gun back into its holster with a look of disgust. "Now what?"

Harlan opened his right hand, ignoring the bolt of pain that went through his fingers at the movement. The freed ghost vanished, not taking the time to retaliate. He had to use his right hand to pry apart the fingers on his left. No matter how hard he concentrated on them, he couldn't make them move. Crying out with pain every time they opened a fraction, he finally managed to free his hand and release the other ghost. It, too, sailed off into the darkness without attacking him.

Harlan tucked both hands in his armpits, desperate to warm them. "I don't know." He forced his attention out—away from himself and his pain—and back to the murderer, who was standing in front of him.

The killer smiled and made a sweeping gesture with both hands. The thick mass of spirits flowed out and away from him in two arcs, converging on Harlan, Charles and Hamilton.

Harlan ducked, but the ghosts ignored him. Instead, they surrounded Hamilton, whirling so thick and fast that Harlan had difficulty seeing him. Hamilton's mouth was open and Harlan thought he was screaming, but the rush and murmur of ghosts was too loud for him to hear anything else. They lifted Hamilton a few feet off the ground, tumbling him wildly in their vortex. One of his arms hit an overhead pipe and snapped away from his body at an unnatural angle. His face was turning blue, like he wasn't getting enough air, like the ghosts were preventing oxygen from reaching his lungs, and his fingertips were already almost as white as Harlan's. Harlan could feel the stygian cold from where he stood.

"No! Stop. What do you want? T-take me. Leave him alone!"

The killer made a subduing motion and the ghosts slowed, letting Hamilton fall to the floor. Harlan heard Hamilton take a huge breath, followed almost immediately by a scream as he jarred his broken arm. In addition to that injury, Harlan suspected, he'd be badly bruised over most of his body.

Hamilton curled in on himself, around his arm.

The killer smiled again and gestured at Charles.

This was the second time he'd pointed to him.

"Wake him up." The killer's voice was raspy and hoarse, as though he hadn't spoken for a long, long time.

"What?" Harlan blinked.

"Wake him up and I'll let this one go." He jerked his head in Hamilton's direction.

He was still surrounded by ghosts, but they didn't seem to be actively attacking him now.

"Why?" The question was out before Harlan could stop himself from asking it.

The killer's only response was to point more emphatically.

"Charles." Harlan knelt beside him, trying to ignore Hamilton's sounds of distress. He lightly patted Charles' cheek. "Charles, please wake up." There was blood in Charles' dark hair, a lot of it. Harlan gently, carefully brushed it aside, trying to find the wound itself.

There was a long, narrow gash above Charles' right ear, but Harlan couldn't see exposed bone. Hopefully that meant the wound wasn't too bad.

Charles groaned, lifting his left arm just off the ground.

Wiping away a tear, Harlan swallowed hard. "Charles, please... Please wake up."

Charles opened his eyes, the corner of his mouth lifting in the faintest of smiles. "Harlan?"

Out of the corner of his eye, Harlan could see the ghosts flickering in and out of sight as Charles' power wavered.

"It's me. Are you—?" He didn't finish his question. Of course Charles wasn't all right. *None* of them were, and the situation would only get worse the longer they were trapped here. "Can you sit up?"

Charles tried to lift his head, then let it fall again. "Dizzy."

"I know, and I'm sorry. I don't think we're supposed to move you, but...I don't think we have a choice right now."

"Help me sit up."

Harlan gave Charles' forehead a brief kiss, immediately regretting this display of affection with the killer watching them.

He slid his arms beneath Charles' shoulders and helped him into a sitting position.

Charles sat with his head slumped almost to his chest, groaning with pain. "Gonna—" He turned and threw up, spattering himself. Breathing shallowly, he wiped his mouth, staring numbly at the man watching them. "What happened?" he mumbled, leaning heavily on Harlan.

"He knocked you out. And now—"

Charles blinked, trying to focus. The ghosts surrounding Hamilton vanished again but quickly reappeared.

The killer laughed, a strangely dry sound, like paper blowing in the wind. "You have no idea what a treasure you've brought me, do you?"

Shifting himself so he was between Charles and the killer again, Harlan shook his head. "I-I'd think he'd be the last person you'd want near you." Maybe if he could get the killer talking, engage him in conversation, he'd be able to buy enough time for...what? Hamilton to spring into action? A rescue? He didn't hold out much hope for either, but he didn't know what else to do.

The killer laughed again, and this time it sounded like a sob. "I want the same thing you do from him."

Harlan blushed, hoping neither of the other two had heard that.

The killer cocked his head and frowned, looking confused. "Do you think I want this?" He gestured at the seething knot of spirits surrounding them.

Considering he'd just seen the man mummify someone's face, his first thought was *Yes*, but he didn't think that wasn't what the man wanted him to say. He stayed quiet and still, waiting for the killer to keep talking, hoping to buy more time for a miracle or something.

"With him...I could be free...just for a while." He pointed up at the ghosts, and for an instant, he reminded Harlan of a painting he'd once seen of a martyr, his eyes drawn up toward Heaven while his body was torn apart.

"You could let them go," Harlan suggested, softly. "You don't need them. You don't need him."

He shook his head, violently. "No. No! I'd die without them. But he could keep me from *seeing* them all the time." He pressed his closed fist to his chest. "I just want a little peace. *You* understand."

Harlan nodded slowly, reluctantly. He *did* understand. If he'd grown up without ghost wards, without the Centre... He shuddered. Why did Charles' power work on him and the killer, when it hadn't worked on the other police medium he'd met? It raised the extremely disturbing possibility that it meant he shared some common bond with this monster, one he didn't share with other mediums.

The killer's voice softened, becoming almost a whine. "I only take the ones who beg for it."

Harlan tried to control his face so he wouldn't show his disgust. None of the ghosts he'd seen had seemed like they'd died voluntarily. "What do you mean?" he asked, not sure he wanted to know the answer.

"The ones...their ghosts, I can *see* them, on the surface. They *want* to be free."

"You mean, you see them while the—" He had to cut himself off. He'd almost said 'ghost vessel'"—the person is still alive?"

He nodded, a look of what might be called gratitude crossing his face. "Yes. Exactly. You understand."

Harlan didn't, hoped he never did, but playing along was the closest thing he had to an idea to save them.

The killer smiled, looking friendly and gentle, and suddenly Harlan could see all too well how he'd gotten close enough to capture his victims. He shivered.

"I saw you watching earlier, when your thug tried to shoot me. You don't know how to make a ghost shield you, do you?"

Harlan shook his head.

"I could teach you. You could learn so much from me."

Harlan nodded, shakily. That part, he didn't have to fake. He was starting to have the barest hint of a plan. He just hoped he was a good enough actor, or looked terrified enough, that the killer wouldn't realize what he was really thinking. He didn't have to fake the terror.

"All you have to do is give him to me."

He sounded so calm, so reasonable, that Harlan actually took a step away from Charles. He shook his head, both in negation and to clear it.

The killer smiled again, almost paternally. "I understand. You care for him. We'll start with something easier. Kill *him*." He pointed to Hamilton.

Harlan's breathing sped up and he fought to keep his hands from shaking. He could do this. He forced himself to nod.

"I know his type. He bullies you and treats you like garbage, doesn't he?"

An almost-genuine nod this time. A few months ago he would've agreed without hesitation. Now...

"Here. I'll help. I'll *always* help you, now." He *blinked,* and suddenly Harlan could see the places where the ghosts were bound to the killer. Some were faint and wispy and looked like they might blow away at any moment, where others were almost as thick and solid as anchor chains.

Without them, I'll die. If he could just sever those links...

The killer held out a hand, and he took another step forward. "There," he purred. He reached up into the tangle of ghost-bonds, selected a fairly weak one and passed the thread to Harlan like he was handing a child a shiny balloon.

Harlan forced himself to reach out and take it, and it immediately wrapped around his wrist, digging in like barbed wire without leaving a physical mark. He bit his lip to keep from crying out, only to be bombarded by what had to be the ghost's memories—triumphs, failures, joys, sorrows. A lifetime compressed into moments and hurled at him, *into* him. Slowly coming back to himself, he realized he'd been sobbing, heavy tears flowing down his cheeks. Even then the memories kept coming, striking his mind at random like static shocks, making it hard to focus on who he was, what he was doing. If it were like that for the killer, all the time, multiplied by... Harlan couldn't tell how many ghosts were bound to him—hundreds? A thousand? No wonder the guy had gone insane.

I'm sorry. He made me do it. He...

There was a flash of bone-deep cold, what Harlan always experienced when he touched the dead, but this was an icy spike that bore straight into his heart as the ghost closed their connection. He gasped, actually worried he might die of shock for an instant before he felt his heart stutter to life again. This was unbearable, but he had to bear it if he wanted to survive...to save Hamilton and Charles.

The killer nodded slowly. "There. It's yours now. It will do as you command." He gestured an invitation at Hamilton.

It all came down to this moment. Everything—the lives of everyone in the room—depended on how convincingly he could sell it. He couldn't even let the ghost know what he was about to do, in case it still felt some lingering loyalty to the killer and warned him.

He stepped towards Hamilton, who had managed to rise to his knees, his broken arm curled against his torso. He shook his head, over and over, wide-eyed but grim. "Don't make me shoot you, kid."

Fuck, if only he could *wink* or something and let Hamilton know he was safe, but he couldn't trust Hamilton's expression wouldn't change and tip off the killer. "Kill"—almost before the word was out of his mouth, the spirit that had tied itself to him sprang forward, eager and fierce as a hunting dog—"*him!*" He whirled, pointing at the killer.

The ghost went from a shimmery human form to a pure black nightmare—jagged rows of razor-sharp teeth, hooked claws sprouting from the ends of its misshapen limbs. It needed no further urging to turn on the one who had killed it, kept it prisoner, tormented it.

For just a moment, Harlan thought it would be enough, that the spirit's rage was strong enough to break through the other ghosts—who, Harlan hoped, would be just as eager to turn on their master, given the opportunity. It smashed through the protective ball of ghosts, sending them spinning and drifting across the vast open space like dandelion fluff.

The ghost had the tip of one spectral claw pressed to the killer's neck, just on the edge of drawing blood, when the killer managed to choke out, "Stop it!"

Immediately the spirits defending him grabbed the attacker, wrapping their 'bodies' around it until it was contained in a whirling sphere of ghosts. Somehow, they still felt reluctant to Harlan, and he hoped he could use that to his advantage.

This was his one chance.

The killer was distracted, watching the ghosts battle. The ones still tied to him began tearing pieces from their former companion, leaving gaping, ragged holes of nothingness. It screamed and fought and twisted but couldn't escape them. Harlan felt every moment of its agony as if it were his own, flinching and crying out as his body, its body, their bodies, were torn apart. He felt it deeper than his bones, but he couldn't allow himself to get distracted. Not now.

Keeping low and hopefully out of the killer's line of sight, Harlan ran straight at the man. He could see a place on the back of his neck where all the ghostly connections, weak or impenetrable, came to a single point. If he could strike it just right...

No. He *had* to.

He tackled the killer and the man fell, taken completely by surprise. Harlan slammed his elbow on the back of the killer's head, hoping to stun him, and the crunch of bone almost made up for the pain that shot up his arm. He *blinked* harder than he ever had before, going deeper than he'd ever dared. The connections glowed so bright that he wanted to close his eyes, but he couldn't look away. He grabbed the bonds at their very roots, slightly alarmed to see his hand sink *into* the killer's flesh, and he could feel them now, knotted around his vertebrae. Pulling the bindings tight with his uninjured hand, he made a violent slashing motion as close to the base as he could get without having to shorten his stroke. He screamed. It felt like smashing his injured wrist against a tree trunk—but he felt it give. The weakest links first, popping free almost immediately, then some of the stronger ones, snapping like broken bow strings. A low, ominous creaking announced that the very strongest connections were weakened. Crying freely, he forced himself to chop at the thickest bonds again...and again.

They gave way with a *boom* that knocked Harlan back several feet and shattered a concrete pillar.

The killer lifted himself to all fours—painfully, Harlan was gratified to see, his nose smashed and bleeding—and snatched at the trailing ectoplasmic threads, desperately trying to gather them back to himself, but the ghosts slipped and darted out of his reach.

Gasping, Harlan flopped over onto his back. With all the strength he could muster, he ordered, "*Kill him.*"

He wasn't sure if the ghosts would obey. Would any of them remain loyal to their captor? Would they attack any human they saw? But it was the first thought that had come to mind.

The ghosts descended en masse, swarming the killer until he was nearly invisible beneath layers of ghosts. The screaming started, and Harlan looked away, closing his eyes. He crawled on three limbs over to Charles, James and Hamilton, who'd been knocked down by the spectral explosion. He tried to crouch over them, protect them with his body, but he was too weak and exhausted. He lay on his side between them and the ghosts destroying their former master. A hand found his and he squeezed it hard, relieved to have something alive to anchor himself to. He suspected it was Charles' but didn't know for sure. His hands were still mostly numb, but with a faint tingle that made him hopeful feeling would return to them eventually.

The attack seemed to take forever, but it was over quickly. The world grew ominously silent and still. Charles moaned, and he could feel Hamilton shift beside him. Harlan forced himself to sit up, to turn around. The killer's body was...gone. Not a drop of blood stained the concrete floor, not a scrap of flesh or clothing remained.

The ghosts wheeled and shimmered above, filling the upper half of the high-ceilinged space.

Swallowing hard, Harlan stared up at them. He could feel them watching him, waiting to see what he would do next. He wondered that himself.

He'd just opened his mouth to speak when a single spirit tore away from the mass and dove at Hamilton, howling.

Your fault! Never looked for me, never helped me.

Harlan scrambled to his feet, taking the full brunt of the ghost's attack in his chest. He staggered back a step, but kept it from reaching the men he was protecting. It howled in his face but swooped back to join the others.

"You're free!" he told them, waving his arms like they were a flock of birds he was shooing. "No one here wants to harm you. You're free."

He felt emotions brushing him, sliding past like cats in the darkness—fear, anguish, rage, confusion.

He felt someone grab his arm and he almost screamed.

"Let's get out of here." It was Hamilton.

Harlan shook his head. He was hurt and exhausted—beyond exhausted—and he just wanted to curl up and cry, but he knew this wasn't finished. He had to see it through to the end. He pulled free of Hamilton's grip and took a step forward.

He tried to *blink,* then realized he'd never stopped. No wonder he had a headache and it was difficult to focus on anything.

He opened a way to the other side, so massive that it made his ears ring. His usual holes were mere doorways. This was a castle gate, massive and booming and empty.

"Go through. Please. You don't belong here, please just…go." He was too tired to convince them, to try and use the bullshit gentling script the Centre had taught him. He'd opened the way, and the rest was up to them.

One ghost broke away from the group, hovered just in front of the opening.

Harlan held his breath, waiting. He didn't want to move or breathe for fear of spooking it into retreating.

It turned to look at Harlan. Its mouth opened and closed, but no sound emerged.

"I'm sorry. I can't hear you." He wasn't sure if his ears were ringing with the sheer effort of keeping such a massive gateway open or if the ghost couldn't make noise.

It pointed to itself, then at the doorway.

Harlan nodded.

The ghost floated closer, extended a spectral arm and touched the portal's edge. There was a moment where the entire world seemed to hold its breath in anticipation, then it glided through and vanished.

The other ghosts began to whisper and shift, roiling above him while they waited to see what had become of their companion.

When it didn't reappear and nothing else happened, the other ghosts began to separate. With each one that passed, the others hesitated a little less before entering.

Slowly at first, in ones and twos, the ghosts departed for the other side. Harlan was sure he heard a few whispers of *thank you*, or fleeting feelings of gratitude when a ghost brushed past him on its way out.

The trickle became a flood, and the mass above him started thinning.

Finally, the building was empty except for Harlan and the other men.

Almost.

Harlan had barely begun closing the doorway when he felt a sharp tug, simultaneously on his wrist and behind his breastbone. A feeling that, if had been a sound, would have been a small, polite cough.

The ghost the killer had given Harlan. It was still attached to him, not free to leave with the others. He felt a moment of desperate panic when he didn't know how to get rid of it, but he wanted it out of him *right now* or he'd be sick. He happened to glance at his wrist, and there was a glowing point that resembled a tiny version of what he'd ripped out of the killer's neck. The connection was thread-thin and smoky. Closing his eyes, he pinched it off. He felt it break, gasping with relief. He was himself again, wholly and alone.

He opened his eyes.

The ghost drifted in front of him, once again a human-shaped apparition. It smiled, bowing its shadowy head as if in thanks. It vanished through the doorway, which collapsed in on itself, leaving the warehouse entirely in the world of the living.

Chapter Twenty-Eight

Hamilton carried James while Harlan supported Charles, who had one arm slung around Harlan's neck.

Hamilton was slightly ahead, and Harlan saw him shift his grip on James so he could raise one hand. "Don't shoot!"

Harlan froze at the words. Did the killer have an accomplice? Had they defeated him, only to fall victim to a second, unknown killer?

He fell back a clumsy step and dragged Charles with him. He made sure Hamilton—who, unlike the rest of them, wore body armour—was between them and the door. There was nothing he could do for James.

"It's Officer Hamilton," an unknown, authoritative voice called out.

Hamilton visibly relaxed at the words.

"Check him, just to be sure."

Curiosity overcame caution and Harlan shifted just enough so he could peer around Hamilton. At first he couldn't make out anything but bright flashes of red, blue and white, lighting the many emergency vehicles and uniformed people surrounding them. All three departments—fire, ambulance and police—were represented, a row of heavily armed police officers making up the first rank and guarding the exit. They stood behind a line of wooden sawhorses.

Two people broke away from the group and approached—one was a uniformed officer with her weapon drawn, the other an unassuming middle-aged East Asian man wearing a sweater under a bulletproof vest. He had his chin tucked almost to his chest, as though he could duck under the chaos around him. He approached James and Hamilton slowly, his backup covering him, and *blinked* in a way Harlan recognized. Harlan assumed he was another police medium.

"They're clean," the strange medium—this must be Benjamin—murmured, barely loud enough to be heard over the activity behind him. His gaze lingered on James' face a little too long and he paled.

Two more uniformed officers hurried forward. One carefully took James from Hamilton, while the other ushered Hamilton back behind the safety of the barricades.

Still supporting Charles, Harlan stepped forward to join them, only for the original officer to firmly plant her palm in the middle of his chest. He was alarmed for a moment, until he noticed the medium was staring at him, his eyes unfocused. Of course—he had to ensure they weren't possessed or otherwise spiritually infected.

After the medium nodded, another officer stepped forward and took Charles from Harlan. Harlan struggled briefly—after going through all of that, he never wanted Charles out of his sight again—but then a paramedic was gently guiding him away from that fucking department store and into an ambulance.

He could see Hamilton sitting in a second ambulance.

James, lying on a gurney, was being loaded into a third.

Harlan was a little surprised that none of the paramedics were visibly reacting to the horrific, mummified patch on James' face, but he reasoned they must get some sort of sensitivity training.

Or maybe they'd seen worse. He shuddered at the thought, watching James' ambulance speed off, the siren wailing.

Charles was also loaded onto a gurney and into an ambulance, which sped away before Harlan could protest that he wanted to go with him.

Harlan couldn't hear what Hamilton was saying, could just see him grimly nodding and shaking his head in response to the questions a plainclothes officer was asking him until the paramedics shooed her away. They wrapped Hamilton in a blanket and started assessing his injuries.

Hamilton caught Harlan's glance and rolled his eyes. He lifted a corner of the blanket and shook his head in mock disgust, flinching when one of the ambulance attendants probed his broken arm.

Harlan was concerned he'd be questioned as well. At this point, he wasn't sure if he could tell someone his own name, never mind a coherent summary of what had happened. He saw Beth, the medium who'd been sent to deal with the ghost in his apartment, running towards his ambulance. She looked ready to kill him. Fortunately, the paramedics intervened for him, cutting her off before she reached him. He'd probably be questioned later, but for now it was a relief to sit quietly and let them examine him.

After carefully checking his wrist and making sure he could move both hands, they gave him an IV. Soon his eyelids felt pleasantly heavy, and he was happy to let them droop shut. The last thing he saw before the gentle darkness overtook him was Hamilton trying to climb out of his ambulance while a paramedic gestured for him to stay put.

* * * *

When he opened his eyes in a hospital room, Harlan was a little disappointed that he didn't see Charles standing over him. Then he remembered how badly hurt Charles was, and he tried to roll out of bed. He needed to see Charles immediately, to find out for himself that he was all right.

A lance of pain shot up his arm and he curled around it protectively. He wasn't a stranger to pain — no one who worked with ghosts was — but he'd never been physically injured like this before. This was a whole new, unexplored plateau of pain, one that he very badly wanted to retreat from and never visit again.

His whole body hurt, a dull ache like he'd overextended every single muscle he had, including several whose existence he hadn't known about until now.

He dimly remembered waking in the middle of the night because he had to pee, stumbling to the bathroom with the help of a nurse, but he'd fallen asleep again as soon as he hit the sheets.

"Careful... You'll pull out your IV." The sound of shuffling papers, then Hamilton was standing at his side.

Harlan had never been so glad to see Hamilton — to see *anyone* — in his life. He opened his mouth to speak, but there were too many thoughts, too many emotions.

"Hey, it's all right. No one expects you to... You went through a lot." Hamilton reached down and awkwardly patted Harlan's hand on the knuckles, below the IV. He had a cut across the bridge of his nose and his jaw was bruised.

"You're okay?" Harlan finally managed. He hardly recognized his voice. It was hoarse and gravelly and sounded decades older than him. His throat hurt, like he'd been screaming, and he wasn't entirely certain he hadn't at some point.

"I'm okay. So are you, and so is Charles. Hell, even James is gonna pull through, they think." He laughed. "Beth might kill you, though. She told me to tell you you're a reckless idiot, and that you owe all three of them drinks for scaring them."

Harlan managed to filter out the important part of what Hamilton said. "You've seen Charles?" There... That was something to focus on, to gather himself enough to concentrate and speak.

"I have. I visited him just before you. He's still asleep. You were asleep earlier, too, but I came to see you as soon as they let me. I've been here most of the night." He grinned, giving Harlan a very light punch on the upper arm. "You did good, kid."

Harlan shrugged, picking at a spot of lint on his blanket. Hamilton's praise meant a lot to him, but he wasn't sure he deserved it. He could see the chair where Hamilton had been sitting, with a magazine tossed carelessly on it.

"Hey." Hamilton placed a hand on Harlan's shoulder. "You *did*."

Harlan nodded. He didn't really believe Hamilton, but he could tell the man was being sincere and he didn't want to argue. "Charles is really okay?" he asked, eager to take Hamilton's attention off himself.

"They gave him a CT scan and said there's no internal damage, but they want to keep him under observation for a few days." He gave Harlan's shoulder a gentle squeeze. "But he's okay. If you'd like, I can ask a nurse for a wheelchair and we can go visit him. He might still be asleep," he warned, "so don't expect too much. They won't want us to bother him or wake him up."

Harlan nodded again, squeezing his eyes tightly shut so he wouldn't cry. He needed to see Charles, so badly that it was an almost physical ache. He needed to be sure Charles was all right, but almost as important, he needed to know how Charles felt about him. If Charles never wanted to see him again, Harlan thought he could survive that, but he wanted to know now, *immediately*, before his feelings for Charles had any more time to grow.

"All right. You wait here." Hamilton chuckled. "I'll see about busting you outta here."

Harlan's eyelids were so heavy. He could close them, just for a moment. Just until Hamilton returned.

He blinked, and the light in his room was completely different. Before, his window had been barely lit, and now sunlight was streaming across the floor onto the empty bed opposite his.

"Hey." Hamilton's voice again.

Harlan felt a hot rush of shame. Hamilton had tried to help him, and he'd fallen asleep like a useless lump. "Sorry."

Hamilton stood, moved to where Harlan could see him without sitting up or turning his head. "No need to apologize. You clearly needed the sleep. But"—he stepped aside with a flourish, revealing a wheelchair—"I've gotten permission to take you on a field trip. A *short* one."

"Thank you." Harlan's voice sounded a little steadier, a little more like himself, but it was still harsh and grating.

Hamilton waved a dismissive hand and helped Harlan into the chair. "You can push your own IV pole."

Harlan nodded.

Outside the relative shelter of his little room, the hustle and bustle and noise of the hospital corridor was overwhelming. Deciding his injuries and ordeal had earned him a little self-indulgence, he gave in to his desire and closed his eyes, hunching over in his wheelchair a little so he'd have less sensory overload. He liked having the IV pole to grip. Having something solid to hold on to, feeling the cool metal warm in his hand, grounded him a little.

Hamilton had to push him one-handed. His left arm was encased in a blindingly white cast. It was already covered in signatures and well-wishes. Clearly Hamilton was well liked and plenty of people had visited him.

The wheelchair stopped, and Hamilton stepped away and knocked on a door.

Harlan felt a nearly physical sense of relief when Charles responded, "Come in."

Hamilton opened the door and wheeled Harlan inside.

Harlan wanted to keep his eyes closed, to stay quiet and still. Now that he was in the same room as Charles, he felt panicky and wanted to leave. This had been a mistake. He shouldn't have come to Charles, not so soon, not right away. He should've left the decision to see him or not up to Charles. God, he was an idiot.

Still, he was there, and he didn't want to look like the coward he knew he was. He opened his eyes, forced himself to look up.

Charles sat up in bed, wincing a little. He smiled when he saw his visitors. "Harlan! I'm so glad to see you. Hamilton said you were okay when I first got to the hospital, but I was still worried. I'd get up, but…" He made a wry face, tapping the white bandage wrapping his partially shaved head. "That, and I'm on some pretty good drugs. I don't think I *could* stand up."

Harlan hoped he wasn't misreading Charles' expression, which seemed to say, 'if only we were alone'.

Seeming to sense this, Hamilton stretched very pointedly. "We-ell…I think I'm going to see if the vending machines have anything new since the last time I checked." Winking at Harlan, he walked out of the room, whistling, and closed the door behind him.

"I'm so glad to see you," Charles said, almost before Hamilton had completely gone.

"Me too." *And that you're glad to see* me, Harlan thought. He hoped Charles couldn't see just how relieved he was.

"Like the new look?" Moving a little stiffly, Charles reached up and rubbed his freshly bald head, careful to avoid the bandages.

"I—"

"Sorry. I was just teasing. I'm definitely not going to keep it this way. Even though it means my manliest scar will get covered up. Well, I haven't actually seen it yet, but I'm assuming there'll be a scar." Charles frowned. "You okay?"

Harlan nodded, his throat tight. "Yeah. I was just...worried about you."

"I'm okay. Still got all my arms and legs—and head, which might be the biggest issue. What's wrong? Are you hurting? I can press this handy-dandy button and summon a nurse to help you back to your room."

Harlan shook his head.

"What is it, then?" Charles looked increasingly worried, which just made Harlan feel worse. "Come closer. I feel weird talking to you way over there."

"I'm...I'm so sorry."

"What?" Charles leaned forward a little, gritting his teeth and hissing in pain. "Sorry? What for?"

Harlan stared down at his lap. "For almost getting you killed. For...for coming back, after, like..."

"Come here."

Harlan looked up at the clear order, surprised.

"I can't go over to you, so you'll just have to come here," Charles added, more gently.

Hands trembling, Harlan wheeled himself over to Charles' bed, but he couldn't bring himself to look up.

"Hey. Did you kill a bunch of people and knock me out?"

Harlan shook his head.

"Well." Harlan felt Charles' fingers pressing lightly beneath his jaw, gently tipping his head up. "You don't have anything to be sorry for then, do you?"

To his shame, Harlan's eyes fill with hot tears and he tried to blink them away, furiously. He shook his head, then looked up at Charles. "But it was my fault you were there. Mine. You wouldn't have been in danger if it hadn't been for me. I never should have brought you. I almost got you killed, and I—"

Charles held up a hand for silence, which Harlan was happy to obey. Making sure he had Harlan's attention, Charles kissed his fingertips, then pressed them against Harlan's forehead. "Sorry if that feels more like a blessing than a kiss, but it's the best I can do right now. I don't blame you. *I promise*, I don't blame you. I blame the crazy asshole who's actually responsible—and he's dead."

Harlan frowned, as if by concentrating really hard he could read every muscle of Charles' face and glean whether or not he was telling the truth. He couldn't, but he wanted to believe, and Charles looked so earnest… "Thank you," he said, barely above a whisper.

Charles extended his hand, not quite able to reach Harlan, so Harlan moved closer and took it. Charles gave it a firm, reassuring squeeze, and Harlan felt strain he hadn't even realized he'd been carrying flow out of him at Charles' touch. He hadn't realized it until now, but he needed that contact to fully, finally believe that Charles was all right, that he was alive and safe and that this wasn't a dream.

Charles yawned, quickly covering his mouth with his free hand. "Sorry. It's these meds they gave me." He jerked his head at the IV. "They make me feel good, but also"—he yawned again—"sleepy."

Harlan nodded. He wasn't sure what was in his own IV, but it didn't seem to be making him drowsy. "I'll let you sleep, then."

"It was really good to see you." Charles gave another squeeze, and Harlan suspected Charles had needed to touch him almost as badly. "And I'll see you again. Later. After I wake up." It teetered on the edge of being a question rather than a statement.

"Of course. If...if you want..."

"I *do*." A third yawn, and Charles' eyes were drifting shut.

Harlan stayed until Charles' breathing slowed and his grip loosened, then he wheeled himself to the door.

Hamilton was leaning on the wall just outside. "Ready to go back, champ?"

Harlan couldn't help grinning. *Champ?* What was next—'sport'? 'Tiger'? "Yeah. Thanks. For taking me to see him."

"Yeah." Hamilton grabbed the back of the wheelchair and pushed Harlan back to his room while Harlan wheeled the IV pole again. Hamilton helped him into bed, tucked him in, then stood awkwardly to the side.

He didn't think he was on the same drugs as Charles, but Harlan *was* starting to feel sleepy. Now he was yawning, and he closed his eyes, just so he wouldn't have to look at Hamilton hovering.

Chapter Twenty-Nine

"Hamilton?"

"Jesus!" Hamilton almost dropped his Styrofoam coffee cup, balancing it at the last second. "I thought you were asleep!"

"Sorry." Harlan hoped Hamilton hadn't seen him smile. It was nice to finally get the drop on his partner, instead of the other way around. "Can...can I ask you something?"

"You just did," Hamilton said with a smirk, as Harlan had suspected he would.

Harlan rolled his eyes.

"Is it about the case?"

Harlan shook his head.

"Yeah, sure, shoot. I think you've earned yourself at least one question from me. Doesn't mean I'll answer, though."

"Why..." Harlan sighed, almost wishing he hadn't asked in the first place. Too late now. He wanted to know more than he was afraid of asking. "Why did you hate me so much when we first started working together?"

Hamilton gave him a sharp look, a brief flash of anger fading into something Harlan couldn't read. "I'm surprised you don't know already." He took a long swallow of his black vending-machine coffee, grimaced and swallowed once more. "Then again, you don't exactly pal around with...well, anyone." He leaned forward, setting the coffee cup on the floor between his feet and resting his elbows on his knees.

He looked as vulnerable as Harlan had ever seen him, and Harlan was determined that, no matter what Hamilton told him, he'd be worthy of that trust.

"I'm trans."

Harlan blinked, not sure what to say.

"I transitioned before I joined this department. I used to work in Calgary. Someone found out, and word got around, and..." Hamilton's fist clenched, and he slowly forced it open again. He was staring at the coffee cup, not looking up at Harlan. "I had to move, to uproot my whole life. I was really scared the same thing was going to happen here. I was just...going through a really shitty time in my life, and I was looking for someone to blame. And then *you* got assigned to me." He shrugged, finally looking up and shooting Harlan a brief grin. "It was a shit assignment—everyone said so—and I couldn't help but feel like I was being punished. I took it out on you and that wasn't fair. So...I'm sorry." He met Harlan's eyes for an uncomfortably long time, almost challenging, then he laughed. "If it helps, I took it out on everyone else, too. A *lot* of people knew I wasn't happy about it. That has nothing to do with me being trans, everything to do with how people have *treated* me when they found out and how I thought you were a symptom of that treatment." It all came out in a rush, and Hamilton was breathing a little heavily by the time he'd finished. He snorted. "Plus, I was kinda an asshole way before I transitioned. Way before I knew I was *trans*!"

"Thank you." Harlan wasn't sure what else to say, but he was genuinely touched that Hamilton would share something so personal. "I hope you don't still see it as a punishment, but…I understand if this isn't what you wanted to do. If you want to become a detective or… I really have no idea what your idea of advancement is. But I understand if it takes you away from me." He'd never really thought about Hamilton's personal or even professional life outside of their work together.

"Nah, you're not so bad. For a while, anyway."

They smiled at each other, a new lightness between them.

"What's your name? Your first name, I mean?"

"What?" Hamilton laughed. "I told you the first day we met!"

Harlan felt his face flush as he desperately thought back to their meeting. *Had* Hamilton told him his name, and he'd simply been too anxious for it to even register?

Hamilton wagged a finger at him. "And anyway, you're over your question limit."

"What?"

"It's Curt."

"That's not what I would've guessed."

Hamilton—Curt—snorted. "What would you have guessed?"

"I don't know."

"Oh, I have something for you." Hamilton held up a stack of pamphlets and tossed them onto Harlan's lap.

He picked them up. They were all for psychic and medium support groups, several specifically for those working with the police. He made a face.

"Yeah, I told them you'd say that, but after what happened, a lot of people are *very interested* in making sure you have someone to talk to."

Harlan shrugged, but held on to the pamphlets. He caught sight of a manila folder under Hamilton's chair.

He sat up. "Is that about the case?"

Hamilton sighed. "Yeah, it is."

"Can I see it?"

"I don't know. You're still healing, so you don't need to be worrying about this shit right now."

"I can't think about anything else." And he couldn't, now that he'd seen Charles.

Hamilton sighed, the sound turning into a chuckle. "Yeah, I can't blame you. I'd be the same in your position. All right. But if that"—he pointed to the heart monitor—"starts going *beep-beep-beep* and a nurse shows up, you're on your own. I had nothing to do with it. I'll eat the folder if I have to. Get rid of the evidence."

"Deal."

"Actually, I have a question, first."

Harlan grinned. "Changing the terms already. Sneaky."

"Yeah? And what're you gonna do about it?"

"Nothing. What's your question?"

Hamilton's jaw tensed. "What that nutjob said, about some people's ghosts being closer to the outside, the people he killed... Do you know what he meant? Have you ever seen anything like that?"

Harlan shook his head. "I think...I think he might've been seeing some sort of pattern, something about all his victims that drew him in, but I didn't see it. It could also just as easily have been random and he convinced himself these people — I don't know — deserved to die, because he'd killed them. I think he had a lot of medium potential and no safe outlet for it. I don't think we'll ever know for sure, and...I'm glad about that." He shuddered, nibbling the tip of his thumb. "I can't imagine what it would be like, seeing what I see and everyone around me thinking I'm crazy or worse, my whole life..." He managed a faint grin. "I'm only surprised there aren't more like him out there."

"Jesus. Fuck. What about the ghosts you saw — the ones that tipped you off in the first place?"

Harlan had wondered the same thing. "Honestly? I have no idea. Maybe he just had too many ghosts to control, and some of them were able to slip free. I think they just sort of drifted to the next closest ghost because they'd already been ripped from where they should have been haunting — if they even would've become ghosts in the first place."

"On that delightful note, our perp's name is — *was* — Samuel Harkness. Born September ninth, 1927."

Harlan frowned. "That's got to be a typo. Right?"

"I thought the same thing, but no, it checks out."

"That would make him almost a hundred! Except for the white hair, he looked barely older than me."

Hamilton shrugged. "That's your department. I just know the facts." He tapped the sheet of paper in front of him. "He's been doing this a long time, and he was *very* patient. Only ever killed one, maybe two people a year. Never escalated. There was nothing to connect the disappearances, and most of the people wouldn't have been missed, anyway." He waved a hand at Harlan's expression. "I'm not saying they wouldn't be missed. I just mean... Never mind. They didn't exactly have people breaking down the police station doors demanding justice. He might never have been caught if it hadn't been for you, meddling kid."

"What?"

"It's a reference...but never mind. You need to watch more TV. He might've kept doing this for decades if you hadn't noticed the pattern." Hamilton cocked his head to the side. "But I think, eventually, it would've caught up to him. Everything's getting digitized, and computers are great at making connections that people might not. Still, you got him off the street."

"It could have been any medium."

"But it wasn't."

"I don't know why."

"You didn't just look at the ghosts and go, 'Oh, there's a problem I have to clean up.' You stopped and wondered what they were doing there."

"Everyone should!" Harlan was a little surprised by his vehemence.

"That's what I told the chief."

"You *what?*" Harlan wanted to burrow under his blankets and hide.

"I told him one of our mediums should've noticed this years ago, and that I thought it was a massive oversight."

Harlan couldn't hold in a small squeak of distress.

Hamilton laughed. "Don't worry. You don't have to teach a seminar or anything. But you could. Maybe at least lay out some ground rules."

"No!" He was fairly certain Hamilton was teasing him, but just in case, he wanted to nip this idea in the bud.

Hamilton held up his hands placatingly, balancing the folder precariously on his lap. "All right, all right. You can think about it for now, while you're stuck here in bed."

Harlan sighed. Now that Hamilton had said it, he really just wanted to be back in his *own* bed.

He thought for a moment, and it struck him for the first time that he meant the bed in his apartment and not the Centre at all. He smiled.

"You should do that more often. It's a good look on you."

Epilogue

"Are you sure you're up for this?"

Harlan couldn't help laughing — he'd been about to say the exact same thing. "I'm sure. And if it's too much for...either one of us, we can always stop. And we're taking it easy. We're at your apartment, not the club." Harlan hadn't been to Charles' place until after their confrontation with Samuel Harkness. He hadn't wanted to impose on Charles by asking if he could come over, and Charles had assumed — probably correctly — that Harlan would be more comfortable in his own space. Charles' injuries had required a lot of bedrest, and it made sense that he'd want to do it in his own bed. Harlan had been delighted when Charles had invited him to share that bed.

"True. All right. If you're *sure*."

"I am. Strip."

"Ooh, so commanding! I like!" Charles obediently took off his T-shirt.

Harlan sat on the bed, watching.

Charles winced once when the movement hurt his head, and Harlan opened his mouth, but Charles stubbornly finished undressing before Harlan could say anything.

Well, he'd gotten himself dressed in the first place, after all. This time Harlan had needed to help him for the first week or so.

"How do you want me?"

"All fours. On the bed." Harlan stood to make room and Charles eagerly obeyed. Harlan could still hardly believe he could give 'orders' to such a strong, confident man and have Charles obey without question. It was a heady feeling.

Honestly, they probably *were* rushing things a little. They'd made cautious, tentative love in the weeks since being released from the hospital—more by using their hands and mouths than what might be called *fucking*, which had seemed much too daunting—but now Charles was restless and eager for the kind of release only Harlan spanking him could provide.

Harlan stood for a moment, just drinking in the sight of Charles, fully exposed in all his hairy glory, waiting for Harlan to begin.

He stroked both his hands up and down Charles' ass cheeks, enjoying the way Charles shivered beneath him, goosebumps following Harlan's touch.

He lifted one hand, gave Charles' ass an extremely light slap. More of a pat, really. Charles moaned. Neither of them fell apart. Encouraged, he struck again, harder. Charles cried out, and Harlan was relieved that he sounded just as pent-up as Harlan felt.

Even though they'd started using toys, both at the club and Harlan's apartment before their injuries, this time Harlan was happy to just use his bare hands. This was, in its own way, a first time, and his hand felt more intimate and natural than having some rubber or leather between them. Just the rhythm of his hands, rising and falling, and the sounds of their breathing seemed to sync up and merge until they were one creature, one flesh. One, and whole. Together. Harlan could nearly feel the sting on his own ass as he raised his left hand and struck again.

They built themselves and each other into a fury until they crescendoed. Harlan slid his hand down between Charles' legs to stroke him while he wrapped his other arm around Charles' waist and pulled him close, possessively, and rutted against the intense heat of Charles' tender ass. Charles didn't take long to come, but Harlan didn't let him go, not yet. He shifted his hand from Charles' cock to his own, quickly finishing himself before allowing Charles to tumble onto the bed, where he rolled onto his back, grinning. He wore an expression of complete and utter satisfaction.

Harlan collapsed beside him, utterly spent.

"Want to watch something?" Charles was already holding the remote.

"Sure." Harlan loved having a TV in the bedroom, and he definitely planned on installing one in his own apartment. Well, with Charles' help.

It was simply so *luxurious*. Decadent. Almost sinful, if Harlan were inclined to think in such terms.

He happily cuddled against Charles' side, grinning to himself as he imagined Charles' freshly reddened ass cheeks rubbing against the sheets with every small movement of his body.

Charles turned the TV on and made a face.

Harlan glanced up, his expression quickly mirroring Charles'.

"Maybe *Criminal Minds* isn't the best choice right now?" Charles said, rubbing his head without seeming to realize he was doing it.

"Maybe not." Harlan reached out and settled his hand on Charles' restless one, stilling it.

Charles closed his fingers around Harlan's, giving them a gentle squeeze in return.

Want to see more from this author? Here's a taster for you to enjoy!

Bound to the Spirits: Cold Blood
T. Strange

Excerpt

Hamilton sighed as he lowered himself into the driver's seat of their police cruiser, settling in much more heavily than usual. "Matthew wants to meet you."

Harlan was relieved that he was already struggling with his seatbelt. It gave him a moment to think about what Hamilton had just said.

Matthew? Do I know a Matthew? Hamilton's—and, by extension, Harlan's—sergeant was named *Matthews*, but Harlan had already met her.

The seatbelt clicked into place. He was out of time.

Hamilton sighed again, this time with an edge of laughter. "Matthew is my..." He mumbled something Harlan couldn't make out. "You haven't met him," he added in his regular speaking voice.

Harlan waited, hoping Hamilton would elaborate, repeat himself or that the words would finally click into place as he ran them over and over in his mind.

Silence. Silence that he had to break if he was going to get anything else.

"Sorry... I didn't quite—"

"Boyfriend!" Too loud this time, loud and sudden enough that it startled Harlan. "Matthew is my *boyfriend*. He wants to meet you." Hamilton slid his gaze over to Harlan, a sly smile on his thin lips. "You *can* say no," he added, making it clear he would prefer that.

Harlan would prefer that as well, so it worked out nicely.

Before Harlan could assure him that he was, of course, in complete agreement, Hamilton shook his head and sighed for a third time that morning. "Nah, I think we're past that. At this point, it would just be a delaying tactic. He's made up his mind."

Harlan glanced sideways at Hamilton. *Is Hamilton actually* blushing? He hadn't thought Hamilton was physically capable of doing that, never mind imagined that it might actually happen.

"And I've met *your* boyfriend," Hamilton shot back, even though Harlan hadn't spoken.

Technically true, but they hadn't exactly met over dinner or another social event. Did life-and-death situations count more or less than sitting down for a meal together?

"And, by the way" — the blush Harlan had probably imagined was gone, and Hamilton was definitely smirking now — "I *knew* I recognized him from somewhere."

Shit. Harlan had been dreading this conversation, hoping it wouldn't happen. He hoped that Hamilton wouldn't connect Charles, Harlan's ghost-repelling boyfriend, to Mr. Moore, owner of Rattling Chains, a formerly haunted BDSM club. Apparently that had been too much to ask for.

Hamilton opened his mouth, started to say something then seemed to reconsider when he saw Harlan's pained expression. "I'm glad you've got someone," he said, just as gruffly as usual, but with a hint of genuine fondness and even warmth. "You don't have a lot of people." He looked away while he took a left-hand turn, then laughed. "Of course you'd meet someone on the job."

Harlan looked down at his lap. Yeah. It was pretty pathetic. Sure, he'd started going to the occasional police-medium group—basically a coffee klatch, not everyone sitting in a circle sharing their feelings the way he'd been dreading—but that was *still* connected to the police. He hadn't even realized that Charles had the same connection. *Fuck.* Somehow, without realizing it, he'd become one of those adults who only lived for his job.

He blinked. *Maybe it isn't just me.*

"What does Matthew do?" he asked, fully expecting he already knew the answer.

He was wrong.

"He's an advertising consultant." Hamilton shrugged. "I don't know what that means, either." He paused, then added, as though he'd read Harlan's mind—more likely his expression—"I did meet him through a case, though."

Harlan wasn't sure if that made him feel better or worse. He didn't know exactly how old Hamilton was, but he guessed his police partner was at least a few years older than he was. Was that what he had to look forward to—all his personal connections coming from his work for the rest of his life? He wasn't sure why it bothered him, but it did. Maybe it was like that for everyone, and he just didn't know—not that there was anyone he could ask.

Maybe Charles... He'd met a few of Charles' friends, more or less in passing. He certainly hadn't sat down and had dinner with any of them, the way Hamilton seemed to be proposing that he do with Matthew. He'd always assumed it was because he and Charles were still fairly new as a couple and—knowing Harlan—Charles hadn't wanted to overwhelm him with a bunch of people all at once—but maybe he'd been wrong. Maybe he just didn't *want* to introduce Harlan to anyone else in his life.

Knowing he was starting to spiral, he was relieved when Hamilton continued.

"I told him you don't do phone calls and you wouldn't want to text someone you don't know"—*Wow, Hamilton really will make a great detective one day*—"so you can just let me know. When *you* decide. Here." He fished a piece of paper out of his breast pocket and handed it to Harlan. "This is Matthew's number so you can give it to Charles. He's invited too, if he'd like." His smirk was back. "I think he still has a choice, unlike you."

"Where are we going today?" Normally Hamilton didn't tell him and he didn't ask, but it was the only change of topic Harlan could think of. "Is it another one of Samuel's ghosts?" Killing the warped medium and serial killer Samuel Harkness had released most of the spirits under his control, but even eight months later they were still finding stragglers like the ones that had led Harlan to their killer in the first place.

Interestingly, Harlan and Hamilton had found—and freed—almost three times as many wanderers as the other three medium pairs put together. It was as if even though he'd never met them, these spirits felt a connection to him for killing the man who had been controlling them.

This part of the job was a lot less glamorous when the ghosts they worked with weren't leading him to a serial killer.

"*Kid,*" Hamilton had laughed after a sweaty, dusty and frustrated Harlan had snapped something along those lines after a very long, hot day crammed in the crawlspace of an old house, trying to coax an especially nervous ghost close enough for him to either grab or calm it down enough for it to cross over on its own, "*that's the job. It's not bringing down bad guys and epic showdowns. It's...this. Hey, you've got a cobweb on your face.*"

Harlan couldn't help feeling that he'd peaked too soon, gotten more police-medium excitement than most of his colleagues got in a lifetime.

Crucially, he'd survived. Most police mediums didn't live long enough to retire.

He still liked his job and found it fulfilling, rewarding and *blah blah*, but he couldn't help feeling a little...let down. Restless, maybe. Not that he wanted to face anything like Samuel ever again! But...*something*. Something more than finding ghost, freeing ghost, next. Day in, day out, week after week. Just a little.

"Nah. Well—not as far as I know," Hamilton amended. "Though apparently this is kinda a weird one."

Harlan couldn't help brightening, sitting forward in his seat a little. In light of what he'd been thinking, 'weird' was good. "Really?"

"Yeah, yeah, keep it in your pants." Hamilton laughed.

"You gonna tell me or is it gonna be a surprise?" Even a few months ago Harlan wouldn't have dared ask for information about the scene they were going to, and he certainly wouldn't have expected an answer.

Now, it was almost like a game between the two of them—if Harlan *really* wanted to know, Hamilton would tell him, and if Hamilton *really* wanted to keep him in the dark until they got there—and Harlan was beginning to think that, sometimes at least, walking in without any preconceptions was helpful—he wouldn't. And, occasionally, Hamilton himself knew very little or nothing about the haunting situation. Harlan was starting to suspect that was one of the reasons Hamilton hadn't filled Harlan in ahead of time in the past. Hamilton didn't like admitting when he didn't know something.

"Mmm, this time I think I'll let you see for yourself. Besides, we're almost there." Hamilton pulled up beside a record store, one of those hipster places that had been popping up in the most gentrified parts of the city. He got out, coming around the other side of the car and opening Harlan's door when he didn't get out immediately.

Harlan stepped onto the sidewalk to take a better look around. Hauntings—the ones not related to violent crime, which he doubted was the case here—tended to be in residential buildings. People died where they lived, not where they bought vinyl.

He glanced across the street—more shops, and they didn't look like they had apartments over them. Neither did the record store or the others around it.

"There's a haunting *here*?"

"I can double-check the address if you'd like," Hamilton offered, smirking a little.

"No. That's fine." As far as Harlan knew, Hamilton had never gotten an address wrong.

Maybe the dispatcher had been wrong?

A young white man stepped out of the shop, waving at them. "Are you with the Graveyard Crew?"

It was a nickname for Toronto police mediums that Harlan didn't really like—and, by the look on Hamilton's face, he didn't care for it either.

Hamilton pointedly glanced down at his uniform and badge. "We're with the police."

"Oh, good! C'mon in. We've been expecting you." He turned and disappeared into the shop.

Harlan shot Hamilton a questioning glance.

Hamilton shrugged one shoulder, extending a hand to say *after you*.

He was suddenly hit by a barrage of noise—apparently the door was surprisingly soundproof. Harlan always thought the music in these types of places sounded bad, but this *was* bad.

Hamilton, never one to fuck around, headed straight to the man who'd welcomed them. "Can you turn the music down? Or off, maybe?" He had to raise his voice to be heard over the din.

The man shook his head. "No! That's the problem." He didn't have Hamilton's loud 'cop voice' and he was practically screaming.

Rolling his eyes, Hamilton motioned Harlan closer. "You go do your woo-woo, and I'll see if I can turn this noise down so we can think straight."

He hurried after the shopkeeper just as Harlan said, "I think they're connected..." He thought he'd figured out just why the music was so awful, because it wasn't just one song playing. It sounded like at least three, maybe as many as five. Harlan didn't know any of them, and at first he'd assumed he was hearing something 'experimental' or something, but after listening for a few minutes, he'd come to a different conclusion.

Shaking his head, Harlan followed the other two men. There was a bank of five record players against one wall, with oversize old—or at least made to look old—headphones hanging from a hook beside each of them. Harlan assumed this was so shoppers could listen to the record they wanted before they bought it.

There was a spinning record on each of them.

He glanced around. There was no one else in the store. *Not exactly surprising.* "How long has this been going on?"

"A few days now." The man extended his hand. "I'm Simon, by the way," he added, his voice a little less shrill now that they were standing closer to him.

Harlan glanced at Simon's hand. Usually Hamilton did this kind of thing, but he wasn't paying attention. "Harlan," he said, shaking for the shortest amount of time he thought he could get away with without seeming rude.

Simon glanced at Hamilton's back.

Fuck. Harlan hated doing introductions. "And this is my partner, Hamilton."

Apparently satisfied, Simon backed off a little. "I called as soon as it started, but they told me I was 'low priority'. And, like, I get it, but…" He opened his arms to gesture at his empty shop.

"Yeah," was the only response Harlan could come up with. He could see both sides of the problem. Obviously, it wasn't great for Simon as a small-business owner — at least Harlan assumed he was the owner, since he was the only one who was here willingly — but by police-medium standards, it was *definitely* low priority. No one was being hurt or driven off or being frightened — just annoyed. Very, very annoyed.

The odd thing was that Harlan hadn't seen any sign of an actual ghost so far, not so much as a sparkle at the edges of his vision.

Hamilton, who'd been bent over one of the record players, abruptly straightened. Harlan could see that he'd been holding something, but he dropped it before Harlan could see what it was.

"Yeah, we tried that," Simon said dryly. "Didn't work."

Harlan wandered closer to Hamilton to see what he'd been doing.

"Unplugged. They're all unplugged." Looking stunned, Hamilton pointed at the cable dangling from each player.

Harlan frowned. He didn't know much about records or record players. A year ago, he never would have asked, but now he trusted Hamilton enough to suggest, "Maybe they don't need to be plugged in all the time? Maybe they can run off a-a battery or something?"

Hamilton blinked thoughtfully. "Maybe." He turned to Simon. "These need power to work, right?"

Simon nodded.

As one, Harlan and Hamilton turned back to the row of spinning records.

"Well, that's creepy," Hamilton said, deadpan.

Harlan nodded. "It is, but it's actually not all that uncommon." He'd almost gotten used to the noise. Barely noticed it anymore.

"Not uncommon?" Hamilton waved a hand at the players.

"Well, not this, specifically... I just mean, ghosts are very good at manipulating energy, especially electricity. They can make electronics — even broken or unplugged ones — turn on, but not usually for this long. It takes a lot out of them to interact with the physical world."

"Like he said, the call came in a few days ago, but no one was able to get to it until now."

Harlan nodded. He hadn't thought Hamilton had been listening when Simon said that, but apparently Hamilton heard *everything*. "That's the weird part. A few hours, maybe. A few days, even if the ghost is only doing it while people are here and resting when it's alone? Very weird."

"Where is the ghost, anyway? I don't know about you, but I'd really like to get outta here."

"That's another weird part."

"Great. *More* weirdness. My favourite."

Harlan ignored him. "I still haven't seen it." He let his eyes slightly un-focus and turned in a slow circle, without looking at anything in particular. His gaze was drawn to a pair of large speakers, one in each of the back corners of the shop. The music was blaring through them, but he could see their power cords hanging limp beside them.

Brushing past Hamilton and Simon, he inspected the turntables. All the headphones were connected.

"The music from the record players is only supposed to play through the headphones, right?"

Simon nodded.

Harlan tried to lift the needle off one of the records. It didn't want to come, and he was afraid he would break it before it finally did, which wasn't helped by Simon making little 'gluhhh!' noises of protest behind him. The record kept spinning—Harlan wasn't sure if that was supposed to happen—but it sounded like there was one less song blasting out of the speakers. "That's something, anyway," he said, quietly enough that the others wouldn't hear. He was making little enough progress otherwise.

He got his fingers under the spinning disc and tried to lift the record off the turntable, but it felt like something heavy was sitting on top of it or like it was glued down. He pulled harder, ignoring Simon's increasingly frantic sounds. He wasn't sure why he was bothering with this — it almost certainly wouldn't solve the haunting — but he was stubbornly hoping that a series of small victories would add up and he'd be able to figure out how to stop it — or at least buy himself time.

Just as he was afraid the record was going to snap in half from the strain, it abruptly sped up. He pulled back with a hiss. Looking down at his hands, he could see a small friction burn on each finger.

"Are you okay?" Hamilton rushed over, and Harlan didn't think he was imagining the way Hamilton's elbow kept brushing his holster. *If only this was a problem Hamilton could solve with his gun.*

"I'm fine." Knowing Hamilton wouldn't let up until he'd seen the damage for himself, Harlan held out his hands.

Hamilton gave them a brief glance, then nodded. "What next?"

What next, indeed? Harlan was asking himself the same question. He just had to *think* for a minute, but it was so hard with all this music playing. When he'd first started working as a police medium, he probably would have stayed, telling himself he had to 'tough it out', but he knew that overstimulating himself would only be counterproductive. "I'm just going to step outside — "

Hamilton and Simon were right behind him. He didn't know how Simon had stayed sane after a few days of this.

Once outside, Harlan stepped around a corner into an alley, stopping where he could still see Hamilton, just in case. Of course, he promptly closed his eyes, but he was relying on the fact that Hamilton could see him too.

The turntables were unplugged. The speakers were unplugged. It had been hard to lift the needle but raising it had stopped the music coming from that turntable. He couldn't tell how new or old any of the records or players were, but the turntables all matched, as though they'd been bought at or near the same time.

He hadn't been able to lift the record off.

Okay... That was the closest thing he had to a clue.

He opened his eyes and walked back to the shop. "Where do you get your records?"

Simon blinked. "Uh...all kinds of places. We order them online. People bring them in to sell or trade..."

Harlan shook his head. "Have you gotten any in the last few days?" Hopefully they hadn't been scattered around the store's stock already and were still sitting in the back waiting for...whatever needed to be done to them before they could be sold.

"Lemme check."

Harlan was afraid they'd have to go back inside so Simon could look at his computer, but he just pulled out his phone and started scrolling through. "Ah, here we go. This woman brought in her dad's old collection. If I'm thinking of the right person—she's not a regular—he passed away recently, and she was clearing out his house. Really sad for her, but great for us. There was some really primo shit."

Harlan and Hamilton exchanged glances. *Bingo.*

Hamilton definitely had an air of *Couldn't you have told us this half an hour ago?* but Harlan was just glad they were making progress.

"I don't suppose you could show us those records?" Harlan asked.

"Ohhhh! Yeah, that probably has something to do with it, eh?"

Harlan steeled himself and went back inside. It was even louder than before, and he groaned when he saw that the needle he'd managed to lift had dropped again, adding another song to the horrible medley.

He and Hamilton followed Simon as he darted them through the store like a hummingbird, flicking through boxes and displays of records and showing them the newest additions. Hamilton glanced at Harlan after each one, and Harlan had to keep shaking his head over and over. None of them held a hint of ghostly sparkle.

"That's all of 'em." Simon slid his phone back into his pocket. "Is this going to take much longer?"

Harlan groaned in the quiet of his mind. They had to be missing something. *He* had to be missing something — but what?

"Hmm." Simon nibbled his lip thoughtfully. "Wait a second. I wasn't actually here the day they came in. Let me call Brianne. She's the one who received them." He flitted outside and had a brief, animated phone call with lots of hand gestures. "Okay, you guys, this might be it." He led them to an office at the back of the store and opened a filing cabinet behind the overflowing desk. "Here we go." He held up a record. It wasn't in a sleeve, was bright blue and didn't have a label. *Definitely weird.*

Harlan, who'd been straining his psychic senses since entering the shop, was nearly blinded by the ghostly sparks shooting from the vinyl. He blinked rapidly, knowing it wouldn't really help because it wasn't his actual vision that was being overwhelmed. He dialed his senses way back — the psychic equivalent of squinting. "Oh, yeah. That's it." He held out his hands.

Simon glanced down at the record he was holding, a strange mix of horror and reverence on his face. He quickly handed it over.

The music stopped.

Simon threw his hands in the air. "Oh, thank *fucking* God!" He immediately looked ashamed for his outburst, but at least Harlan and Hamilton weren't customers. Harlan also thought he was entitled to at *least* that after putting up with the non-stop blended music for days.

Hamilton grinned at Harlan and gave him a little golf clap.

Harlan turned away from both of them, concentrating on the disc. *Come out,* he told the spirit sternly. He was not in the mood for messing around with this haunting any longer, even if it was quiet now.

A long-haired young white man wearing clothes that looked like they were from the sixties or seventies slowly materialized. His arms were crossed and he looked very unimpressed. "Dude, you're like, *majorly* harshing the vibe in here."

Harlan wasn't surprised that the ghost didn't look old. It was pretty common for the deceased to appear as younger versions of themselves. "Good. The vibe is harshed. What were you *doing*?" He wasn't usually this abrupt with ghosts, but he could feel a major headache coming on and didn't feel like holding the ghost's hand. Besides, anyone—living or dead—who would do something *this* annoying probably needed a firm touch.

The ghost sighed heavily. "I asked, like, a *million* times for them to put on the records I wanted to listen to, but everyone just ignored me. Then I realized I could do it myself. I realized I could listen to *all* my favourites, *all* at once." He grinned dopily.

"I'm Harlan. I'm a medium, and I'm here to help you pass on today." Emphasis on *today*. "What's your name?" Harlan wasn't sure why, but he hated introductions a lot less with ghosts than with living people. He also tended to remember their names more easily. Though he also didn't have to remember their names for very *long*.

"Groovy. I'm Mike." He held out a hand, but Harlan didn't take it. He *could* have given him a handshake—unlike non-mediums, whose hands would have gone right through—but he already had enough nerve damage from touching ghosts, and he didn't want to add more for something so pointless.

Mike didn't seem offended and slowly pulled his hand back.

"It's time for you to go," Harlan told him solemnly.

"But I haven't listened to—"

"You do realize you're going to...a good place, right?" Harlan didn't like saying 'heaven,' and he didn't think it was entirely accurate. "You'll be able to listen to all the music you want."

"You mean it?"

"I mean it," Harlan agreed gently. He could afford to be gentle now that he was this close to sending the idiot on.

"Groovy," Mike said again.

Harlan opened the veil, blinking at the bright swirl of colours on the other side. He'd never seen a portal quite so...psychedelic. He was sure Mike was going to be just fine.

After one final glance back at the record store, Mike stepped through to his final resting place. Harlan wasn't sure if he imagined a sudden swell of sitar music as the vortex closed behind Mike.

Harlan took a deep, steadying breath, then turned back to Simon and Hamilton—who, he realized uncomfortably, had apparently just been standing there watching him the whole time. "He's gone," he assured Simon. "But you should make sure this gets back to its rightful owner."

"The dead guy?"

"No. His daughter. He had his ashes mixed in with the vinyl, and either she didn't know or she got it mixed up with the others. It looks like it didn't get a label by mistake." Or she'd just thought it was creepy and wanted to get rid of it.

Hamilton took a surreptitious step back. Harlan didn't think he'd even touched it.

"Cool…" Simon said.

Harlan could see him wiping his hands on his pants as if the ashes had left some kind of residue.

Mentally rolling his eyes at both of them, he handed the blue record back to Simon, who took it—though he held it at arm's length, like it was a dead rat.

"Do you still have that Advil in your car?" Harlan asked Hamilton, both because his head was killing him and because he wanted to get out of there.

"Yeah, I think so." Hamilton turned to Simon. "Feel free to call if you have any more problems, but you should be good to go." He barely waited for Simon's answering, 'Thank you!' before striding toward the front door with Harlan hurrying to keep up with him.

There was plenty of Advil in the cruiser, but the only thing to drink was a miraculously unfinished cup of Tim Horton's coffee Hamilton had gotten before work. It was unpleasantly warm—worse than actually being cold—and Harlan didn't like Tim Horton's coffee, even when it was fresh. He was pretty sure that made him a

Bad Canadian, but it was true. But he gulped it down, only grimacing a little at the taste. "Thanks."

"You know, we could've stopped somewhere and gotten you something to drink," Hamilton laughed, shaking his head as he popped the pill bottle back in the glove compartment and started the car.

"Yeah, but..." He couldn't explain that he'd, for some reason, decided using the coffee was a kind of personal challenge, because that sounded stupid, even to him. He grinned, changing the subject. "Well, you were right. That was a weird one."

Sign up for our newsletter and find out about all our romance book releases, eBook sales and promotions, sneak peeks and FREE romance books!

About the Author

T. Strange didn't want to learn how to read, but literacy prevailed and she hasn't stopped reading—or writing—since. She's been published since 2013, and she writes M/M romance in multiple genres, including paranormal and BDSM. T.'s other interests include cross stitching, gardening, watching terrible horror movies, playing video games, and finding injured pigeons to rescue. Originally from White Rock, BC, she lives on the Canadian prairies, where she shares her home with her wife, cats, guinea pigs and other creatures of all shapes and sizes. She's very easy to bribe with free food and drinks—especially wine.

T. Strange loves to hear from readers. You can find her contact information, website details and author profile page at https://www.pride-publishing.com

Made in the USA
Monee, IL
19 February 2022